MOUNTAIN WOMAN

MOUNTAIN WOMAN

HOW SHE DEFIED THE ODDS IN THE TIME OF THE MOUNTAIN MEN

A Novel

GREGORY J. LALIRE

THORNDIKE PRESS
A part of Gale, a Cengage Company

LIBRARY OF CONGRESS CIP DATA ON FILE.
CATALOGUING IN PUBLICATION FOR THIS BOOK
IS AVAILABLE FROM THE LIBRARY OF CONGRESS.

ISBN-13: 979-8-88578-347-7 (softcover alk. paper)

Published in 2023 by arrangement with Gregory Jean Lalire.

For Montana Lovers I Have Known

PROLOGUE

I was once known as Little Bit. I'm still, at seventy years old, not so big. I was born and raised in the Bitterroot Valley, which extends south nearly one hundred miles from Missoula, Montana, to Lost Trail Pass on the border of Montana and Idaho. At its widest point, east to west, the valley is little more than twenty miles, and it averages only seven to ten miles wide. For most of human time on earth, white people, of which I am a mighty pale and small representative, have not occupied this beautiful and sacred (at least in my mind) place. In 1805–06, when William Clark and Meriwether Lewis explored here, it was home to the Salish (commonly referred to as Flathead) Indians, whose families inhabited most tributaries of the Bitterroot River.

Afterward, employees of the Canadian-based Hudson's Bay Company entered the Bitterroot Valley from the north to find furs and trade with the area Indians. A dozen of the employees who came in 1823–24 were Iroquois Indians who had been introduced to Christianity, and they decided to stay. They married Salish women, and the tribe adopted them. In spring 1841, after requests in the 1830s from four separate Salish delegations, Father Pierre-Jean De Smet trekked to the valley from St. Louis. He and two other Jesuit missionaries, Gregorio Mengarini and Nicholas Point, established St. Mary's Mission, the first permanent white settlement in what would become Montana.

Before the missionaries came, American trappers and explorers passed through the valley, sometimes as individuals but more often as company men. They rarely stayed long, for they were anything but settlers. They would by their nature move on to trap and hunt game elsewhere in the Rockies. They needed to be as strong and hardy as bears and often just as brutish if they wanted to survive in the difficult, dangerous, and violent Western wilderness. Removed from the restrictions of civilization, these males were a breed apart, real and rugged by necessity but also romanticized in American mythology. They were the mountain men.

But back to the Bitterroot Valley. Father De Smet and the other Jesuits believed it would be easier to convert the Salish without the bad influence of the outside world, but white pagans could not be kept out of the valley. Neither could the Blackfeet, the traditional enemies of the Salish, who raided from the north. The original St. Mary's closed in 1850, the property purchased by one John Owen, who built a trading post he named Fort Owen. Because of St. Mary's Mission and Fort Owen, this site came to be labeled the "cradle of Montana civilization." I was a young adult at the post, but when I was a babe in the wilderness, my actual cradle was located above the valley inside a warm tepee belonging to Bet Hex, a good friend of the Salish. She was referred to as Woman Who Roams the Mountains or Pale Woman Who Lives in Mountains Alone and was also once tagged the White Woman Who Never Dies. But, of course, she did die as every living thing must, civilized or not. Her death was sorrowful, but I was not sorry that she did not live to see the removal of the Bitterroot Salish people north to the Jocko Reservation (later called the Flathead Reservation). I never left the valley myself, but I never amounted to much, adjusting too easily as I did to a world filled with towns, industry, commotion, and all the other trappings of civilization.

While what follows covers Bet Hex's entire life, I have tried to focus on the most important times and dramatic moments. That's only natural, I suppose. Her life started in the 18th century, and most of her wild adventures came before she turned forty. Because I wasn't born until 1831, I either didn't witness most of those adventures or was too young to remember them. Therefore, I have relied in many instances on things she told me or that I heard from several of her friends, most notably a Salish man I came to call Uncle Schweeleh. After Bet gave birth to me at age thirty-eight, she began to settle down, as much as a woman like her could. I must stress that this is not *my* story. In fact, for the most part, I avoid using the singular first-person pronoun; instead, referring to myself as "Little Bit." Certainly, I have chosen to keep "Bathsheba" out of this story as much as possible, for Bet Hex disapproved when Father Anthony Ravalli baptized me under that name in 1846. I write this "life history" for one reason and one reason only: To commemorate a female of the wild frontier, the

one and only Mountain Woman — my
mother.

— Little Bit (aka Bathsheba Hex)
Stevensville, Montana
September 26, 1901

CHAPTER ONE

Bet Hex lived from day to day — the only way to survive in the wilds of the early West — but always kept an eye to the future, not so much for her own sake but for mine. She was a good mother, after all, and I was that future, something to live for, someone to carry forth her goodness and feminine strength ("calm power," she called it) after she was gone. But she still found time, most frequently on long winter nights, for remembering. Not one to readily reveal details of her early life, she did share with me remembrances, both good and bad, that she figured could benefit me immediately or down the long, winding path to physical, cognitive, and spiritual maturity. I remember how her remembrances often centered on the Three F's — family, frontier, and fire. Sometimes a couple of other F's snuck in there, too — fornication and fate. But allow me now to fade from *her* story, as I do not make an appearance until much later.

Bet Hex was born a little less than a year after (her estimate) Kentucky was admitted as the fifteenth state of the Union on June 1, 1792. Her unplanned, premature candle-light birth in a backwoods Kentucky cabin in 1793 had caused Mama Hex (my grand-mother Martha, but I'll call her what Bet called her) to break out in burning fever and Pappy Hex (my grandfather Samuel) to go into the hills to fetch ice from a secret cave. Bet had heard the story so many times, she thought she remembered the event herself. What little Pappy Hex found in the ice cave turned to slush before he got home, but Mama Hex's fever broke anyway. While still delirious, she named her fourth daughter Crystal. Once on her feet again, she changed it to Betty, after the name of a spinster sister who was said by the menfolk to be "cold as ice" and even a witch.

Aunt Betty spoke out against militiamen, drinking men, and the idea of a wrathful God, spoke up for small children, Shawnee Indians, and a female Great Spirit, and sup-posedly conjured up fire, famine, and pesti-lence with her witchcraft. Aunt Betty lived with the Hex family, and Little Betty grew to love her more than her parents, her brothers, or her sisters. Pappy Hex, who drank to excess and angered easily, mumbled curses at Aunt Betty and probably would have cast her out of the log cabin he built had he not partially believed she could turn him into a toad or a jackass. He settled for making accusations against Aunt Betty to his wife and neighbors and insisting the entire Hex family call the youngest member Little Bet and then Bet, but never Betty. "Bet be best, you bet," Pappy Hex insisted. "Living be a gamble anyways you regard it. The odds be better she grow up if she ain't mistook for no hag-witch." Mama Hex as always agreed with him, and their other three daughters and five sons obeyed their wishes. "Bet" it was. Only Aunt Betty saw things differently as was her way. She failed to cooperate, insisting on calling her youngest niece "Betty II."

Bet Hex recalled Mama Hex telling her a thousand times of that "most inconvenient and difficult" winter birth in the darkness before dawn — so different from those of her brothers and sisters, who apparently all slid out of the womb into the summer sunshine on Sundays right after morning prayer meetings. Oh, how Mama Hex hated to miss her communal prayers or her nightly prayers or her morning prayers. Her knees got plumb worn out praying. Bet was a bright child. At age three, she issued a blanket apology to her mother. "Sorry I hatch," young Bet said after seeing a baby bird break out of its shell. Her mother let the remark pass without correction or comment. But Bet's older brothers and sisters periodically teased Bet about it through the years and called her "Bet the Baby Bird."

Not that Mama Hex ever neglected her duties as a mother any more than she did her duties as a wife or her duties to God. Bet mostly pictured Mama Hex cooking hams and potatoes in an open hearth with hissing and sizzling wet wood while smoke from the defective chimney swirled through her gray hair. When the family acquired a beehive stove, the children took turns burning their fingers on it, and Mama Hex would apply gobs of churned butter, though even young Bet figured out a cool cloth worked better. Pappy Hex had a devil of a time, sober or not, keeping his corn pipe lit, and he couldn't relight it without burning his fingers. His slash-and-burn techniques for clearing fields in forests were equally faulty and caused everything from singed eyebrows to swollen splotchy skin to, at least on one occasion, blisters on his red neck and bare chest. Aunt Betty said he was dumber than a bag of rocks and half the time couldn't see a hole in a ladder.

The day the hungry Shawnees came raiding, Mama Hex hid the children in the root cellar, Aunt Betty fed the Indians cornbread, and Pappy Hex, from his seat on a backyard stump, fired his old musket twice. The first time he pulled the trigger, flame and smoke burst from the barrel; the second time, the gun blew up in his face, knocking him backward and out cold. While the Shawnees were busy eating, Aunt Betty led her sister and the children out the back door and through the woods to Fort Harrod. Pappy Hex, left behind, survived by not moving a muscle while the Shawnees put the torch to the cabin, the outhouse, and the pigpen. The raiders soon moved on to burn out the neighbors, in the process killing one man and abusing his wife. All the other settlers, including Pappy Hex, eventually found refuge at the fort, over which thick clouds of hazy smoke hung for three days and nights.

The savages were all destructive fire starters, Pappy Hex said. That was a generalization stemming from his bitterness, and he was bitter about many people besides Native arsonists, including whiskey taxmen, land speculators, horse traders, politicians, preachers, lawyers, the elite, the overeducated, the overcivilized, and his censorious spinster sister-in-law Betty. At the turn of the 19th century, Samuel Hex ended his association with the state. "Land's sake!" he cried. "This ain't my land no more." He finally cast Aunt Betty aside (by then convinced she was more vixen than witch), packed up the Old Lady, as he called wife Martha, and the seven surviving Hex children (smallpox had claimed two of the sons) and followed in fellow Kentuckian Daniel Boone's footsteps — leaving the United States of America for what was then part of Spanish Louisiana (just prior to President Jefferson's Louisiana Purchase). Traveling on the trail west, growing up forty-five miles west of St. Louis in the Femme Osage settlement (so named for a young woman of that tribe stoned to death for helping a white captive boy escape) and then in Boonville, Missouri Territory, and later living far from family on the Great Plains and in the Shining Mountains, Bet had observed that Indians were indeed incendiary, but not only to burn out settlers or because they were uncontrollable pyromaniacs.

They used fire as a weapon, offensive and defensive, against both the white man and other Indians. Bet had seen the Sioux light the grassy plains to deprive their Crow and

Pawnee enemies of hiding places, to set up the ambush of white traders, to signal their Cheyenne and Arapaho allies to join them for a fight or a hunt, and to screen themselves when escaping a large enemy war party. More often, she had seen Plains Indians and mountain Indians, too, set fires for better hunting — to force bison, elk, and deer into open areas where they made easier targets; to drive the big game over cliffs or into rivers and box canyons; to bring bears, rabbits, and raccoons out of hiding; to improve the foraging conditions for the animals they intended to kill and eat; to clear trails to better reach the game. Bet remembered fires that were hundreds of miles across that served the Native hunters well. The nonhunters, the Indian women, also had reason to use fire. It led, either that season or the next, to the growth of seed plants, berry plants, and tree nuts for a better yield during gathering time, and it promoted the growth of deer grass, bear grass, hazel, willow, and other basket-making materials.

In both Kentucky and Missouri, Bet had felt constricted and unvalued by her unsympathetic parents and conspicuously different from her unimaginative, conforming brothers and sisters. She had run away from home a number of times but never got far — failures she attributed to her fear of "red Indians," her lack of self-sufficiency, and her poor survival skills in the woods. In summer 1819, with Mama Hex long gone to her reward and Pappy Hex still trying to drink himself to death, Bet had run away from Boonville for the last time. She wasn't young, maybe twenty-six (she wasn't big on counting her birthdays) and had finally figured out she was in no way fit for domestic life with her motherless family or with any of the several settlers who asked for her hand in marriage. She was unsettled and liked it that way.

She jumped at the chance to leave the rutted land behind, climb aboard the steamer *Western Engineer,* and head up the Missouri River to Fort Lisa, established seven years earlier by Missouri Fur Company trader Manuel Lisa. On this trip Lisa was taking his third wife, Mary, to spend the winter with him at the fort, and indeed Mary became the first white woman to land in that middle Missouri country. Bet, who went in the capacity of Mary's personal servant companion, was the second, although she hid what female curves she had in loose men's clothes and was hardly recognized as such by Lisa's men. Manuel paid much closer attention to her skinny form, which might have proved a problem if Mary hadn't been so tolerant of her enterprising and very rich husband.

Explorer Major Stephen H. Long was around for a while and spoke of a great expedition to the Yellowstone River, but as far as Bet remembered, he never actually got there. Lisa in the meantime was reaching out to all potential western Indian trading partners and in previous years had dealt with the Arapaho Nation. When he sent out a hunting party in November to reconnect with the Arapahos, Bet went along because she promised to do the cooking. The group couldn't find any Arapahos, but the Arapahos found them, stealing half their horses and their cook. A tall, brawny raider, with a scalp lock and the rest of his hair long and braided, scooped Bet onto his pony and stroked her irresistible yellow hair as he rode west into the wind.

It was love at first sight for Red Elk, and for Bet it was, in short time, first love. By the first moon of the new year — the Snow Blows Like Spirits in the Wind — they were in the foothills of the Rocky Mountains living in a cozy tepee in a small winter camp away from his disapproving parents and extended family who had recently arranged a marriage to a good Arapaho girl. Red Elk had rejected the arrangement, as he did not care for his would-be parents-in-law, for a squaw more interested in her ceremonial quillwork than him, or for having children and other obligations just yet. All he wanted now was this wild woman with the yellow hair who did not behave like a frightened captive. Bet thought she might marry Red Elk someday, but in the meantime, she was boiling bison tongues and tending to the other needs of her young man and couldn't imagine any woman back in civilized Boonville being as happy as her.

During the fifth moon — the Moon When the Ponies Shed Their Shaggy Hair — they left the sheltered foothills for the Plains, where grass was growing again, the bison herds were congregating for the calving season, and Arapahos were planning communal hunts. It turned out that Red Elk, as nonconforming as he was in matters of courtship and marriage, was a die-hard traditionalist when it came to hunting buffalo and raiding, fighting, and counting coup on his people's enemies. He wanted to do all those things with a small group of friends, no women allowed. He might as well have told Bet: *There's a time for us courting with a buffalo robe over our heads.*

It's over. This is the season when an Arapaho man must prove himself worthy of the respect of his tribesmen. You are free to gather roots, berries, vegetable plants, and nuts with the Arapaho women till the first snow comes. Then it will be our time again, and I shall have many new buffalo robes for us to bundle under. Of course, he couldn't say all that in English, but he made it clear enough with forceful Arapaho words, elaborate gestures, and sign language, some of which would have been judged as vulgar back in Boonville.

Bet might have been a white female captive, but that didn't mean she would readily accept all orders. When they were alone together in their tepee in the foothills, she did everything Red Elk asked her to do — and he did a few things she wanted him to do. Not now. She had nothing against being a gatherer, but the Arapaho women had something against her — they either treated her as a slave or ignored her. The one exception was the elderly medicine woman who gave Bet enough horehound leaves to kill the seed growing inside her. This so-called healer had been instructed to do so by Red Elk. Bet took her medicine to show Red Elk how much she loved him and for the sake of their free-spirited ways. Only trouble was, he wasn't much in the mood for love and kept going away to be one of the boys.

One day during the Moon When the Hot Weather Begins, Red Elk put war paint on his face, his body, and his favorite horse and rode off with two other young braves to steal horses from a Pawnee village. Bet fidgeted for no more than an hour and then deserted the women, riding after the trio on a pony from the herd of Red Elk's father — the animal would have gone to the good Arapaho girl's family anyway had the arranged marriage gone through. She wanted to prove to the man who had chosen her that she was a strong-minded woman of a different color and far more interesting than any Arapaho squaw.

Two days out on the Plains she caught up with Red Elk, who was none too pleased when she snuck up on him and his two raiding partners and caused all three to nearly jump out of their moccasins. Nevertheless, they allowed her to ride with them, or rather the other two men raced out ahead while Red Elk followed their tracks and Bet followed the swishing tail of Red Elk's horse. She had no wish to be a warrior woman, but she believed she was capable of stealing horses and, more importantly, that she should be with her man, or at least directly behind him.

By deadly coincidence, while this tiny Arapaho horse-raiding party neared the enemy's closest village, a much larger band of Pawnee raiders was setting out to strike a camp of Lakota buffalo hunters. Since the Arapahos were allied with the Lakotas, the Pawnee warriors had no problem with a change in target. Red Elk's two friends saw them too late and were felled by a dozen arrows each. With the odds drastically in favor of the enemy, Red Elk, who was brave but not foolish, turned his horse full circle to make a run for it. That sudden movement, or perhaps the war yelps of the fast-approaching Pawnees, caused Bet's pony to rear up and throw her to the ground. She was on her backside watching Red Elk gallop off to safety when a passing arrow creased her right cheek.

One Pawnee discovered that she was female and white before the others could unleash more arrows at her. She was spared and taken to the village, where a medicine woman treated her wound and nobody tried to abuse her. She was not their enemy. The Pawnees had long traded with the French and had become peaceful trading partners with the Americans. Right now, though, she was the only American present and not a very grateful one. Besides not thanking the Pawnees for rescuing her from the Arapahos, she told them she had willingly gone on the raid with the great warrior Red Elk and was much pleased he had escaped to steal their horses another day. "Do with me as you wish," she boldly told her captors, "for I am Arapaho in my heart." It wasn't that she was particularly brave, more so that she was stubborn and foolish and full of loyalty to her first lover, never mind that he had bolted without her.

Despite Bet's poor attitude, the Pawnee women provided her with all the food she could eat, dressed her in a painted buffalo robe, and placed flowers in her hair. Meanwhile the men collected four types of wood — willow, elder, cottonwood, and elm — and built a scaffold. A silver-haired French-Canadian trader who happened to be in camp knew enough English to explain to her that each wood represented a point on the compass and a sacred animal. She expressed relief that no noose dangled on the scaffold, since she feared the Pawnees might want to hang her Arapaho-loving self. The Frenchman said the Pawnees never hanged anyone but did place their dead onto scaffolds. "Who died?" she asked. The Frenchman shook his head. He would say no more.

What happened at the Pawnee village two days later shocked Bet. The Pawnees put her on the scaffold, stripped off the painted buffalo robe they had put on her earlier, and painted her body — the left side black to represent the night, the right side red to represent the day, more specifically the Morning Star. Below her the men were smoking tobacco and the women were changing into brighter clothes. Four tribal holy men climbed onto the scaffold and seemed to be blessing her in their own way. But then they stood her upright and tied her spread-eagled to the scaffold. She was still in that position when the rays of the morning sun shone upon her black and red body. In a pit below her she saw an offering of buffalo meat. She found this curious, but her curiosity turned to pure terror when a warrior appeared with bow in hand. He fitted it with an arrow. Clearly, he intended to shoot an arrow into her, and his aim was for her heart, not her cheek.

The Frenchman interrupted what he later referred to as the Pawnee Morning Star Sacrifice ceremony by firing his pistol into the air. Once he had everyone's attention, he insisted that the ceremony would not ensure fertile crops or great victories since the girl to be sacrificed was *not* an enemy but a full-blooded American woman. The holy men were divided on this matter, some arguing she was too tainted in body and spirit to be considered an American friend while others contended her death would surely bring on the wrath of the big chief in Washington. The Pawnee people argued among themselves as Bet struggled against her restraints. The next part of the ceremony called for a chosen warrior to cut a hole in the *dead* girl's already pierced heart, smear her blood on his face, and let the rest of it fall in a stream onto the buffalo meat below. The people would then eat the consecrated meat and praise Morning Star and Mother Corn as they made merry by dancing, singing, acting out mock battles, and engaging in licentious acts. That never happened because the holy men finally agreed that others could be found who were more suitable for human sacrifice and because the Frenchman proposed a trade that pleased the principal chief — a musket, a packhorse, and a plug of baccy for the pale-blooded squaw.

The Frenchman's name was Louis Pierre Coquerel; he was an ancient *voyageur,* at least twice her age, and admitted to already having at least a dozen wives. "Always room for one more," he told her. She repeated many times one of the few French words she knew: *Non.* The man was older than her father — that is, if Pappy Hex were still alive back in Missouri — and like him, Louis Pierre had trouble keeping his pipe lit and his whiskey jug full. No, she would never marry him in any Christian way or any Indian way for that matter. Nevertheless, this nomad had saved her life. In return she spent five years on the tramp with him on horseback, on foot, and in canoes, while his wives, mostly Indians and half-bloods, stayed in their respective homes and saw him infrequently at best. She in turn never ran into Red Elk, who would always occupy special places in her heart and loins but who in each year of separation seemed increasingly selfish and close-minded.

Monsieur Coquerel never pretended to be a gentleman or a second father, but he was mostly gentle and fatherly, and those times he was not, he was easy to dodge. He jokingly referred to her not as his mistress but as Mistress of the Shining Mountains. He taught her to hunt and trap, to trade and gamble (she won her first pipe tomahawk from a Dakota chief he did business with), and to survive in the wilderness with or without him. That was good, because one day in the remote north border country his heart gave out on him while he was carrying three ninety-pound bundles of fur over portage. She lowered his body into the river as he had requested and then carried all three bundles herself. Anyway, that was how she remembered it. And, though her time with the Frenchman was a blur of days both tedious and menacing, she also remembered her year's long sadness afterward that only ended once she had indulged in the excesses of a mountain man rendezvous in 1826.

She told me only a few basics about that summer rendezvous at Cache Valley in what would become Utah. There, as was the norm at these annual events, anything went. The fur trappers met there with friendly Indians and William Ashley's pack train from St. Louis because it was their business — a way to get their beaver pelts to market and obtain supplies for the coming year. But they mixed business with pleasure, and for most of them the pleasure came first. They guzzled medicine water as if they wouldn't see it again for a year, which was sometimes the case, and showed off their dash-fire by fighting with each other and fornicating with willing Indian women. Bet Hex hadn't been so willing, but as perhaps the only white woman within one thousand miles, she was in unreasonable demand, and after drowning a year's worth of sorrow with watered-down whiskey that flowed like an endless river, she had joined fully in the debauch at Cache Valley. She never hated herself for attending, but she vowed to stay sober and more discriminating about her male partners after that. Never again did she show up at rendezvous.

CHAPTER TWO

After her one and only rendezvous, Bet Hex wanted to get away from everyone. Loaded with supplies obtained, one way or another, from mountain men, she set out alone from Cache Valley. She had no desire to make her way back east to Missouri to reconnect with any surviving family members or to meet any so-called civilized white men. At the same time, she had no wish to go to Arapaho country to try to rekindle the flame that was Red Elk. The Great Plains, where the buffalo roamed and were stalked by Arapahos, Sioux, and others, did not interest her, for hunting was not in her blood, and neither did the Rocky Mountain streams where beaver worked to live and trappers worked to profit, for only sheer desperation could ever make her trap.

She had a vague notion to head to the north border country where the late Louis Pierre Coquerel had taught her all the necessary wilderness-survival skills. On her trek, she stalled at the Clark Fork River that flowed generally northwest across what would become western Montana, and after several days of self-reflection staring into the rushing water, she had a change of heart. She decided, like Sacagawea of the Lewis and Clark Expedition, she must see the Pacific Ocean. With a relentless determination that came to rule her every action, she made her way westward to Lolo Pass, through which Lewis, Clark, and Sacagawea had traveled both coming and going. There she stalled again, for on a rainy night at her no-fire camp, she met a handsome, friendly man, her first Salish acquaintance. His name was Schweeleh.

She had heard of the Salish by their other name — Flatheads. That was the translation of Têtes-Plates, the name given to them by French fur traders. But Schweeleh's head was normal and shapely, and in Bet's opinion, his well-cut nose, fine cheekbones, tender lips, and chiseled chin gave him a face to match. His English was limited, and she knew nothing of his language. But his eyes, like brown saucers, looked her over from coonskin cap to quilled moccasins. They said a lot, but unlike the eyes of many men, they not only saw her but also saw what her own eyes were seeing. Mostly with sign language he explained that his people being called Flatheads was a case of mistaken identity, for nobody in the tribe practiced head flattening. "Salish I am," he said. "Means 'the People.' " When he smiled, she replied, "I like people."

He indicated, not in a boastful way, that he had come to the pass in the mountains to do a rain dance of his own invention because it was a time of drought for his village in the valley. He had learned by his experience that his rain dance was most effective when performed in the high country, particularly this pass. He pointed to the sky and shook his head, and then pointed west toward the other side of the pass before motioning with his hands to show her that the rain needed to go through the pass to reach the east side of the Bitterroot Mountains. Then he laughed. But it was no joke. His rain dance had worked. He took her hands and swung her around in circles, their moccasins splashing water as high as the tops of their leggings while the hard rain pounded their heads and shoulders. Dancing in the rain was not something done back in civilized white society where dancing was confined to taverns, barns, and ballrooms. "I fell in love with Schweeleh while we were going around in circles," she would later recall.

What happened next was that Schweeleh led her into a shelter he'd fashioned with saplings, leaves, small branches, and two beaver pelts. Inside, they made love in ways Bet Hex had never made love before or even imagined. That was all she said about that first of many mutually satisfying intimacies between her and her Salish savior. She had removed her coonskin cap, let down her hair, and given him all of her, and he had given her all of him. Neither demanded anything then or later, and she never regretted her time spent with Schweeleh.

From the beginning, the tender looks, ardent broken sentences in two languages, and lovemaking came with intermingling laughter. Beginning that first rainy night, she called him "Flat Head" because he was so fun to tease and, in the same spirit, he called her "Flat Chest" at first. He was some years younger than her but had already had his fill of Salish girls lacking in any concept of chastity, conversation, or consequence. After she and Schweeleh had shared several campfires, she showed him how she bound her bosom to minimize it in an unexplored and savage land. When she knew him better, minimizing became more difficult to

35

do, and he started to call her, all in good nature, "Double Mountain Woman" and later "Pretty Pale Face," even though by then she had lost the last of her whiteness and gained a furrow in her brow. Meanwhile she took to calling him "Strong Head" not so much because two arrows had bounced off his forehead during a Blackfeet ambush but because he was both willful and willing and the wisest young man she had ever met. Of course, he was no longer young, but he wore his wisdom well and his lips were still tender.

Since Lewis and Clark, the Salish had continued to trade in peace with other white men, mostly employees of the British Hudson's Bay Company who showed up to rub out as many beaver as they could to dishearten American trappers. Nevertheless, the Salish had never encountered a white woman until Schweeleh brought her from Lolo Pass to his village in the valley. The people had made her feel special that first time and ever since. The unthreatened women and elderly men all spoke well of Schweeleh and her, whether in Salish, French, English, or sign language.

Some had tried blandishments to lure her to their village permanently. Always, though, she could stay only so long, even when

Schweeleh was present, before she needed to head back alone to the mountains. For many moons in her many mountain camps, she wondered what flaw in her character made her turn away from Indian villages as she had from white settlements. But then she put that negative thinking behind her. She came to know herself and to accept what she had become or perhaps what she had always been beneath her once pale skin.

She belonged to the Bitterroot. She loved the high country and the valley with all five of her senses. She loved animals more than people, trees more than animals, waterfalls more than trees, and mountains more than everything else. The Place of the Bitterroot was good to her, so good that she only ventured across the Bitterroot Mountains twice — once when she again got the notion that she wanted to see the Pacific Ocean before she died and once when an excitable young Nez Perce buffalo hunter, Yellow Bull, convinced her to come home with him to meet his mother, a village matriarch who in a recurring vision had seen her son marry a non-Indian girl.

On the first of those occasions, Bet never reached the ocean because an early winter storm left her snow-blind and stranded for weeks. On the second, she reached the Nez

Perce village, but the mother found Bet too old, too independent, and too headstrong to make a good squaw and told her son that it must have been a *different* white woman in her vision. Yellow Bull spent five days and nights with Bet before he decided he must obey his mother's wishes and look for a second white girl. Bet told him he wasn't likely to find one this side of St. Louis, but she made no effort to sway him. She had come to Nez Perce country for adventure, not for matrimony, and besides, Yellow Bull was too much of a mama's boy to suit her tastes for as long as a week. Schweeleh, as always, was in the back of her mind and occupying at least half her heart. She returned to the Bitterroot alone.

For reasons not entirely clear, Bet Hex then began to make her solo camps near but not in the Bitterroot (valley or mountains). No doubt the traditional-minded Schweeleh still enjoyed her company and wanted her as his friend but did not wish to take this yellow-haired woman as his wife. At the same time, the independent-minded Bet must have had mixed feelings about making him her husband or having any man share her camps permanently. By living just north and east of the Bitterroot, on the modest mountain slopes on the other side of the Clark Fork River, she kept some distance between herself and Schweeleh but was still close enough to some of her old haunts to visit them on occasion. That's one explanation, anyway.

At this juncture, allow me to intrude on Bet Hex's story for just a moment to make this point: She told me, her only surviving child, what she wanted to tell me, leaving out many of the details about her life before I was born. As a good mother, she waited until I had gone through my puberty rites in a Salish women's lodge before starting to reveal certain secrets that would have disturbed a younger girl, and it was not until I was twenty-five that I learned who my actual father was. I have utilized at this late date every bit of information provided to me by my mother and certain others to present my case that Bet Hex deserves to be remembered in the Bitterroot and beyond.

A word of warning: While we have now, like it or not, entered the 20th century, I feel young children today can still be shocked by things they hear or read about, and I see no reason to burden youngsters with certain hard facts of life they aren't equipped to handle. Therefore, I request that you read on only if you have come of age and can handle the truth. End of my intrusion! I take you now back to 1830 when Bet Hex was about thirty-seven and neither she nor anyone else on the planet could conceive of me.

Her one-person camp that year was some twenty miles from the confluence of the northward-flowing Bitterroot River and the Clark Fork. Her tepee, whose door opened east toward the rising sun, stood unflinchingly on an unnamed mountain that might have been seen by westbound Lewis and Clark in September 1805 when their expedition stopped at Travelers' Rest before crossing the Bitterroot Mountains. This camp and two earlier camps farther east had sheltered her through two winters, one hailstorm, two lightning strikes, and countless burning sun days. Her latest residence seemed safer than the previous two because it was farther from Blackfeet country. Still, those ominous warriors in black moccasins had sometimes passed by to steal horses from or settle old scores with their enemies, the Kootenais to the northwest and the Nez Perces farther west. The Blackfeet had never found her camp, but they hadn't been looking for it either. They seemed to view her as one of their untouchable spirits in disguise, and it was understood that spirits could roam the earth forever without ever needing to take shelter in a tepee.

Downslope from her tepee was a small creek with a fallen log that had been a good crossing place in time of flood — many moons ago. This year, the creek was running low — not enough snow had fallen in the mountains over the winter to produce a decent spring runoff. Still, there was plenty of water to drink and enough for a sit-down cold bath. She had no complaints. She was alone in April, which the Salish called "The Lovemaking" month, at least according to her old Salish lover, Schweeleh. But that didn't bother her either. Mid-spring, by herself, she did what she knew the Salish Indians were doing wherever they were — gathering the nutritious ripened bitterroot. She worked hard with her antler-handled digging stick and relished peeling off the brownish-red skin and exposing the red "heart" that some Indian diggers removed because of its bitterness but that she savored. "Good food and good medicine," the Salish healer Otter Woman once said of the bitterroot. "The heart is good for the heart."

Bet's heart felt good, and so did her stomach. Two nights in a row she feasted on bitterroot boiled in broth from the flesh of blue grouse and uttered a Salish prayer of thanks to whatever spirits were responsible for shoots, greens, bulbs, and especially roots. The days began running hotter than usual during May, the "Bitterroot" month to Schweeleh and the Salish, and the "Moon When the Ponies Shed Their Shaggy Hair" to Red Elk and the Arapahos. "Moon when the Hot Weather Begins," is what Red Elk had called June, but this year in the Bitterroot, the scorching heat of June days suggested July, "Moon When the Buffalo Bellow," or late July, "Moon When the Chokecherries Begin to Ripen." Bet began to wonder if the drought would continue through "Moon When the Geese Shed Their Feathers," "Moon of Drying Grass," and "Moon of Falling Leaves." That would take her to November, "Moon When the Rivers Start to Freeze." And surely there would still be enough water then for her creek to freeze as well. That's what she told herself one early June night when she was sweating like a horse she no longer had. But then she gently scolded herself: "How silly of me to be thinking of the cold and freezing water again when summer hasn't even arrived. I may as well enjoy the heat while I can."

The enjoyment didn't last long. Wildfire season usually came in July and August, but this year it began a month earlier, as Bet found out in a most appalling fashion. Her contentment came to a swift end when she was rudely awakened from a midmorning nap one unseasonably warm June day. Actually, her misery had begun the night before, when Man rather than Mother Nature intruded on her pleasant little camp. She never forgot the horror of that episode in her life, and even after all these years, I can still feel my mother's pain. Yet, as fate would have it, I wouldn't be here today had it not been for what she called "The Ignoble Incident."

CHAPTER THREE

What happened that night kept her from sleeping. She was too cold, so she pulled the hide blanket to her chin and then the wool blanket. Instantly, she became too hot and kicked off the blankets. Soon she was cold again. And the cycle continued — hot, cold, hot, cold. Her eyes kept opening and closing. Either way, the visions she saw in the darkness were bloody and terrifying. She cried softly but didn't scream. Even when she was young, she never woke up screaming from nightmares of hobgoblins and boogeymen, since she knew how Pappy Hex hated to have his precious sleep disturbed and how Mama Hex hated such foolishness. "If you must have a fright, girl," she'd once said, "have it at a reasonable hour over something real like being forcibly seized by red savages, fatally mauled by a black bear, or stuck dead by lightning." Bet, in the middle of her most frightful night at age thirty-seven, found herself finally replying to her mother: "Can't you see. Can't you see. This is real, all too real. *He* was no mythical monster!"

Just before dawn, with her eyelids sticky from tears, a fitful sleep came. It lasted two hours at most. She woke up choking and coughing with her left hand covering her mouth and the right one clutching her throat. Smoke poured through the open flaps of her tepee. Her right hand shot up to pinch her nostrils shut, and she listened to a rhythmic crackling that grew louder. She recognized it. Time to move.

She rolled naked away from her blankets and crawled like a lizard below the smoke. She paused when she came to a man's beaver felt hat. The hatband held a clay pipe and a blue ostrich feather. She snorted and kept going, crushing the hat with a hand and then a knee. Outside, she raised her head and tried to peer in all directions at once through the eerie midmorning darkness. Haze permeated the mountainside and smoke blew in from the west like the darkest storm clouds. She spotted only a hint of sky, an orange glow around the choking sun. She didn't see fire, but she heard it, smelled it, tasted it. Lightning had struck again. Somewhere above. Wildfire was spreading like itself. She must keep moving.

Her world had been ablaze before, though never this early in the year. Birds flew. Large mammals ran. Small mammals burrowed into the ground or sought shelter under rocks. None of them just sat there waiting to be overcome. In another life she might have been a mammal with wings — something bat-like. Now she was a medium-sized land animal without wings but with legs as hard as steel traps. She pushed herself up, her feet churning before her knees cleared the ground. She sprinted blindly, covering less than twenty feet before tripping on one of the camp stumps she thought she knew so well. She tumbled now, down the slope, kicking up dirt, dust, sticks, and stones — a one-woman avalanche. She finally stopped rolling when she dropped into the creek bed and smashed against the redheaded mountain man who lay facedown in a trickle of water, his swagger long gone, all life drained out of him, his bare buttocks stone cold still. She pulled away from his body and rose onto her knees.

"No, I won't pray, goddammit," she told the smoky sky. "Not for that son of a bitch, not for me, not for anybody human!"

She quickly stood but took the time to wipe traces of mud from her kneecaps before she stepped over his bloodied, caved-in skull and ran with the scant current toward the sunbaked valley floor. The creek stones felt round and flat and pleasantly cold against the soles of her feet.

At the quiet waterfall where she had bathed during a wetter time, she let the drops run into her cupped palms and drank as if her belly burned. She glanced back and saw the last of her tepee poles collapse into devouring flames.

For a moment she thought of her possessions inside — all lost. She turned away. No sense dwelling on it, any of it. Sheet-like flames were advancing toward the creek like a pack of thirsty red foxes. She would not look back again. No home was meant to be forever. She fast-walked down the creek, flapping her arms like a bird released from a cage. She needed to work the stiffness out. Most birds built new nests every year, sometimes twice a year if they flew south. Her feet would fly south to the Bitterroot Place; she would put up a new tepee in a fresh camp that, she hoped, would provide more shelter. And she would forget in time . . . maybe. Now, she just needed to cover ground, on foot since she owned no grain-fed horse or Indian pony. The burning tepee behind her had the memory stains of the redheaded mountain man who had invaded her camp with his .69-caliber musket and butcher knife, paid for his intrusion by getting his head deeply dented, and then wormed his way down to the unnamed creek to die alone.

She kept her head. She would not be driven mad. The lightning strike and fire might be a blessing, she decided. Fire cleared tired brush, leaving room for new grasses and shrubs that attracted wild animals. And those lodgepole pines had waited years for enough blazing heat to open their cones and release their seeds. Without fire, the lodgepoles would die of old age with no new generation to replace them. She slowed down, with the immediate danger safely behind her. As she walked, she touched her warm belly and felt the not unfamiliar sensation of a seed growing inside her. God knows (and the devil, too, if either of those immortal beings existed) it was *not* something she had asked for and perhaps nothing would come of it. But what if something did? "The horror!" screamed a thousand voices inside her head. "What a wicked woman!" screamed a thousand more. Perhaps one of the voices was that of her late Mama Hex. She wasn't sure. Never mind them. Her voice was the only one that mattered out here.

"If you want to grow, grow!" she said defiantly, staring at her navel. It could be a blessing, she told herself, even if the seed planter was lying dead in a creek with leaping flames ready to consume his repulsive flesh.

She turned away from the creek at the fallen log. She counted twenty-one steps through the bushes and then pushed aside earth and brush to uncover her cache pit — a five-foot hole in the ground lined with dried prairie grass, bark, and a buffalo hide. Inside were food, a change of clothes, her backup pipe tomahawk, a sheet-metal frying pan, a tin cup, and a cradleboard. Everything was bone dry. She lowered herself into the pit and loaded the cradleboard with three rawhide bags of pemmican — elk jerky mixed with melted fat and dried chokecherries — and a parfleche packed with the dried taproots of recently ripened bitterroot.

She dropped to her knees in the pit as if before a church altar and found herself praying, not to the Christian God, whomever that was, but to the creator god of the Salish, Amotken, who she knew to be a kind, elderly gentleman who listened to women. From five hairs on Amotken's head, he created five young women who he considered daughters and asked them what they wanted to be. They gave five different answers — Mother of Wickedness and Cruelty, Mother of Goodness, Mother of the Earth, Mother of Fire, and Mother of Water. Amotken did as they asked, and to prevent any female bickering he decreed that they would take turns ruling the world, starting with the No. 1 Mother. This would all happen on a godly timescale, unfathomable to human beings whose time on earth was severely limited. Schweeleh, who preferred not to question his people's creation mythology, contended that the Mother of Wickedness and Cruelty was still very much in command. It seemed to Bet Hex on this onerous day that the Mother of Fire must be lending the No. 1 Mother a helping hand.

Just two nights ago she had savored bitterroot boiled in broth. Now she had the taste of death in her mouth and ash in her throat. The arrival of the redheaded mountain man and then the red-hot fire was like a double damnation. She wondered if the Mothers had singled her out for some reason or if the Salish guardian spirits had forsaken her. Not for long, though, for she had no time to concern herself with the doings of unseen immortal beings, supreme or

50

otherwise. Nothing mattered now except survival, and she could only count on herself. She was no farmer and a fair hunter at best, but she excelled at gathering and trading for what she couldn't gather. Those skills had saved her during starving times. They would have to get her through this time, too.

Rawhide ties on the sides of the cradleboard allowed her to attach the pipe tomahawk and pan. It crossed her mind that this cradleboard she had won gambling might be needed in three-quarters of a year to carry an actual infant. That thought didn't fill her with horror — the civilized voices inside her head were already growing faint — but it made her nervous. She quickly draped the buffalo hide over the entire works and lifted it out of the pit. To worry too far ahead about what might happen was to start dying before you were called away.

She patted her flat belly once and with her middle finger scooped a powdery residue from her navel — ash. She sighed for as long as she could hold her breath and then quickly dressed, slipping her shirt, two doeskins laced loosely together, over her head; stepping into her breechclout and leggings, both held up by the same leather belt; and sliding her feet into her second pair of moccasins. Next, she stuffed most of her long yellow hair inside her coonskin cap. No skirts and dresses for her. Looking like an Indian man or a mountain man gone Indian had its advantages when strangers saw her from a distance — often when they got closer, too.

At times, yanking off her cap and letting down her hair had served her well upon encountering the rare traveler who wouldn't think of scalping a woman or interfering with a female spirit. A few times, she had lifted the flaps of her breechclout and loosened her belt — by choice. But that wasn't the way it had been with the red-headed mountain man with a caved-in skull in the creek. She had offered no encouragement. He had wanted his way with a squaw and then had stumbled onto her and considered himself the luckiest man in the West, right up until the moment she got hold of her principal pipe tomahawk and struck his thick skull with its head, using both the war-like iron cutting edge side and the peaceful pipe bowl side. The hickory stem of that tomahawk pipe must have burned to nothing by now, but that was for the best. She could never again have put it to her lips and smoked it. Besides, she possessed this other pipe tomahawk, one she needed to break in if she was ever to regain peace of mind.

I have already mentioned that what I am putting down on paper here is based on things my mother told me and things I learned from several people who knew her. Call it oral tradition. As far as I know, Bet Hex never wrote letters, kept diaries, crafted poems about nature, or even made out a shopping list. But once, and only once, she wrote something substantial and asked me not to show it to anyone until after her death. Why did she write it? Perhaps it helped her get a gut-wrenching pain at least temporarily out of her system. Perhaps she wanted me to know the full extent of her horror but couldn't say the words out loud. Perhaps she wanted to set the record straight for future generations of curious and nosy people. In any case, here it is, Bet Hex's true personal account (in full, lightly edited for spelling and punctuation) of what happened the night before the first fire of 1830:

THE IGNOBLE INCIDENT

I smell him before I see him on a warm spring night. His scent is of rotgut and rotting guts. I open my eyes to a musket under my nose. He orders me to stand. I'm glad I slept in my clothes. He is big like a bear. He takes off his felt hat adorned with a corn pipe and a blue ostrich feather. He tickles my nostrils with the feather, but when I don't laugh, he tosses the hat aside.

"Won't need that," he tells me, running a hand through his tangled red hair that curls at his shoulders. His red beard goes every which way like it wants to escape his weather-beaten face. At full height the top of my coonskin cap only reaches his chest. He looks me over, flashing his yellow buckteeth in what might pass for a grin. He lays his musket and possibles bag down gently and then draws a butcher knife still coated in blood — animal blood, I hope — and presses the blade under my chin. In a second he could slit my throat from ear to ear, but I feel more disgust than fear; he can't even keep his knife clean.

He tears off my coonskin cap to free my yellow hair and then grabs a handful in a tight fist. My hair is the color of his teeth. Now fear takes over. He might want to scalp me — but not immediately. He releases my hair, pulls away the knife, and nibbles on my neck, hard enough to hurt. What big teeth he has.

"Where you come from, mister?" I ask him because I want this dumb brute to talk instead of do what he's doing or whatever else he has in mind.

"Hell," he says. The nibbling stops, the squeezing begins, and he squeezes like the devil — a bear hug that would make a grizzly jealous. "Bug's Boy country. Another narrow escape."

"I didn't hear you ride up."

"Ain't been riding. I had me two horses. A redskin stole one in the Spotted Foot Mountains. The other one run off 'cause of lightning."

"There's sure been some of that, mister." He stops squeezing, and I exhale. "You looking for your horse?"

"I be looking for any damn horse. It ain't healthy to be afoot in Bug's Boy country. Them Blackfeet be the devil's children. They got scores to settle with me, and me with them. It pleasure me to kill them murdering savages."

"I don't have a horse. You looking for beaver, too?"

"Not for the last fortnight."

"But you have been trapping some?"

"Some? Pshaw! Better'n ten years I been sucking in the same air as my old pard Hawk. We been birds of a feather, two peas in a pod, singular blood brothers! No two men take more prime plews than us, kill more bears and Indians than us, drink more tanglefoot than us, have more squaws than us. Ain't it a wonder me and my partner never crossed paths with you before this occasion!"

A blessing, I think. He jerks his head down for another nibble, a mass of his red hair whipping my face, his darker red beard tickling my throat. Yes, I must keep him talking.

"You working for an American or British fur company?"

"For our own selves. We likes to trap on our own hook. We ain't company men."

"I can see that now."

"We goes where the beaver is, and we knows fat cow from poor bull. We been to cricks where the beaver be so thick was no need to trap 'em — just clubbed 'em till they went under. Me and Hawk be free trappers. Wagh! We has hair of the bear. We don't need nobody else."

He starts squeezing again, though, like he might need me for something.

"Me neither, mister. I'm free, too. Don't want any attachments. Understand?"

He just grunts.

"Mind letting go? I ain't delicate, but I do break."

He doesn't ease off, presses me so tight my face squashes against his buckskin shirt. The man can squeeze and talk at the same time. "Ain't no easy living where the beaver is. We was setting and checking our traps at dawn and dusk and layin' hidden in the light of day on account of the Bug's Boys. Them red savages stole our plews four times, near raised our hair more than that. Hawk saved my life once; I saved his three times, last time with my musket when I plugged a Bug's Boy 'bout to take his scalp. Hawk owes me."

"Sure," I mumble, 'cause my mouth can't open fully. I taste his buckskin. "Where's your partner now? Where's Hawk?"

"Don't need him now. Don't need him no more — not never. He become a hindrance to our operations."

He lets go of me completely so he can spit on the blade of his knife and clean off the blood. Now I'm not so sure it is animal blood. He wipes the blade on his pant leg. I think about running, but this is my tepee, my home. He's the one who must go.

"When you throw in with a man in the mountains, it's got to be death till you part," he declares, shaking his fist like a righteous man of the cloth. "Hawk know'd that. Damn his rotten hide!"

My mind forms a picture. This bear of a man quarreled with his partner and then knifed him, turning him into wolf meat. I figure I'm lucky to be standing on my own two feet. He's not squeezing or nibbling now, but I can't back away 'cause his right paw rests heavy on my left hip. Without hardly trying, he has me feeling lopsided all over.

"Damn that Fallen Leaf, too," he yells. "She be more to blame."

"Fallen Leaf?"

"Crow bait!"

"Come again?"

"He give her some red beads and other foofaraw, and she give him herself. She be hell-bent on making Hawk a squaw man in her village and dropping a parcel of half-breeds."

"So your partner is alive?"

"He ain't nothing like dead. Last I seen him, he and that Crow squaw was going belly-to-belly at the water hole at Travelers' Rest."

"I know it — that is, I know the place. Lewis and Clark stopped there and named it."

"She wasn't given Hawk no rest."

"Does Hawk want rest?"

"Having squaws be natural as breathing out here. Being a squaw man ain't, not when you got a partner. His mind ain't right. She ain't no beauty, but she gots a frenzied passion for dog faces." He pauses to rip knots out of his matted red beard, and his cheeks redden like plump tomatoes. "Damn her redskin ways. She done put a spell on him."

"Women can do that, I've heard."

"Shut your bone." He slaps my cheek so

58

hard it twists my neck. "You don't know nothing 'bout it. Me and my old pard was blood thick till he bedded that demanding squaw and got altogether stingy 'bout her."

I keep quiet, figuring it's safer.

"I come here looking for more'n a horse," he tells me, and his eyes say just what.

"You need a meal?"

"I come here to catch a squaw for my own self."

"I'm no squaw."

"You bet you ain't. I don't want no squaw no more, see. I found me a better water hole."

"Look, I'm not what you're looking for. I've been baked by the sun too long; I'm leathery."

"You're what I found. You're the crazy white bitch who runs around in the Rocky Mountains. Heard tell of you. Thought it was fool's talk . . . till now."

I keep my head up, look him square in the eye. His left one is bloodshot. I'm desperate to discourage his predatory devilment. "My name is Bet Hex. I'm from Kentucky. Who are you?"

"I be the man with the knife." He puts the blade to my throat again. "And you gonna do what I want."

"How about some pemmican, or I can make a cookfire and . . ."

He doesn't answer. He grins that awful grin,

dips the knife, and returns to nibbling my neck. His whiskey breath is hot like fire. His whiskers aren't tickling anymore; they're pricking. When he tires of acting gentle, he latches onto my hair again, draws me close, and bites my nose. I don't scream or cry; that might only encourage him to bite some more. He licks the blood trickling from my nostrils. I suppose he's still gentler than a solitary male grizzly. But I wouldn't bet on it.

"You taste like fresh meat," he says, smacking his lips.

"No," I tell him. "I'm old and . . ."

"Not too old. I'm done talking."

"No, wait. I . . . I don't even know your name."

"You never will, crazy white bitch."

His hands slide down to my breechclout, and he cuts it loose. I try to knee him where it will hurt him most and scratch his eyes out at the same time. He screams but keeps coming, driving me down onto my back and landing so hard on my chest I lose my breath.

"I could slit your throat and cut out your innards to make it look like the Bug's Boys done it," he says, running the blade across my wounded nose.

I don't doubt it. But his knife moves to my shirt and he starts cutting that off. Better my clothes than me, I tell myself, but then he sticks me a little in the right breast. And he keeps prodding my flesh around the collarbone while his other hand tugs down his buckskin breeches, turned black and hard from rain, grease, and blood. When they get caught on his ankles, he loses patience. "Wagh, wagh, wagh!" he shouts, spraying spit and sweat as he grinds against my middle.

The knife falls out of his hand. I reach for it, but he interrupts his violation by kneeling on my wrist and slapping my face. He's panting so hard he can't pick up where he left off, so he slaps me again. I spit in his face. He lets up on me and rises onto his haunches. His tongue shoots out, reptile-like, and gathers up my spittle that's running down his left cheek. I try to slide out from under him, but he lays a paw on my hip and flips me over onto my belly like I'm a sack of flour.

"You is as white back there as my sainted mother," he says, but that vision doesn't slow him down any. He smacks me twice, once on each buttock. "Now you getting ripe redder." He flops on top of me. We both squeal. He starts grinding again, but it isn't doing either of us much good. Nothing is happening down below like he wants it to, so he strikes my back, yanks my hair back, and picks up his butcher knife. I think for sure he will now scalp me and hang my yellow hair on the tip of his musket. Instead, he holds the knife much lower as if it is an extension of him and shoves it inside me, handle first, which I suppose is an act of consideration on his part. Apparently it also excites him, because at some point the knife is out and he's back in thrusting with his own instrument. On the fourth thrust, he plants his seed.

He lies there, atop me, heavy and still like a fallen fir tree. I can't move out from under him. My body is trapped by the great weight. But my head is light, as if it might at any second float off through the smoke hole. The sun is up early and sends beams through the tepee door to make my yellow hair shine like fool's gold and his yellow buckteeth glow like buttercups. I have time to think about the red-headed man lying on top of me. I give him a name: Sunshine. I have plans for Sunshine.

He starts to doze but catches himself at first snore. He pushes hard on the small of my back to get off me. I think he might leave. Instead he sits on the back of my thighs. And he's not done yet. He finds his knife again and begins pricking my left buttock.

"That's enough, Sunshine," I tell him. "I'm not a pincushion."

"Shut up, crazy white bitch. You want me to stick the sharp point where the sun do not never shine?"

"I reckon not. Why not be nice."

"What?"

"N-i-c-e. Nice. You be nice to me and I'll be nice to you."

"I could kill you. Who would know?"

"You made that clear. Why do that? Wouldn't that be a waste?"

He stops pricking with the knife. I can hear him thinking. Thud, thud, thud . . .

"You and me, Sunshine, should head over to my blanket bed and have a smoke. Wouldn't that be nice?"

"Smoke?"

"Sure. I got a kind of peace pipe."

"Squaws, pale or red, don't smoke with men."

"Come on to my bed. We'll smoke and then . . ."

"Don't tell me what to do or I'll cut out your tongue."

"What do you have to lose? After we smoke you can do whatever you want to me. Take me this way or any way you want me."

"You bet I will. This way, that way, every damn way. I'm a free trapper."

"Sure you are, Sunshine, and I'm a free woman."

When he stands up, I raise my backside and wiggle my hips as I crawl to my blankets. I feel his penetrating glare and know I have him hooked. He plods after me. I turn onto my back because that's the position I want, right next to my pipe tomahawk. I think he might complain and tell me some other way to lie. But his trap stays shut. He keeps coming, the grin back on his face. The knife drops out of his hand, maybe accidentally, maybe not. But he doesn't stop to pick it up. I offer him the pipe tomahawk, but he doesn't look up from where his eyes are fixed — right between my hard thighs.

"I told you men don't smoke with squaws," he says. "Anyhow I don't want no smoke." He stands over me, continuing to stare for a half minute. His britches are still tangled at his ankles. Under other circumstances I might find that amusing. He takes the time to remove them the rest of the way and then pounces like a panther.

He grinds and grunts — but not for long this time. I grab him by his red beard to pull his head down. Maybe he thinks I'm being nice. I'm not. I strike him with the pipe tomahawk on the side of the head. He groans but isn't stunned. He's still on top. I deliver another blow . . . and then another. He groans and I keep striking till he falls to one side of me. He's moaning now. I quickly get on my knees, line up the cutting edge of the tomahawk with his temple, and land the hardest blow yet. I think how I once killed a snake the same way. The redheaded man looks dead, too. I back away on my knees and toss my weapon aside. He stirs and groans. Mama Hex warned me you cannot kill the devil.

I don't hit him again. Maybe I don't figure there's any point — he'll either die or he won't. Or maybe my arm is just tired. He crawls toward the glimmer of moonlight like a red-headed reptile. I don't see how he can find the open door with so much blood in his eyes. But he does. He leaves a trail of blood behind him as he goes out. I don't follow. I take one look out the door and see him still crawling in the shadows, heading downhill toward the creek. Maybe he'll make it, maybe not, but I know he won't be back in my tepee.

My nose hurts, and hurts more when I touch the tip. I look myself over. I see blood on my hands, my arms, my chest. I don't know if it's his blood or mine. I wipe it off with the leather britches he left behind. Tossing the britches into the dry fire ring takes the last of my energy. I try to sleep. Impossible. It goes like this. I feel chills. I feel heat. I feel too full. I feel too empty. I cry as if I have been saving tears for years. I am in and out of my blankets. It is dawn before I am in position to rest — curled up on my left side with one hand between my knees and the other caressing the precious neck he didn't slice open. I think of it all as a nightmare, and then, with eyelids as heavy as cannonballs, I fall asleep in the fetal position. What a time for a nap! But it doesn't last. In short order I am coughing and choking on smoke. Crackle. Crackle. The dry bush behind my tepee is burning. I have awakened to another nightmare. The smoke fills my tepee. I can't see the door, but I know where it is, and so I head in that direction, crawling fast after a dead man.

CHAPTER FOUR

Bet Hex marched south through the tiny, heated valley below her destroyed campsite. She crossed many creeks, most too dry for comfort, until she reached the Cokahlarish-kit, the river of the road to the buffalo. Blackfeet Indians named it, and they guarded it like white men guarded gold. She spotted the tail end of a band moving eastward, more likely looking for fresh air than fresh meat. She didn't fear the Black-feet the way everyone she knew did, but she would never call out to them unless they spotted her first, in which case she would wail like a screech owl since the Blackfeet saw owls as evil spirits that brought misfor-tune to the living. This time she stayed silent and hidden behind a larch with vibrant green needles and pinkish-purple female cones. She could only hope it would survive the wildfire heading its way.

After she saw the last of the moccasin

heels, she dashed off in the opposite direction, heading downstream. The river was low; rocks she had never seen before showed their round tops and she jumped from rock to rock like a mountain goat. By late afternoon she had reached the spot where the Cokahlarishkit ran into the Clark Fork River. Eating pemmican on the move, she followed this larger river through a heavily wooded valley her Salish Indian friends called *Im-i-sul-étiku,* which meant "by the cold, chilling waters."

"These waters are hot as hell right now," she told her aching feet.

Some Salish, showing their morbid sense of humor, said a better translation was "the place chilled with fear," since Blackfeet considered it the ideal spot for ambushes. French trappers passing through discovered so many Salish skulls and bones that they named the narrow canyon *Porte de l'Enfer,* or Hell Gate. As she passed through, curling and twisting smoke followed her, sticking mostly to the ridges and sides of the mountains but sometimes creeping toward her like the dark fingers of strangers. Her clammy feet whimpered like small dogs. "Hell Gate for damn sure," she said to them, and she made them move faster. Her feet, especially the left one, had never toughened up enough to suit her in all these years of roaming. She seldom received their full cooperation and could not trust them to act in her best interests. They blistered and faltered too easily. In contrast, her thighs and calves were sturdy and rugged, but also untrustworthy, for they were willing to march to her death in silence. She only measured distance in terms of how her knees and lungs behaved, and they were still behaving well.

Even with low water, the Clark Fork posed a problem if she wanted to keep going south without getting the goods in her cradleboard wet. But she remembered her Salish friends stashed a bullboat in a willow grove just beyond where the Clark Fork received the northern-flowing Bitterroot River. She located the compact craft — willow branches bent into the shape of a bowl and covered by a bull buffalo hide with the hair still on — and paddled across, the boat spinning all the while like a wooden top. On the far bank, she hid the boat in the bushes and plopped down on stones that were usually wet. She sighed, thankful to have reached before darkness the Place of the Bitterroot, named for the small pink flower with the nourishing roots. White people said that explorer Meriwether Lewis discovered the bitterroot plant, but for generations the Salish had been harvesting the roots and feasting on these delicacies. She had been doing the same for half a dozen years. The Salish believed that an animating power in the universe surged through everything in this wondrous place, and though she found all religions suspicious, trying to maintain her disbelief here had always challenged her.

She removed her cradleboard and lay down on the rocks. There had been no sunset and there would be no stars. She fell asleep dreaming of bitterroots — the roots and the flowers — and the people with a spiritual connection to them. Those were practically her people now. Sometimes she forgot that. Self-reliance only went so far, and so did denying the biggest problem for woman or man living alone in the mountains — loneliness.

A hooting owl and other night noises woke her. Fitful flashes in the northern Bitterroots caught her attention — lightning strikes without rain falling. Telltale smoke let her know that fire burned there, too, in her beloved high country, which had always meant a feeling of rapture more than simply a remote, rocky place near the clouds. She had lived in other unsettled (at least by white people) spots, high and low, clear to the High Plains, but she always came back here, her heart and the rest of her — except maybe her left foot — guided by sacred mountain light. The wall of rugged granite peaks that usually comforted her now loomed over her like an unbroken row of gigantic hungry vultures. The smoke clouds might have been playing tricks on her, but those ugly birds began all at once to flap their wings. Years of surviving on the edge had served to minimize her fear of death, but this vision unnerved her — vultures scavenging at an hour when only owls and bats should have been out. As easily as night follows day, mountain gloom had replaced mountain glory.

She jerked her head down, sending sweat flying from her forehead. She scooped up her cradleboard and put it on her back as she ran in the darkness. She thought far ahead once more to the Moon When the Rivers Start to Freeze, November, which created ice patches inside her head and provided some relief even as balls of sweat tumbled from her armpits. But she wondered if five or six moons would be enough time for her to forget her bloody, bone-dry nameless creek.

All that thinking and wondering distracted her and she forgot to keep an eye on her unreliable feet. She stumbled and fell to her knees, skinning the left one. Instead of continuing to fight the darkness, she lay back down for a few more hours of broken sleep. She rose with the sun and trod lightly on the land out of habit if not respect, but now the land burned rudely above her and behind her. The smoke caught up to her and danced circles around her. The parched and drooping brown grass turned to charred stubble. Her footprints would be buried in ash if she didn't move faster.

"At least," she told a watchful mule deer in the distance, "the fire and smoke keep away the mosquitoes and flies."

A clap of thunder made the mule deer's ears move in two different directions at once before the skittish animal took a bounding leap in its chosen direction — away from her. The deer disappeared into a hillside thicket, but she listened to the clatter of its hooves until another thunderclap drowned them out and turned her head. An enormous bird appeared, its wings spanning the sky between two mountain peaks. The wings beat fiercely, generating yet another loud, rainless storm. Lightning flashed from the creature's eyes, and dark clouds rolled out of its beak like sinister laughter. Vultures were mere fleas compared to this mythical creature, the Thunderbird.

"You are real then?" she asked, hardly believing her own eyes. No answer came, but she hadn't expected one. Some questions out here never got answered. Many Indians had told her of the Thunderbird, though they never agreed on its exact appearance or its true nature. A Sioux medicine man she met on the Upper Missouri during her time with the Arapahos told her that a Thunderbird came with each of the four directions but the one out of the West was by far the mightiest. She squinted into the powerful wind and barely made out two crooked horns sprouting from its head and red feathers all about its powerful beak. It wore a red zigzag lightning bolt on its broad back. Its wings, glowing crimson at the tips, flapped harder, fanning the fires.

She had heard Indians talk of Thunderbirds as being sacred, spiritual, shapeshifters, tricksters, protectors, predators, contrarians, creators, and destroyers. The Sioux medicine man had stressed at the very least the Thunderbird's dual nature — it generated rain that gave life to people, plants, and the earth; it brought hailstones and flood that destroyed the same. Well, this Thunderbird out of the West seemed ornery, delivering thunder, lightning, and fire without a drop of rain. Could it be part of the Great Spirit or the Great Mystery of Creation? Indians credited activity on earth they could not explain to animal spirits. Not so strange. She had heard white people speak of angry gods and her own mother tell of one God acting in mysterious ways.

The Thunderbird suddenly turned upside down, showed its tail feathers, and flew backward until it disappeared. She tried not to take it personally, but that wasn't easy to do when you lived the solitary life. Meanwhile, the storm blew itself out and the Place of the Bitterroot became quiet. She took a deep breath, and when her lungs didn't fill with smoke, she walked on, mostly staring at her weary feet but on occasion glancing nervously at the sky over the serrated peaks. For many hours she listened to the rhythm of her steps while squashing the complaints of her feet. She rested infrequently and gnawed pemmican on the move through a day that had little sun but was still hot. With again no sunset or stars to guide her, time escaped her. But when her lungs heaved and her knees buckled simultaneously, she stopped in the late afternoon or the night, whatever it was. Prepared to collapse on the spot, she noticed an inviting rocky ledge and made her feet go that much farther. With her last bit of strength, she clambered onto the ledge and found herself facing a cave entrance. It was new to her, but she stooped her head and entered without hesitation, knowing the cozy shelter would cool her.

Inside the cave she removed her cradleboard, flopped stomach first against a smooth rock bed, and folded up her coonskin cap for a pillow. She slept until dawn, but not so deeply that she didn't remember visits from three bear cubs, two jaybirds, a flying squirrel, a fawn, a family of little brown bats, a great horned owl, an assortment of spiders, the shadow of a Thunderbird, and the lifeless stare of a redheaded man. Nights could be like that, whether in a cave or a tepee or under open sky. Smoke stayed out of the cave, but she smelled it when she peered out, looking in vain for the rising sun. She retreated to the rear of the cave where the low ceiling with funnel-shaped spiderwebs made it necessary to crawl. She liked that sometimes — smaller spaces. And she could live with spiders. She decided she wasn't hungry enough to look in the cradleboard for food or revitalized enough to start walking just yet. She couldn't imagine a better shelter from the heat of day or from the agony of the soles of her feet. "This day," she said to a long-legged spider on the cave wall, "is best spent on my stomach."

Although she had never made anything but a cookfire or a winter fire to warm her bones, Bet had roamed on land that fire had changed, for better or worse, for more than fifteen years. Most of the fires she had known were intentionally ignited by the Indian tribes rather than by the Thunderbirds. But now things were different. The grasses and trees were burning in every direction in the high country where no Indians lived. The fire, she could sense even when the smoke hid it or now when she was inside this cave, was out of control, working its way downward to the lower grasslands like a hungry beast. Whether Thunderbirds or gods or any other supernatural beings were behind it or not, the intense burning was lightning caused. It would not stop until a hard rain fell, and that was highly unlikely in this time of drought.

Most Indians set purpose fires and tried to control them. Bet's Salish friend Schweeleh, who she now admitted she wanted to see, said that his people had never set a fire in the wrong season or let one rage destructively. His name meant "Water

Snake," and several times he had found hidden springs for her when she was thirsty and provided food when she was hungry. Once she had thought of him as her savior, but despite all their shared campfires she had never called him, or any man, *her* man. It had never been her wish to live in his village or to depend on him too much. It was all right to go to him now, she told herself, for she hadn't seen him in more than a dozen moons, since before the drought.

She remembered during a Moon of Drying Grass when they fell asleep in each other's arms while their circle of fire was still glowing and then didn't awaken until the flames rose on three sides of them. Instead of fleeing with her, Schweeleh stood his ground, calmly studied the flames, and then executed the personal rain dance that he had developed without any tribal support. It worked just as it had the night they first met at Lolo Pass. The Water Snake knew what he was doing. So much rain fell that the brushfire drowned in minutes and their campsite became a pool deep enough to please an actual water snake. Hours later, when they were on high ground laughing and flirting, she teased him, saying if he had been an ordinary Indian instead of one blessed with a Water Spirit, he would have caused the first uncontrolled fire in the history of the Salish people. That had stopped both his laughter, for his sense of humor stretched only so far, and his flirting, for his sense of responsibility to his tribe was enormous. "I must go take up the bow before I anger the spirits," he told her. "The enemies of my people grow near." His knees were known to tingle when Blackfeet were around. In any event, he had left her half-dressed in a meadow of blue flowers and ridden like the wind to his village. And, as she now recalled while lying on her stomach in her dry cave, that was the last time Schweeleh had touched her with his good heart and strong hands.

She reflected on other campfires, too, and other men — some Indian, some white, some half-bloods, two blacks, one brown. Shared campfires were good as long as the other party was invited, didn't drink himself rotten-mean, or overstay his welcome. Unshared campfires were good, too. Most of her campfires during the past half-dozen years in the mountains had been unshared, often remote, some lonely, some not, and in all but a few instances providing warmth inside her as well as out. Unshared campfires, though, tended to all blur together and burn out quickly in her mind. On this day on her stomach, she wanted to remember only shared campfires, and her memories belonged to her entire body.

But then her mind, like an Indian contrary, went off in the opposite direction. She remembered the recent non-campfire event, the Ignoble Incident — too disturbing to allow for rest or normal breathing. She turned onto her side, her back, her other side, but no position could relieve the pressure in her head or the discomfort in her body. She sat up and her head banged against the rock ceiling. Dazed, she rolled out of her suddenly suffocating spot to where the cave opened wider. Still, she didn't have enough space to breathe. She screamed, something she had not done in the presence of the redheaded mountain man who never gave his name. No fire had been made; he had not wanted a hot meal or coffee and had not tried to warm her up with words. He had entered her tepee at daybreak as uninvited as death. His hair was blood red; his mangy beard was blood red; his face was blood red. She saw it all once more — all the rushing blood. He was burning from the inside out.

She crossed her legs Indian style, and then crossed her arms at her chest. She had known her share of mountain men, and her one rendezvous in the Cache Valley crossed her mind. As drunk and crude as those fur trappers there had been, not one had been vicious mean like the redheaded bastard who invaded her tepee. The horror scene with the redheaded mountain man played out in her head once again. She made herself recall every word spoken, every action in detail because if she pushed the truth aside now, she knew it would resurface later in bits and pieces of inaccurate, convoluted, and painful memory. She might even come to doubt whether she had been justified in killing him. She couldn't allow that to happen.

She nodded off to sleep while sitting up. When she awoke an hour later, she was still sitting like a stone, her arms and legs tightly crossed. She was glad *not* to be crawling or lying as dead as mutton. It took her awhile to find her bearings. When she did, she smiled. It was nice to be in a dark cave, maybe one no man had been in since prehistoric times. She felt safe. But her feet had gone to sleep and balked at waking up. She rubbed them through her moccasins and then rose slowly, thinking how troublesome her feet could be. She would have done better thinking about her head, which struck the low ceiling so hard that she dropped to her knees.

"You got me," she said, wiping her watery eyes. "But I'm still *not* praying."

Now she did begin to crawl, anxious to find her coonskin cap. She stopped abruptly when her head butted a cave wall. The pain shot straight to her neck. She uttered a half dozen damns and one drawn-out "tarnation," the way Pappy Hex used to say it when his pipe wouldn't stay lit or he couldn't locate his stashed-away bottle of whiskey. But then she laughed at herself, and the more her head throbbed, the more she laughed. She thought she might die laughing. She remembered her brothers and sisters tickling her mercilessly in the Kentucky cabin just because she was the youngest and still running around shirtless. "Never fear, Betty II," Aunt Betty used to tell her. "Laughter is almost never fatal, not even in the long run." Her aunt was no doubt right, Bet decided. Something else must have rubbed out the prehistoric cavemen. Something else would surely kill her, too.

She needn't have worried. Her happy tears turned bitter soon enough, and it was only her laughter that died. Seeing the boiling-hot bearded face of the redheaded man in a dark corner of the cave was what did it. She realized that remembering every detail of his appearance and actions was damn easy. Forgetting would be the hard part, the impossible part. His bloodshot eyes pierced holes in her flesh as he bared his ferocious yellow teeth. What an ugly vision, uglier than all the swooping vultures on earth. He was pure evil, but he was not Satan. He was not immortal. Although the violent scene at her old camp kept playing out in her mind, she now allowed herself to picture what she had missed the first time at the nearly dry creek — seeing bits of the mountain man's blackened flesh peeling away, smelling his tendons and muscles burning. Killing and skinning animals had never come as easy for her as it did for the mountain men she knew, but she had done her share of both to survive. And that man with the fiery hair and face, the one she called Sunshine, had been worse than any four-legged animal she had known. To kill something did not make one evil.

"He got what was coming to him," she said, pounding a fist against the cave wall. "That crazy white bastard needed to die." She opened her fist and kissed her bleeding knuckles. "A mountain woman's gotta do what a mountain woman's gotta do."

If she had a motto to live by, that was it.

The man had deserved to be punished swiftly and severely, and she wasn't one to count on God to do the punishing later on. The lightning fire that consumed him had merely added a touch of extra justice, compliments of some greater power — nature, the white man's God, or the Indians' Thunderbird.

CHAPTER FIVE

She had settled everything in her head, but in a flash all became unsettled. She didn't know why. Maybe, like the dead man said, she was crazy. The cave walls that had been sheltering and comforting her began to close in on her. She needed to move again under the open sky — now!

She put on the loaded cradleboard and rushed like a panicked humpback mole to the cave entrance. The outside provided no immediate relief. The smoke and the clouds melded, blocking out any blue. Worse, fire had spread like lava, blocking her exit. Its crackles sounded like vile laughter. Flames licked up the tall pine trees. The heat caused her to shield her face, and her feet shuffled backward without consulting her mind. In her predicament, she questioned herself all over again. Had she really needed to kill the redheaded mountain man? Had something evil inside her triggered her brutal act of vengeance? Was God or some spirit of the mountains now punishing her? Mama Hex's God had been more about divine retribution than forgiveness.

"Beware," Mama Hex told all her children when they misbehaved. "Better folks than us have burned in hell."

"Or frozen in heaven," Aunt Betty would counter. "The notion that we will feel hot and cold when we're gone is preposterous."

Bet shook her head; she didn't need to hear from either woman at the moment. She needed a way out; she wanted to live. She reprimanded herself for acting helpless. She was neither a wan white woman cultured to insignificance because no red-blooded man possessed her, nor a beaten-down squaw doing the constant bidding of some me-first buffalo hunter. Still, for a moment, she wished her Salish friend Schweeleh would appear to do his rain dance. In the next moment she wished he had taught her the rain dance so she could put out the fire herself. And then she remembered a distant time when she saw her Arapaho lover Red Elk and other tribesmen build a fire, spread the glowing coals, and then do a high-stepping dance on them until they had stomped out the fire. Finally, she said to hell with dancing, and she ran and leaped into the fire as if being chased by the devil himself.

She expected the worst, envisioning burns over ninety percent of her body and Mama Hex bathing her in butter, freshly churned in the world of the dead. With no clear path, she closed her eyes and plowed ahead like a blind buffalo. Somehow, she made it through the flames without feeling pain or becoming scorched. Upon opening her eyes, a clear road, familiar to her, showed itself at her feet. Had a miracle unfolded? She considered the possibility that nothing could harm her, that she would safely walk this land for all eternity. Vulnerability and invincibility were like the two sides of a coin she kept flipping in her head.

When she sat down to remove a pebble, she discovered a burn blister spread across her left heel and both moccasins blackened. She sighed but choked on smoke. She was hot clear through, and she ached for water. No time for further rest. She ignored her throbbing feet and twitching calves, smacked her iron thighs, and stood on surprisingly shaky ground. She walked gingerly now, barely able to stay a step ahead of the trailing smoke.

"Neither the Thunderbird nor the giant

vultures nor the ghost of Sunshine can catch me," she shouted, trying to recapture her invincibility. "I have transformed into the great long-legged Water Bird. I'll find the powerful Water Snake and we'll mate and become immortal."

She even sounded a little crazy to herself. What she found immediately were the tracks and dung of animals, large and small. She followed animal sign to a water hole known to her and the Indians, but it was dried up, and she needed to get on her knees to squeeze powdered mud to wet her lips.

"I'm a poor excuse for a water bird," she admitted, laughing even as she licked her blistered lips with a swollen tongue. "A mountain woman is what I am and will always be. It doesn't make me a crazy bitch, dammit. I got a right to talk to myself. I got a right to protect myself. I got a right to . . . find water."

Once she was back in her walking rhythm with her thighs leading the rest of her legs, she reconfirmed that being a mountain woman was good enough for her. She was as stubborn, independent, and resourceful as any mountain man. She knew how to survive in a man's world — an animal's world, really. She knew what could get her killed. For years she had withstood every danger, every threat that crossed her path. The lightning fires — like the drought, the heat of day, the loneliness of night, the precipices, the grizzly bears, the wolf packs, the Blackfeet, the mountain men, the angry Indian spirits, the forsaken God, and the long-ago floods — called for caution, not fear. Self-reliant and strong of mind and body, that was what Betty II had become. Aunt Betty would be proud of her — a comforting thought now, as it had been for each of her years roaming the mountain west. With renewed confidence, she strode off the main trail to a stone ledge from which dripped, in slow but harmonious rhythm, almost cool water. She knelt in front of it, positioned her wide-open mouth, and patiently waited for each precious drop to fall on her tongue.

Her thirst nearly quenched and her resolve strengthened, she scanned the horizon in all directions looking for any wisps of smoke or sign of the Thunderbird. Seeing nothing that threatened or frightened her, she licked her lips and pushed on, passing a series of small caves.

"Not enough water, not enough shelter, not far enough away," she said to a turkey vulture that appeared out of nowhere and circled above her. This one, she was almost certain, was real, not a vision. "I can outlast you and your bigger brothers, too!"

From now on she would leave the caves to the wild beasts. If worse came to worst she knew she could set a course down to the Bitterroot River, which always had some water, drought notwithstanding. What she wanted was suitable fresh ground to set up a new tepee, and she knew she would find it sooner or later — she always did. She returned to the main trail that largely ran parallel to the river and headed south up the valley. She saw in the baked dry soil many prints of unshod Salish ponies and the lines where they had pulled the travois. She was anticipating a good tepee site in the mountains up one of the side canyons, but sticking to this valley road would surely bring her first to Schweeleh's village, and that thought, though kept in the back of her mind, was pleasurable.

While she generally knew the lay of this land, she had never set up a tepee this far up the valley. The site she envisioned must be near running water or a spring, protected from the west wind, far from fire and smoke, high enough to be above the pathways of migrating people but not so high as to cause her to freeze up alone come winter. She would not rush her search. The right-size trees for tepee poles grew all along the mountainsides; she simply had to reach the ones out of the fire range. But she would need buffalo hides to stretch over the pole frame, food, tobacco, extra clothing, a second pair of moccasins, and a backup weapon, preferably another pipe tomahawk. To acquire these things, she must rely on her trading and gambling skills, her valuable yellow hair, and a natural magnetism that made people want to give her gifts. It would take time, how long she didn't know, nor did it matter. Her life had become almost timeless, and timelessness was on her side. Yes, snow days and cold nights would come as they always had, but no time soon. With so much heat on her tail she could no more imagine an early winter than she could President Andrew Jackson showing up for a tour of the Place of the Bitterroot.

The familiar ground she walked on wore a brown disguise, and the jagged tops of the mountains to the west still partially hid behind a veil of smoke. Sweat beads rolled from her chin, ran down from her armpits, pooled on her palms, and swished around inside her breechclout. For a time all she could think about was her legs in motion, putting one foot down and then the other, advancing — or was it retreating? — step by step. But her brain refused to accept the tedium of fatigue, and in defiance of her feet again soon bristled with energy. When Meriwether Lewis and William Clark traveled across this same area three decades earlier on their way to the Far Ocean, they had encountered ten fires: three caused by lightning, seven by Indians. She had heard this tabulation from a traveling half-blood called Halahtookit, whose name meant Daytime Smoke. Halahtookit, who had blue eyes and reddish hair, claimed to be a product of an Indian-style marriage between Clark and a Nez Perce woman. Bet believed him about the fires but not so much about his father. Her Salish friend Schweeleh also told of a black-haired, dark-eyed uncle of his named Willie Tonka who had claimed to be Clark's son. This uncle's captivating Salish mother, according to Schweeleh, had known many good husbands, like William Clark, and produced an equal number of fine sons, including Uncle Willie Tonka. Schweeleh said he looked like his late uncle. Bet liked that story, true or not, because when she was at loose ends, it made her feel connected to something besides the no-man's-land where she lived. Stories like that, along with her own stories about Aunt

Betty, sustained her.

"Many happy campfires," she shouted to a passing blue bird, also headed south.

Schweeleh had jumped to the front of her mind. She savored thoughts of her old friend but had to cut them short. The smoke that had been trailing her now partially enveloped her. Was there no end to it? She must have slowed down, or else the wind had kicked up at her back. "Land's sake!" she shouted, using Pappy Hex's favorite exclamation for the first time in years. "Not time to think of happy campfires." She demanded that her blackened moccasins move faster. Since Lewis and Clark had passed this way the fire and smoke had returned each summer, but never this early or with such fierceness. She also knew that fires in the western mountains had been going on for thousands of years before the white man, let alone the white woman, arrived. And before the Indians ignited them, ancient lightning did it. Lightning was striking again, perhaps harder than ever, as if to prove it was king of the fires. Nobody claimed Clark was the father of fire.

Her mood changed again when she was sure she was walking where the fire and smoke had not yet visited. She breathed deeply but easily and smiled with each step.

Her stride, boosted by hope, lengthened. She could not imagine being happier anywhere else on earth. She confirmed in her wandering mind that her new home site must be in the mountains of the Bitterroot, and no matter what, she must never leave the Bitterroot again. In the meantime, though, seeing Schweeleh in the valley would provide immediate gratification.

Schweeleh was no mama's boy like that Nez Perce buffalo hunter Yellow Bull, who had lured her that one time to the other side of the Bitterroot Mountains. Schweeleh was his own man, a rare one who understood and accepted that her ways and her thinking were unlike those of other women, red or white. She thought she could hear her heart keeping the beat for her footsteps as she approached the bend in the Bitterroot River where she expected to find the village. But her heart sank and her feet dragged as she drew closer. She saw no tepees, only holes in the dirt, one broken pole, campfire rings, cooking pits, and half-buried elk bones. The bent blades of grass and patterns in the dirt told her that the Salish ponies and dogs had dragged the travois further up the valley. The Blackfeet, unless desperate for ponies or scalps, rarely came this far south. The wildfires might.

She would grit her teeth and keep walking, for the village had to be somewhere, and no matter what threats they faced, the Salish would never desert the Place of the Bitterroot.

Long after the sun went down, she was still following the lodge trail until she stumbled onto a corral of sleeping ponies and sighed so hard that a spotted stallion whinnied. She assured him that she was no Blackfeet raider out to steal him. She had ridden her share of horses, and they were dear to her heart like most four-legged creatures, but she didn't want to get anywhere so fast that she would need to ride. Besides, owning a horse would only be another mouth to feed, and most any man in this country would be tempted to take it away from her.

"I go everywhere on my own legs like you do, boy," she told the stallion. "Of course, I only have two."

A little beyond the corral she came to skin tepees and then several conical cedar bark houses on wooden frames and a long ceremonial lodge. One of the houses had a white cross over the door. She figured Schweeleh, an altogether traditional fellow, must be in one of the tepees, maybe even dreaming of her. All the tepees looked alike, and her feet were screaming. Finding him would keep till morning.

She entered the ceremonial lodge, struggled out of her cradleboard, and dropped off to sleep on a grass mat where she knew some Salish kneeled and prayed to the white man's God, much as Mama Hex used to do at the Sunday prayer meetings in Kentucky. Bet never prayed at night or anytime to any god, not once in the seventeen years since leaving Boonville, Missouri Territory, and heading up the Missouri River with fur trader Manuel Lisa and his third wife. She had encountered enough frontier horrors — from nature and man — to realize that praying made no more sense than wishing upon a star or wearing a bear-claw necklace to keep smallpox at bay. The white God, she imagined, was more likely female than male and not of a mind to keep watch on the wild side of the Missouri River where there were no preachers or churches to resist the works of the devil.

Chapter Six

Bet Hex slept until midmorning, interrupted only once by nightmare — a great red bear biting off her head. When she emerged from the ceremonial lodge, the sun was bright and hard. She saw children playing games with strings, sticks, and rings and women butchering, cooking, washing, tending to young children, and shooing away the older ones. She saw no man. A woman stepped forward, crossed her arms, and stared — a stare as dark as her raven-black hair. She wore a two-skin dress decorated front and back with deer tails, with a tightly cinched beaded belt drawing in a wisp of a waist. She looked too young to be a mother of any of the children.

"You want Schweeleh," she said, sniffing as if Bet smelled bad. "He no here."

Bet struggled to remember the young woman's name, but she remembered those eyes that flickered in darkness like moth wings. The woman put her hands on her wide hips and explained in broken English and sign language that Schweeleh had gone with the other hunters on a fifteen-day journey to reach the grassy plains on the other side of the river of the Red Paint (the Missouri) in search of buffalo. That made sense because the Salish shamans and animal spirits rarely could summon buffalo into the Place of the Bitterroot. But Bet hung her head at the news because, besides the one nightmare, she had dreamed about shared campfires through the night.

Instead of speaking of her disappointment, she raised her chin and corrected the dark-eyed woman: "The journey to the hunting place takes but ten days."

If she had been a boastful woman, she could have added that two times she had made the trip with Schweeleh and the other hunters, and that one of those times they had barely escaped thrashings from the more numerous and better-armed Blackfeet. The perpetual warfare between the two tribes stemmed largely from two facts of life — the Blackfeet refused to share the buffalo, and killing Salish kept the Blackfeet warriors alert and in good training for slaying more formidable foes. The other woman sat down on a log and shook her head, before

97

explaining with elaborate hand signals that the men did not follow the usual People's Trail, but took a less direct, more southerly route.

"To avoid the Blackfeet?" Bet asked, knowing how much even brave Salish warriors, let alone this woman, feared their tribe's traditional enemy.

"Avoid . . ." The woman shot her arms into the air and made noises more like a cannonball exploding than a raging fire. She stared far off while twisting the beads on her necklace. Worry lines on her forehead made her look older than her years, but she was younger than Bet, much younger.

"Yes," Bet said, taking a seat on the log. "Many fires out there. Like hell on earth."

The woman looked confused. Bet wasn't sure if the Salish even had a word for hell, but she shouted "Hell!" anyway, as if saying the word louder would make Dark Eyes understand better. Perhaps the recently arrived Christian Indians among the Salish had taught this woman the true meaning of hell. Dark Eyes raised her hands and pressed the palms together at her chest as if preparing to pray. But then she yanked out from the top of her dress a dried-up white bog orchid that she clutched as a good luck charm. The woman's eyes grew moist and reddened, though her lips and tongue stayed dry and brown. It dawned on Bet that Dark Eyes was worried to tears over one of the hunters.

"You know me," Bet said, taking off her coonskin cap to give the woman a better look. "And you know I know Schweeleh."

"Schweeleh," the woman whispered, and then she sniffed her white bog orchid.

"I know I have seen you before when your village was to the north."

The woman nodded once and reached out with her left hand, the one not holding the orchid. She touched Bet's yellow hair, half stroking it and half twisting the ends. "Pretty."

"Thank you, I think. Ouch. How well do you know Schweeleh?"

The woman jerked back her hand as if she had touched fire. Her eyes lost their wet redness, but they didn't turn back to dark. She kissed the orchid and stuffed it back in her dress. Her chest heaved.

"At least the rivers and creeks will be low for the men to cross safely," Bet said, as much to reassure herself as to comfort the woman on the log.

The woman stood abruptly, wiped a chunk of bark off the seat of her dress, and, with a look of defiance, placed her hands on her hips again. "Ponies, hunters swim good," she practically shouted.

Bet had seen Schweeleh swim many times, mostly when he was buck naked, but she said nothing more. For two men to fight over one woman was foolish but understandable, since men fought over most anything. But she saw no reason for two women to fight over one man. Besides, Schweeleh was too wise to let a silly, worrying woman like Dark Eyes latch on to his buckskins.

"He no here, no here," the Indian woman said again, stomping her right moccasin with each word. As she walked off, she looked back, her eyes now red like fire. "You go."

Salish people as a rule were hospitable. This female was an exception, but jealousy could do that. Salish women were no more immune to the green-eyed monster than were the ladies of St. Louis or Louisville. None of them wanted to stay single long. What Salish woman wouldn't want the most eligible single man in the village for her very own? Dark Eyes joined a long list. But Schweeleh had rejected them all no matter how hard they tried to shine for him. Bet chuckled at that fact and then tried to remember without success the last time she had made that kind of sound. She stretched toward the sky and found herself blinded by the high noon sun. Just like that she remembered the name of the rejected wide-hipped Indian woman — Spukani, which meant "Sun." That unsettled Bet some, because the sun had obvious power and appeared each day to deliver light and heat to the miniscule human beings beneath it. But what power could Spukani possibly have?

"Damn silly woman," Bet muttered to a curious spotted dog that kept its distance but wagged its tail. As she started for the heart of the village, she waved to the children, some of whom recognized her from her coonskin cap, yellow hair, and breechclout. No Indian mother looked like her. "I am not going anywhere just yet," she told a little girl who was biting one of her braids while peeking out from behind the narrow backside of her older sister. "And hello to you, too. Don't be shy. I'm *not* really a stranger, and I am *not* a strange man. My moccasins may be black from fire, but I'm no Blackfeet."

When the little girl smiled, Bet thought it might be nice to one day put her own infant instead of food and supplies inside her cradleboard. Yes, it would be another mouth to feed, but a baby was not a horse. She

101

rubbed her belly, thinking the seed might still be growing inside her. Either that or she was hungry.

The two sisters took her to their secret place where the flowers of the arrowleaf balsamroot created a yellow glow. The older girl and then the younger one each handed her a green arrow-shaped leaf to eat raw. "If I ever have a baby girl," she told them as she chewed. "I want her to be like you, both of you." She pointed to them and then tapped her belly. Of course, they could have no idea what she was talking about. Maybe they thought she was thanking them for the plant food. Anyway, they giggled. With or without Schweeleh, she would stay awhile. Many others in the village knew of her and liked her, and she wanted to renew their acquaintances before she went off alone to the mountains. Besides that, she had important business to transact.

Nobody turned her away. She visited in the tepees of unthreatened women and elderly men, some of whom remembered the visiting French fur traders who called them Têtes-Plates or when Lewis and Clark passed by and called them either Flatheads or Tushepaus (the people with shaved heads). Their kindness boosted her spirits.

She could do without Schweeleh, of course, but that didn't mean she had to like it.

As she suspected, the current village site was only a few weeks old. With lightning flashes and ominous smoke appearing in the northern sky daily at the old site, the women, elderly men, children, and several braves left behind had moved their village south as a preventative measure. Left Hand, one of the elderly men who knew far more English words than Bet did Salish words, told her this; he had once been a fighting Salish with the scars on his face to prove it, but now he stood with difficulty to greet her and wore a cross around his withered neck — more for the cross's pleasing shape than what it stood for. Those who remained in the village, he said, would neither sit in place waiting for fire to consume them nor starve to death waiting for the buffalo meat to arrive. He added that when the young buffalo hunters returned, they would have to search for the village; in the meantime, he would delight in protecting the squaws from the Blackfeet. He gave her a toothless grin and most of his pemmican, since chewing it proved too difficult for him.

"We do what we must do — like you, Pale Woman Who Lives in Mountains Alone," Left Hand said, using a nickname well known to the friendly Salish, Kootenais, and Pend d'Oreilles, and possibly even to the disagreeable Blackfeet. It sounded better than "Crazy White Bitch Who Runs Around the Rockies."

"You have a good heart, Left Hand."

"You have teeth strong and good, Pale Woman Who Lives in Mountains Alone."

She smiled back and thanked him. He raised his trembling, bony right hand as if to touch her front teeth. She moved her face closer, but he touched her cheek instead.

"I am no longer pale, Left Hand," she said. She slipped off her coonskin cap, and his right hand steadied as it stroked her hair for nearly a minute.

"Your hair is still yellow," the old man stated. "Like the sunflower."

"It's funny you touch me with only your right hand."

"Right hand for love and friendship. Left hand for hunting and war."

She thought it would be better if he was called "Right Hand," but names didn't matter that much. She gave his right hand a squeeze and he gave her a stalk of wild rhubarb and tobacco from a plot he still tended — using both hands, he admitted.

Left Hand was hardly the only one to admire her yellow hair in the next few days.

She acquired a good supply of tangy bitter-roots, wild carrots, and *pstchelu* (white roots), as well as a pair of moccasins, by clipping off locks and trading them to villagers of both sexes who wanted yellow hair for religious, superstitious, or sentimental reasons without resorting to scalping her. She had the hair to spare, and it was good as gold. She was unwilling to trade any more of her than that, which was just as well since many of these Salish were better Christians than her, and most of the others, by tribal custom, frowned upon adulterous and even premarital sexual relations. With Schweeleh everything was different. They hardly needed words for their mind-to-mind communication, and their bodies merged as naturally as a couple of jackrabbits. But Schweeleh was far away. Her time in the village now was all business.

Her gambling with the old men proved the most productive. They liked to watch her adeptly toss the beaver-tooth dice by hand like a man instead of in a basket like the Salish women did. They believed the trickster spirit Coyote had sent her and that they must lose to her or else face much greater losses in the days to come. She put her hair, her moccasins, her buffalo robe, and her only pipe tomahawk on the line but lost nothing. She won much tobacco, or rather a mixture of white man's tobacco and *kinnikinnick,* a horn for keeping herbs, a buffalo bladder water pouch, a pair of elk-skin mittens, skins for a tepee cover, and even another breechclout. The old men laughed even as they lost, for they had accumulated many things they could spare, especially to such an unusual player. She kissed each old man on his leathery forehead for being such a good loser.

One squinty-eyed gentleman who watched instead of gambled decided for Bet's own protection to give her a small American flag that Lewis and Clark had given him. He apologized for the hole in the center of the flag made by a Blackfeet arrow. She promised to wear the flag close to her heart and stuck it into her deerskin shirt. These people, with the exception of the jealous Spukani, treated her right. But her cradleboard grew heavy and could hold nothing more, and every fiber of her body twitched after four days of mostly sitting around in the village. She did not want to overstay her welcome. She wanted to find her own home.

CHAPTER SEVEN

On the fifth day in the Salish village, she said her goodbyes quickly to the elderly men and unthreatened women, while the children followed her to the southern edge of the village as if she were the Pied Piper. None other than Spukani ran after her and called her back. The wide-hipped, dark-eyed woman offered no apology, but she bowed and then begged Bet to come listen to Joseph Logan speak before God at the long ceremonial lodge. Unhappy memories of the prayer meetings back in Kentucky and her recent encounter with the repulsive redheaded man (why had God, if there was a God, permitted such a man to live so long?) surfaced like belligerent snapping turtles and she tried to shake them out of her head. But the boys and girls tugged at her shirtsleeves and leggings until she relented. Curiosity won out as much as the pleas of Spukani and the children. The only white people she had encountered in the past decade were mountain men, and she had seen one too many of them. A cross-bearing missionary would be something different.

Joseph Logan stood tall before a packed house, his skin as dark as his white man's trousers. Spukani explained that the God-fearing man was an educated Eastern Indian, one of a dozen Iroquois *engagés* of the Hudson's Bay Company who had come to the Bitterroots to trap beaver and then stayed on to marry Salish women. The tribe, suffering from a shortage of healthy young men because of war with the Blackfeet, had adopted them all. Most of these Iroquois husbands, however, had not come to fight. They had introduced the Salish to Catholicism and told of white men in black robes who wore crosses and taught people of all races how to know God and to live in a better place after death. The most prominent of the Iroquois was Joseph Logan, who had chosen for his wife Spukani's sister Sakaam, which meant "Moon."

Bet listened to Joseph Logan give personal testimony in both English and Salish to how he had killed many Americans and their Indian allies until he found salvation, physically and spiritually, first in Upper Canada and now in the Place of the Bitterroot. He spoke of the one and only true God and the religion of miracles preached by the fair-skinned Black Robes, who he promised would one day come to this place from the American city of St. Louis to save more souls, as had been prophesied by the great Salish medicine man, Shining Shirt. Joseph Logan's audience looked spellbound. He led the people in Catholic chants, songs, and prayers that he said must be learned to perfection. Creator god Amotken and the five Mothers, old animal spirits, and Salish shamans, he insisted, were no longer strong enough to keep Blackfeet, disease, and fire out of the Place of the Bitterroot; it was now up to the Catholic saints. He seemed to lose his audience somewhat, though, when he spoke of good and evil, heaven and hell.

Bet saw the confusion on Spukani's face. "Schweeleh would never stand for this," Bet told her. "He thinks white man's white-god religion eats at an Indian's soul. No matter how hard the times, he will believe in the ancient spirit helpers, in particular his Water Snake Spirit."

Spukani nodded, but her mind seemed far away, and not on any kind of religion.

Bet's mind was on other things, too —

like leaving. She stood up and then bent down to lift her weighty cradleboard once more.

"He ask me marry," Spukani said. "I say no."

"What? Who?"

"Joseph."

"Oh, him."

"No marry. Schweeleh too much here." Spukani pounded a fist over her heart.

"Oh. I see."

"He next ask her." Spukani pointed to the front row, where her sister Sakaam sat at Joseph Logan's feet, letting everyone know she already knew all the chants.

"Some men will do that."

"Schweeleh no ask you?"

"To marry him? Well, no, but he understands me and . . ."

"He ask me maybe."

Bet suppressed a chuckle but said nothing.

"You go now, yes?"

"I've been trying to go. This was your idea."

"Joseph Logan."

"Yes, the good Catholic. What about him?"

"His idea."

Bet shrugged and walked out. She took a deep breath of air that was not as clean as she wanted. At least the traces of smoke were from fire contained in rings of stone. She looked for any children, but they all must have returned to their family tepees.

"Now I go find my own home," she said to her feet.

This time she made it a half-mile out of the village when a horseman caught up with her to give her his blessings. It was Joseph Logan.

"I'm afraid I am not seized by white man's religion," she confessed.

Her admission did not put him off. Joseph Logan slid off his pony, stood too close for comfort, put hands on each of her shoulders, and stared at her with owl eyes. In perfect English he told her that while receiving his education in England he had met the king and many fair-skinned ladies, none of whom possessed her strong character and admirable features.

"I remind you perhaps of Sakaam, your wife?" Bet asked.

"Not at all. Do you mind?" Without waiting for an answer, he removed her coonskin cap and studied what remained of her yellow hair after all her trading. "Sakaam is my fourth wife."

"Sakaam knows this?"

"Yes. The other three are far away where

the sun rises. Sakaam understands. She knows I find women impossible to resist and am opposed to divorce for religious reasons."

He stroked her hair, but she pulled away and demanded her cap back. He twirled the cap on one finger. She had once seen a Sioux warrior do such a thing with the scalp of a Pawnee.

"You could stay and . . . well, many women find me impossible to resist."

"Spukani did, and I do."

"You do what, mysterious Pale Woman Who Lives in Mountains Alone?"

He put the cap back in place on her head, but while doing so drew her close to him, too close for talking. She squirmed but stopped when she thought that might be giving him pleasure.

"Why not take that load off your back?" He removed her cradleboard without asking and placed it on the ground. "Isn't that better?" He stood up and then in quick order rubbed her shoulders, her back, and the tops of her buttocks.

"You had better resist, Joseph Logan — not do anything you'll regret."

"I don't regret anything I do. And whatever I do, God will forgive me. You palefaces have a most forgiving, loving God."

"Not me."

"All the better. Heathen love is fine by me."

She debated whether to warn him again or knee him. Before she could decide, he knelt down and untied the pipe tomahawk from the side of the cradleboard. He looked it over closely, running his fingers up and down the handle and then inspecting the two-sided end — the cutting edge and the bowl.

"Excellent craftsmanship," he said, standing again and brushing the tip to his lips. "You smoke this often?"

"That's one of its uses."

"Interesting. Did you know that Lewis and Clark gave the Flatheads three such pipe tomahawks as gifts, but the Blackfeet later stole all of them?"

"Too bad. I'd like to obtain a second one."

"One isn't enough? I understand. You're the kind of female who wants two of everything. Two Indian braves perchance? Yes, I heard about you and Schweeleh."

"From Spukani, no doubt. She wants him to be her man."

"Ridiculous, isn't it? He is too old and set in the ancient Flathead ways. He puts his faith in a water snake instead of God."

"And I put my faith in Schweeleh, mister."

"Now you are being as ridiculous as Spu-kani. A woman like you deserves better."

"You better not even think it, mister."

"Call me Joseph . . . please."

"Give me back my pipe tomahawk, mister. I will never smoke with you."

"Look, your Flathead savage is with the hunters. They won't be back for many days and nights." He handed the pipe tomahawk to her. "See, I can be nice. I'll help you mount up. You can ride back with me. You really don't want to go away." He reached down and tried to scoop her off her feet. She pried his fingers off her as if they were deer ticks.

He wasn't going to give up that easily. He reached out and grabbed the front of her shirt. The small American flag that the squinty-eyed elder had given her fell out. Joseph Logan noticed and stopped grab-bing. He was curious. While he bent down to pick up the flag, she took one step back, raised her pipe tomahawk, and chopped the air in the small space between them. He threw up his hands as if a she-bear was about to attack, stumbled backward, tripped over a root, and landed on the seat of his white man trousers.

"Sometimes I smoke with it," she said, still cutting at the dry air. "Sometimes I kill with it."

"You . . . you must be crazy."

"I've been called that before. I'm leaving. You aren't going to try to stop me, are you, mister?"

"God, no! Go now, you crazy heathen."

"When I'm ready. You sit still." She made three more swipes with her pipe tomahawk just above his head. He sat still. "You want to act nice to someone, you act nice to your wife — the one who is right here where the sun sets."

"Sure, sure. Stop swinging that bloody thing."

"When I'm ready."

She took one last swing that caused him to duck his head and cover up. He didn't look up again, which was good or she might have struck him for real. He kept his head bowed while she snatched the flag from his hand. It would be dark soon. She considered spending the night alone in the long ceremonial lodge just to show this holy Iroquois she was free to do what she wanted. But she knew Sakaam would want her gone at once, and Spukani would want her gone before Schweeleh returned from the buffalo hunt. Maybe those two Salish sisters didn't matter much to her, but they mattered far more than Joseph Logan.

■ ■ ■ ■

She walked slowly south along the river all night listening to coyotes howl and owls hoot and then removed the cradleboard and rested on a pine needle bed in a snug rock crevice during the heat of day. At dusk she walked again without thinking, like an animal operating on instinct, until she knew in her heart and her back if not her legs that she had gone far enough. She could not sleep and rested for only two hours after dawn before leaving the Bitterroot River behind and following an inviting creek whose steady flow teemed with trout. That was a good sign, but she left them alone for now. She didn't know how much further she must go, and it was enough to know they were there. The creek defied the drought. How different it looked from her old creek, the one with almost no flow and fully contaminated by a dead man. She promised herself a cleansing bath in the new creek's cooling water, maybe as soon as that evening if all went well.

She followed up the canyon what was no more than a deer and elk trail, never losing sight of the creek as she rose above it toward the high country. Along the way she plucked a few wild strawberries beginning to ripen and noted the abundance of serviceberry bushes that promised fine picking in the weeks to come. High up but not too high, she came to a beaver-made pond lined on one side by downed trees — some with their bark already off, others with bark ready to peel — that could be made into fine twelve-foot tepee poles. On the far side she took twenty paces from the shoreline and reached a level clearing sheltered by three boulders and a single mature pine that had stout needles, red bark, and a sweet scent. She removed her cradleboard and leaned it against the trunk. She arched her back like a cat and stretched her arms high. She saw a square of blue sky through the upper branches and took a deep breath, filling her lungs with the air she loved. She didn't cough. No smoke. No fire. No sniff of Indians, friendly or otherwise. No sniff of mountain men. And, of course, no sniff of civilization.

"This is my place," she said, kissing the pine trunk that smelled so good. Then she planted her tiny American flag between the second and third boulders.

As the sun went down behind the mountains at her back, she began naming things, which went against her nature since everything was temporary and things with names were harder to forget. Her creek became Lost Trout Creek, her pond Beaverhead Lake, her tree Lonesome Pine, and the site Three Boulder. White men loved the naming game — claiming things for self or country. But she couldn't help herself. She was as delighted as a little girl given a beautiful cloth doll to talk to at night. She had once been that little girl. The gift giver Aunt Betty. "For someone to tell your hopes and dreams to when I'm not around," her aunt had said, knowing how impossible it was to talk hopes and dreams with her folks or her less imaginative brothers and sisters. The pretty doll, which never got any name besides Dolly, had burned up with the family log cabin during the Shawnee raid. Funny, though, in these mountains it wasn't hard to keep talking to the absent Dolly or to Aunt Betty or to a suitable substitute.

"I am home," she said to a chunky, prominently crested blue-and-gray jay that landed on a low branch of Lonesome Pine. "Like it or not."

The jay opened its long, straight bill and spoke back, not noisily but with the soft clicks, chucks, and whirrs of its whisper song. She knew what Schweeleh would do at this moment. Never having taken to the white man's religion, he would raise his chin high and thank both his personal Water Snake Spirit and Amotken, his people's pre-Christian gentlemanly god who dwelled in heaven solitary, for this bountiful land that provided his friend Pretty Pale Face with everything she needed to stay well. She loved her Strong Head almost as much as she loved the wild land and her freedom, and she admitted as much to the jay, whom she imagined had been sent to earth by Amotken to keep an eye on old Bet.

CHAPTER EIGHT

Bet Hex found contentment at her bountiful Three Boulder. The Moon When the Hot Weather Begins ran hot to the end, with the Moon When the Buffalo Bellow in hot pursuit. But she knew it was far more scorching below — heat that steamed the valley during the day merely shimmered at her high home, and whenever she started to sweat, she went to the nearby water to cool her body. Sometimes she swam leisurely or floated on her back in soothing, turquoise-colored Beaverhead Lake, which she shared with a beaver family. She loved to watch them glide slowly along the surface, their black noses and tops of their heads showing while their flat tails acted as rudders. Other times she lounged on an underwater rock in Lost Trout Creek and let her body soak as the running water pressed against the small of her back. The fins and tails of trout brushed against her toes, ankles, and calves, and sometimes the trout lay low in her shadow and then darted out to catch flies in the sunbeam that always struck the surface of her favorite pool at midafternoon.

The fish became little friends, although she only named one of them — Bent Rainbow. She fashioned a spear, but for several moons only used it on the frogs, for she could not befriend everything, and their roasted crunchy legs went well with mashed mushrooms, roots, and berries. She smoked her pipe tomahawk often, but no more than every two weeks did she use the sharp edge on a visiting cottontail or squirrel for a meal of meat. Like Schweeleh did, she thanked the frogs, rabbit, and squirrels for their sacrifices.

The Moon When the Chokecherries Begin to Ripen arrived without rain, but at her fingertips was plenty of water for one. "Or two," she said on her lonely nights, when she would wonder why Schweeleh, returned from the buffalo hunt, did not come find her in her mountain tepee. Come dawn, though, she stopped thinking of him, and went about her daily tasks and experienced her small pleasures — all the things that took on a greater importance because they were hers alone. She would never let loneliness swallow her up.

She took her time fashioning her tepee — smaller than her last one but snug and comfortable, the entrance facing east toward the rising sun as usual. She had exactly the right amount of hides to complete it and exactly the right amount of space inside to move around without feeling any emptiness. Pappy Hex used to say a man's home was his castle, but the family's overcrowded log cabin in Kentucky wouldn't have been more than a decrepit hut without Mama Hex, who took full charge of it. She even made him light his corn pipe outside. "A woman's home is her tepee," Bet told an invading mouse whose presence was actually not unwelcome.

She established her cache beyond the third boulder and kept it full of food. With a round stone, she mashed serviceberries, dried them in the sun, and stored them away for leaner times. She developed a craving for moose tongue and heart, remembering when she was up north and male moose, their antlers covered in velvet, appeared at their fattest in willow-rich swampy areas. Later, in the rutting season, they would chase after females and lose weight. In particular she remembered partaking in a Kootenai first-foods feast and watching a narrow-shouldered boy roast the fleshy outer layer of antlers over hot coals because he believed that this dish would give him the strength of a grown man — for war and for love. To think of it made her laugh, which startled the resident bird. Louis Pierre Coquerel had once identified the type — a Steller's jay, intelligent, inquisitive, bold, and a shameless camp intruder, who hopped about on its long legs looking for food with a certain informal dignity.

"What makes me want moose now?" she asked the bird, whom she named Jay Talker. "Moose are hard to kill. I have never killed a moose and would not kill a moose should one visit the high country, which they don't."

Jay Talker talked back as usual, though his beak was full of her chokecherries.

When the clustered huckleberries ripened, she forgot about moose meat and no longer craved animal flesh of any kind. She picked and ate three times a day from the brambles that formed a thick, woody semicircle above her tepee. The love of black huckleberries was rooted in her, and one afternoon when she knelt to pick, her hands suddenly came together, folded in a prayer position. A prayer of thanks for this bountiful mountainside made some sense, but it so startled her that she rose quickly and walked to a different bush. Jay Talker hung close during her walking meals, fluttering from branch to branch and chattering in pointless fashion, or so she thought. Finally, she caught on to his message, and she followed the bird for a mile up the mountain slope to where a three-year-old fire had cut a swath through the lodgepoles and created a sun-blessed patch of young bushes bursting with the sweetest berries she had ever tasted.

She ate more than her fill and then filled her coonskin cap. Wanting to take home more than that, she removed her shirt, turned it inside out, and fashioned a buckskin carrier. Huckleberry stains on her clothing were fine with her. Jay Talker kept his eye on her the whole time while chatting up a storm. She couldn't tell if she amused the bird or he was irritated because she hadn't thanked him for finding huckleberry heaven. For some reason, though far from any human eyes, she became self-conscious about being bare-chested. She interrupted her picking to study her breasts, which were swollen and tender to her touch. When she finally resumed picking, fatigue set in and her lower back began to ache.

"I'll just have to come back tomorrow," she told the bird.

She stuffed a handful of berries into her

mouth and started back for her tepee. Immediately she felt nauseated and spit out the chewed fruit as if it were poison. And then she began retching. Before she could stand up straight and walk again, she coated a young bush with blue vomit. She knew the reason; it was *not* from eating too many huckleberries.

Through most of the Moon When the Geese Shed Their Feathers she gathered and ate fresh a variety of other berries — raspberries, gooseberries, willow berries, buffalo berries, silver berries — and vomited every day but still gained weight. She felt better in body and head after discovering along the creek fibrous, brown-skinned osha roots that she both chewed and made into tea. Poison hemlock, which she once confused with osha with near deadly results, grew only a few feet away, but she had learned to distinguish between them using a smell test that Schweeleh had taught her. He had taught her so much about survival in the mountains, things that even her old French companion Coquerel had not known, but she had taught him a few things, too, like how a woman could want her freedom and unalloyed pleasures as much as he did.

Her old Arapaho lover Red Elk had told

her that late July was the Moon When the Chokecherries Begin to Ripen, but in the Bitterroot Mountains, early September was when chokecherries ripened, turning from red to purple-black. She didn't like their taste directly off the bush; they left a furry sensation on her teeth. Unlike huckleberries or serviceberries, chokecherries had pits, and those were acidic and poisonous. She didn't need Schweeleh or any other Indians to tell her it was unwise to swallow the pits. After she collected the berries that showed no red, she used a stone pestle to mash the whole fruit — pulp, skin, and pits — and then molded the pulp into cakes that she set out to dry in the sun and wind before putting them in her cache. In the winter they tasted sweeter.

She started to understand Jay Talker a little better. At least she understood when he wanted her to go with him. After the last of the unpicked huckleberries had dried out and withered, the bird led her further north to a forest of white-bark pine. He perched on a branch and she stood perfectly still beneath him as they watched a slightly larger gray bird that flashed black and white in the wing and tail. With its daggerlike bill this bird ripped open white-bark pine cones and plucked out seeds, eating some on the spot but carrying off most of them in its bulging throat to bury in the ground, three to five seeds in each chosen location.

"Yes," she said to Jay Talker. "I have seen them before. Schweeleh told me that William Clark and Meriwether Lewis also saw these birds on their journey. I think they are endearing, the way their beaks swipe at the ground to make holes for their food and how they then carefully cover them with soil. They are like me; they want to be prepared for the Moon When the Snow Blows Like Spirits in the Wind — for no matter how hot it is now, we all know the cold will come."

Jay Talker muttered something but didn't move from his branch.

"You want these seeds yourself, don't you?" Bet asked. "Well, be my guest. I don't think that other bird will mind. See how many cones hang in the trees."

Jay Talker whistled and then flew off slowly in a series of circles, until she followed him. Instead of going to the cones in the trees, he went to the other bird's caches and dug up the stored seeds. He had a good memory for where they were, but he didn't gobble up the pea-sized seeds. He left some for her to collect. She felt guilty about taking the seeds, but she wanted them badly.

She knew they were nutritious and that she was no longer eating only for herself. Schweeleh had once told her that eating the seeds gave him energy, something he had learned from watching bears gobble them up before retiring to their holes for winter. The bears, Schweeleh said, either climbed trees to get the cones or else raided the seeds, or pine nuts as he called them, that the dagger-beaked birds buried and red squirrels also stashed in hollow logs, tree cavities, and underground burrows.

"Why is it whenever I think about what I know, I think of him — I think of Schweeleh?" she said to Jay Talker as she placed a seed between her teeth and nibbled at it like a rodent.

When she felt the ground tremble beneath her, she gulped down the seed and stopped thinking of Schweeleh. A large brown bear with blond-tipped fur on its back and a hump on its shoulders rumbled into the white-bark woods. She had seen such bears take down a wounded elk, devour a winter-killed bison, catch salmon running a river, and even feast on eggs from an eagle's nest, but mostly she knew them as hunters of berries and nuts. At the Cache Valley rendez-vous she attended, every last fur trapper spoke of close, sometimes deadly encounters with these powerful beasts and how bullets never stopped them right away, only made them mad. The trappers told her it was foolish to roam the mountains without a firearm, but she had made it through all these years without ever being attacked by a brown bear or a smaller black one. She didn't want her first time to be now, though, and this big fellow might not be in the mood for sharing white-bark pine seeds with her. She retreated with her handful of stolen seeds. Jay Talker issued a husky scream at the bear and then flew after her. She took one nervous glance back and was relieved to see the bear clawing at already disturbed ground, not showing the slightest interest in her.

For the rest of September, the Moon of Drying Grass according to her adopted Arapaho calendar, she competed with the squirrels and bears for nuts. For something more substantial, she began to use her spear on the fish of Lost Trout Creek, even spearing Bent Rainbow one day while aiming for a smaller one with no name. She thanked her special trout as it cooked and then gobbled it up, surprised to find it so tasty — her best meal since establishing her home at Three Boulder. Jay Talker chattered steadily by day, and she invented her own translations in her head before chattering back. It made for conversations that always centered on a subject of her choice, whether it be the lingering hot weather, the sun, the moon, the stars, mountain scenery, Lonesome Pine, wildflowers, berry picking, gambling, trading, swimming, trout, squirrels, rabbits, owls, eagles, bears, frog legs, Thunderbirds, bird and human babies, the God of Mama Hex and the Christian Salish, the traditional Salish animal spirits, her Dolly, her Aunt Betty, or shared campfires. She avoided only a few unpleasant topics — loneliness, sickness, death, war, violence, and the redheaded mountain man.

"I know most persons, but not you Mr. Jay Talker, would say that disturbing and menacing cogitations must lurk in the mind of anyone who shuns civilization and doubly so for me since I am *not* a man. Talking to a bird doesn't make me crazy, does it?"

Without hesitation Jay Talker answered, but with a question of his own. Her translation: "Talking to a mountain woman doesn't make *me* crazy, does it?"

Her chosen high country seemed blessed even without rain — no lightning strikes, no burning forests, no clouds of smoke, no unwanted visitors. Mountains had a way of making where you were born and raised of no consequence. Like your equals — all the wild animals of the forest — you had to rely on your own skills and instincts to make a go of it and then hope for your share of good luck. The only fires she saw, she started herself. She struck her C-shaped steel against flint to create a shower of sparks over a twist of dry grass, and once it caught, she gently blew on the glowing spot to produce a tiny flame. In that fashion she lit her tomahawk pipe every evening and boiled water several times a week in the ring of stones at the center of her tepee. What smoke she created rose up through the smoke flaps of her tepee like trained black birds. She liked creating fire and smoke she could manage.

October, the Moon of Falling Leaves, arrived in a heated state, and for a few days she could put off making fires for warmth at night. She also began putting off stretching out on her buffalo hide, because falling asleep didn't come easily. Once Jay Talker had retired to some dense thicket for the night and she had finished her smoke, the troublesome thoughts more easily suppressed in daylight entered her head like stampeding buffalo. The hooting and screeching owls didn't help. Recurring questions peppered her brain as she paced both inside and outside her tepee.

Did anything remain of the redheaded mountain man after the fire reached the old nameless creek? Had anyone stumbled on, say, his cracked skull or his pelvic bones? Had anyone missed him when he didn't show up at the annual rendezvous in Cache Valley or Pierre's Hole or wherever it was being held this year? Did he have family back in the settlements waiting for him to finally emerge from the wilderness? Was his longtime trapping partner, the one called Hawk, enjoying campfires with the Crow woman or was Hawk relentlessly looking for him? By now wouldn't Hawk have assumed the Blackfeet had finally caught up to Sunshine and taken his bloody red scalp? Would she ever fall asleep again without thinking what the redheaded mountain man had done to her and what she had done to him in return? Did she really want to have a baby in five moons? Would she be able to separate the child from that man?

When all the questions kept her awake too long and curling up on her buffalo hide failed to help, she would stand up and dance the dances of Indians she had known — sun dances, moon shadow dances, rain dances, jump dances, spirit dances, bear dances, blue jay dances, and spider dances.

Even if she interpreted them wrong and moved incorrectly, it mattered not at all. She even invented two of her own dances. In one, a boulder dance, she twirled around the three boulders as if they were three men — Red Elk the Arapaho, Yellow Bull the Nez Perce, and Schweeleh the Salish — and occasionally bumped her hips against their rock-hard bodies. In the other one, a Lonesome Pine dance, her tall silent partner was that great tree and she both squeezed it and rubbed up against it. This last dance was her most private one. She couldn't imagine doing it in daylight or in front of anyone, not even her jay friend. With her strong legs and great stamina, dancing all night seemed like a real possibility many times, but at some point after midnight, her feet always kicked up a fuss and she would collapse and need to crawl to her blankets.

One unseasonably hot night, the dancing made her more sweaty than sleepy and she danced over to Beaverhead Lake. The beavers were awake, working hard at dragging fresh branches to a pile next to their lodge. They were stockpiling sticks and logs before the lake froze. She stripped off her clothes and plunged into the water. It was too cold for a leisurely float on her back, so she kicked hard and slapped at the water with her arms while the beavers slapped their tails all around her.

She had been coming to the lake for months without trying to harm them, but they still kept their distance. She didn't blame them. The fancy hats worn from St. Louis to Philadelphia and across the ocean in London, England, and Paris, France, were called "beavers" because they were made of felted beaver fur. To get a plew, you needed a dead beaver. That was what lured soft, sober palefaces to the Shining Mountains and metamorphosed them into sinewy, sunburnt mountain men. She'd trapped and skinned her share of beaver with Louis Pierre Coquerel, but those days died with him. While plews might still fetch $5 a pound in St Louis, she didn't care a lick about money, let alone a heap of it, or going to the city, let alone some backwoods settlement in Missouri.

What kept her in the mountains was *not* killing beaver but swimming with them — the freedom of movement and the freedom to choose their society over human society. She wondered if to all beavers west of the Mississippi, humans were suspected fur trappers. While Schweeleh considered them the wisest of all animals, those web-footed rodents were not as clever as they looked on the surface. They couldn't even tell a vicious, redheaded mountain man from a friendly yellow-haired mountain woman. But then, as she knew all too well, a mountain woman was also quite capable of killing.

"Do not fear, my friends," she announced after pausing in the middle of the lake to catch her breath. Her teeth chattered. Her hands were purple. Her legs were like blocks of ice. She felt the little one forming inside her start to shiver. "This is my last swim of the year in your lake."

As she swam in place she looked up and saw the man's face on the moon looking down on her. He seemed to be sneering, but she kept looking back until the clouds blotted him out. Thunderclaps sent the beavers back to their stick houses. She expected to see lightning dance across the sky and bolt in her direction — perhaps to jolt her out of the water or to strike Lonesome Pine and start a fire that would engulf the peaceful paradise that was Three Boulder. But the sky failed to illuminate. A few not-so-bright stars winked at each other between the clouds as if sharing a private joke. She wondered if the Thunderbirds were playing tricks on her. And then she felt a drop, two drops, three . . .

"I can't believe it," she cried out. "I might get wet!"

She laughed at herself. Maybe she had performed the rain dance better than she thought. The chill of the lake was forgotten. The first rain since the Moon When the Ponies Shed Their Shaggy Hair — May — fell lightly on her head, and when she pointed her nose at a star, the rain tickled her nostrils and caressed her cheeks like a gentle lover. She had never felt more awake, more alive. She swam to the far shore and then back, gliding through the water like a great fish. She climbed out, arched her back, and threw her arms out wide, wanting to feel the rain on her throat, her bosom, her belly.

It didn't last, but it was a start. When the rain stopped, she started shaking all over and ran back to her tepee, where she wrapped herself in her buffalo hide. The troubling questions were gone, but her mind tingled like her body; she was not ready for sleep. She worked her steel and flint to light a juniper smudge, filling her tepee with her own sweet-smelling smoke. She then offered tobacco to the Salish animal spirits in the hope that they would come to her and use their clairvoyant powers. She wanted to know if this was the end of drought, lightning, and wildfires.

The spirits didn't answer, but Jay Talker made a rare night appearance and whistled at her. She poked her head out of the tepee flap, and he whistled again before laughing with open beak. Coyotes, the Salish believed, were the primary jokesters, but jays also had playful senses of humor when in the mood, as well as deceptive power. They liked to show off their talent for deception. Maybe the resident jay had made like the mythical Thunderbird and produced the thunder earlier. Could Jay Talker also have produced the rain? Well, he would have to do that again before she nicknamed him The Rainmaker; otherwise, he would be The Jokester Jay at best. She stepped out of her tepee and told him that, and he talked back in his usual way. He told her she could no more understand a jay's way than she could learn to fly. Anyway, that was her translation.

"Why are you here?" she asked him. "I mean, why are you awake at this hour?"

Jay Talker just stared. She rewrapped her robe more tightly around her middle, and the bird whistled once more before flying off.

She felt the temperature dropping as she stood there watching the moon play hide and seek with the fast-moving clouds. It looked like more rain. Instead, a snowflake fluttered down and landed on her nose. Another joke? It hardly seemed cold enough, but this was high country. Most years, the snow would already be piling up. In any case, she wasn't going to stay outside to see if a real snow would occur. Even if she wasn't sleepy, she thought the little one inside her must be.

"Goodnight, moon," she said as she turned to go inside.

"Whoa there," said a deep voice.

No translation was needed, but how could that be? The resident jay sounded just like a human male.

"Is this another joke?" she asked, hoping to hear another whistle or bird talk.

"No joke."

She jumped this time and then froze. The words were human talk all right, the talk of a man. Unless she had gone mad, she heard him breathing hard, as if he had run up her mountain. Of course, panting could mean other things. She didn't turn to look. She wasn't taking any chances. She darted through the flaps and went right to where she had left her pipe tomahawk. She wouldn't be asking the camp invader if he cared for a smoke. She whirled around, holding the ax blade side in ready position while trying to keep the robe closed around her middle. This time, she would give it to him before he gave it to her. She needed to protect more than herself now. She had killed one man. The second one would be easier, but even if it wasn't, she could do it. Men always underestimated her strength. She all of a sudden felt like a she-bear whose cub had been threatened.

"I smell smoke from far below. Juniper, right? I knew it must be you. Glad to find you *not* on fire, Pretty Pale Face."

Bet was glad, too, glad all over. The familiarity came through this time. It wasn't just any man's voice. She did not lower the pipe tomahawk but turned the end around so that the bowl of the pipe faced the entrance. Her arm trembled, but not as much as her knees, and not from anything like fear.

"But *I am* on fire," she said in a tone she had not used for many moons. Her robe opened on its own and she let it tumble to her feet. "Come in, come in. I thought you'd never get here."

CHAPTER NINE

Had she truly been waiting all this time for Schweeleh to return from the buffalo hunt, hear of her visit to his migrating village in the valley, and then seek her out in the mountains? It seemed that way now that he was inside her tepee, and she told him how hard it had been to wait and how empty her heart had been without her Strong Head. She liked to be alone, but sometimes it was nice to have a man around who could share in her solitude. She tried to kiss him on the lips, but he turned his sagacious face and she barely got to peck his cheek. She shrugged. There would be plenty of time for locking lips later. He told her to get dressed.

"You taking me somewhere?" she asked.

"No," he said. "You cover."

She shrugged again, but then put on all her clothes. "You like me better like this, do you?" she teased.

"Yes," he said.

She suspected that Schweeleh had finally come to see her because he hungered for her touch but wanted to show some brave Salish restraint. She spread out the new buffalo robe he'd brought her and invited him to sit on it for a smoke. He hesitated for a moment but then sat, facing her. She loved the way he crossed his long legs and flattened both hands against his knees. They passed the pipe tomahawk back and forth many times without speaking. That was not unusual, but their eyes never quite met, and each time she held the pipe to her lips, he would press down on both knees until they were within an inch of the robe.

"Did something go wrong on the hunt?" she asked.

He shook his head and didn't take the pipe the next time she tried to hand it to him.

"Trouble with the Blackfeet? The wild-fires? Finding buffalo?"

His head moved three times from side to side.

"Tell me more."

"No Blackfeet. Many buffalo. Easy to kill. Easy to cook with fire so close."

She laughed as if he had told a joke. But her Strong Head stayed stone-faced.

"Like you've always said, fire can do good

and do bad — like us." She thought that might make him smile, but no luck. She took an extra turn on the pipe tomahawk. "Those mighty Thunderbirds have sure been busy whipping up lightning without rain, although I did feel a few welcome drops earlier tonight when I was in the water. And listen to this. Back when I was walking up the valley, I saw one of them flapping its enormous wings over the mountaintops, you know, an actual genuine Thunderbird . . . I think."

"Your eyes getting sharp like Indian eyes."

"I suppose. You didn't ask, but I came to the Place of the Bitterroot to see you, sweet one. Well, also because a wildfire burned me out of my home up north. And fire caused your women and old men to move your village while you were away on the hunt. But, of course, you know that now. I don't know why I'm talking so much. I can't help it. Maybe it's because I haven't talked to anyone for many moons, except a jaybird who . . ." A sudden vision of the redheaded mountain man's bestial face made her cringe and bite her tongue. She could see those ugly lips move: *I could kill you. Who would know?* She shook all over and crossed her arms to at least control that part of her. Schweeleh didn't notice; he was looking down between his crossed legs, which he had twisted to the side so that his toes were pointing toward the tepee door. "Or maybe it's because you aren't doing any talking — or kissing and squeezing, either. Not that I necessarily want you to jump into anything, you understand . . . I mean, I'd like you to talk to me some with our clothes on."

He nodded solemnly. "I been home."

"Is that all you have to say?"

"I been home much many days."

"Right. But you took your sweet time coming to see me. Was I that hard to find? I didn't try to cover up my tracks or hide my smoke or anything like that."

"You make nice home."

"Yes, I like it much better than my last one. This might be my best home since I've been out on my own, before that, too. And that's a hell of a lot of years, my friend."

"I too have much many years. With so many years, we change."

"Well, you're still looking good, Strong Head." She touched his nearest knee and moved in for a proper kiss on his finely curved lips. This time he suddenly dipped his chin and her lips barely grazed his forehead.

"Land's sake!" she said. "You never objected when I made the first move before.

143

Now you do? Is that what you mean by change?"

"I don't know. Maybe. Yes."

"I'll wait, then. Whenever you feel up to it."

Silence.

"Talking is fine," she added.

More silence. She puffed hard on the pipe tomahawk, and he watched the good smoke fill the tepee. She felt full of good fire, but he must be willing to let her show it to him. She waited, thinking something must be wrong — with her, with him, with the world. A series of spasms in her belly diverted her attention. The little one inside her was kicking or perhaps coughing. She tossed the pipe tomahawk aside. She imagined Schweeleh somehow knew what the redheaded mountain man had done to her and what she had in turn done to Sunshine. She couldn't help glancing at her covered belly.

"Have I really changed?" she asked softly. "My hair is still yellow. You always loved my hair. Your people still love my hair."

"I want son," he blurted out.

"What?" She shifted uneasily on the buffalo robe, finally raising her knees and hugging them. They had never talked of such things before. They had spoken a little about love but mostly about freedom. Twice when she was much younger a man's seed had grown inside her, but never his, and neither seed had grown for long. Once it stopped when an Arapaho medicine woman gave her a skullcap potion; the other time it stopped when she jumped off a cliff three times.

"Son carry forward old Salish ways," he said.

"I have nothing against that, not anymore. So, I guess in that regard, I've changed, too."

She thought he would see that her belly had changed, but he couldn't. She wasn't hiding anything, but she wasn't going to tell him, either.

"Son no have yellow hair. Must be full Salish."

She released her knees and kicked out her legs. One of her feet caught him hard on the hip.

"I anger you," he said. "I much sorry."

"I suppose a yellow-haired daughter wouldn't do, either?"

"You no speak of children."

"True enough. It's a recent development. No doubt a redheaded child, male or female, wouldn't suit a Salish thinker like yourself."

"You mean head of fire?"

"Exactly. But don't you worry, Strong Head. Whatever you do next, there is no danger of me having your baby."

He finally looked her in the eye, but it was only a look of puzzlement.

"Don't ask me to explain anything. You can trust your yellow-haired woman when I say all this talk of babies can be forgotten tonight. You came all this way to find me in my new home. And here I am — found! Never mind our differences. Never mind our changes. Never mind the rest of the world. We can still make a happy campfire together."

As far as she was concerned the wait was over. She knelt before him, placed both hands on his chest, pushed him onto his back, climbed on top of him, and pressed herself as flat as she could against him, breechclout to breechclout, belly be damned. Not hearing any complaints and losing all restraint, she began to grind and crush as if she were a rock pestle and he were so much corn in a hollowed-out hardwood mortar. It took her several minutes to realize that instead of responding to her frantic passion he was just lying there like the buffalo hide he gave her.

"Would you prefer to be on top?" she asked, for that was the way they had always talked to each other in their tender moments.

He shook his head.

She thought of the little one inside her again. "Maybe side to side?"

He stood up, which was a definitive answer, and not wanting to look so far up at him, she stood, too.

"What if I no come to you on mountain?" he asked, shuffling his moccasins.

"Well, we wouldn't be together like this. But you did come, and you brought me this beautiful buffalo robe, and here we are."

"You no wait for me in village."

"I needed to make myself a home."

"You no come back."

"I thought about it many times. But I've been busy here. The Moon When the Rivers Start to Freeze will be here soon, and I need to . . ." She was not one to lie or make excuses for her behavior, so she stopped talking. The truth was she had never once seriously considered leaving her safe paradise in the high country despite bouts of loneliness. If she didn't see anyone, nobody could harm her. Maybe in the spring she would have emerged from her hideaway home like a she-bear coming out of hibernation.

"You never want home in my village."

"That's true. I don't want to live in *any* village. I've told you that. I thought you understood, sweet one."

"You no change."

"I am the way I am. You always liked that."

She pressed her lips to his and tried to engulf his tongue, but it thrashed about like a beaver's tail. His tongue escaped. He withdrew. With arms crossed he paced in a circle around the firepit, her saliva dripping from his lower lip. She became dizzy watching him.

"You good here," he finally said. "This I am glad to see."

"But are you glad to see me?"

"You always make my heart glad."

"I'm glad you are glad, Strong Head. So, are we going to stretch out on that glorious buffalo robe you brought me and revel in our gladness?"

"Is not the skin enough for you?"

"No. I want the man, the gentle man, who comes with it."

"I come here to talk."

"Like I said, talk is good, too. Speak your piece, sweet one."

"Hunting, we see fire halfway to Red Paint, what you call Missouri River. No harm, but Mandan medicine man say it is sign. He say it is end for Mandan, Arikara,

Lakota, Blackfeet, Flathead, and all people of the setting sun. He say white man bring fire like he bring the killing pox."

"Lightning caused the fires. White man can't make lightning."

"Many kinds of lightning."

"Anyway, the fires are gone now, and the heat will go soon. It is near the end of the drought season, not the end of the Indian."

"Not end," he agreed. "Have sons."

"And daughters."

"But white men will have more."

"Yes. With a little help from white women."

"I see fire and worry it is end for you."

"But I'm *not* an Indian."

"Not a Salish."

"That's right. Not an Arapaho, not a Nez Perce, not a Kootenai, not a Sioux, not a Mandan, not a . . ."

"You have all this." He uncrossed his arms and opened them wide.

"And my yellow hair, too."

"I no worry about you."

"No worry. But thanks anyway."

She walked into his arms. He squeezed her tight, and she squeezed back, harder.

"You are who you are," he said.

"I have always said that."

"Who you will always be."

149

"Most likely. A mountain woman to the end."

"I change. Not who I was."

"So you've suggested. But not noticeably, not to me, not when you hold me like this."

"I change."

"I believe you, sweet one. Mind telling me how?"

"I take wife."

"Eh . . . I don't follow you, Strong Head. You want to get married?"

"I take wife."

"Oh." His fingers no longer pressed firmly against her backbone. She felt as if she were falling backward even though he had not let go completely. "Now I'm following a little better. And I'm not so sure I like it. You've already taken a wife."

"Yes."

"Do I know her?"

"You know Spukani."

She could hear of wars and tortures and massacres and epidemics and burning land without being shocked. But his news floored her; she collapsed onto the buffalo robe. She felt ashamed she could not take the news standing on her own two feet. But in another moment, she was beyond shame or needing to appear strong. She turned onto her belly and buried her face in the sweet-smelling fur.

She did not question him; that was not her way. But he said he owed her an explanation before he left. It took a while. He naturally wanted to please his grandfather and father, neither of whom was still living, and other ancestors. Their spirits and even older animal spirits, including his guardian Water Snake Spirit, had spoken to him with one voice: *We have always welcomed the white man since Lewis and Clark visited our ancestral lands, but she is wrong for our Salish son. This woman who roams in our mountains might be a Pretty Pale Face, but she is a paleface touched by contrary spirits and unwilling to accept the tribal ways or the duties of a proper Salish wife and mother.*

"So, your ancestors and spirits like my yellow hair but don't want a bunch of half-bloods running around with yellow hair flowing in the wind?" Bet said, interrupting Schweeleh and his damn *voice*. She couldn't imagine Spukani interrupting him, at least not for the first twelve or thirteen moons of their marriage.

"They no mention yellow-hair children," Schweeleh said. "Spukani say . . ."

"Oh, so she talked about me?"

151

"I have much many talks with . . ."

"It wouldn't surprise me if she told you I was no good. We had a talk when I was in the village. She has had an eye on you for a long time, and clearly she saw me as her rival for your everlasting affection. I didn't see her that way. I thought I knew you, and she . . . well, she might be the kind of black-haired, obedient woman your ancestors would want, but I never thought she was what you wanted."

"I change."

"So you keep saying."

"On buffalo hunt I see much many fires, more fires than my people see in all years since Amotken create Earth Mother. We meet Old Bear, great Mandan medicine man, and he say burning fires mean we lose our power, have few more days — that it is end . . ."

"The end for his people, your people, and all Indians. I know. You told me."

"Must not end, I also tell you. I want wife, family. You no want husband, family."

"Unlike Spukani."

"Young sister Sakaam married. Not Spukani. No good."

"And now she is — nice of you to be so obliging. I hope Joe what's-his-name, Sakaam's God-fearing Iroquois husband, gave you and Spukani a splendid Christian marriage ceremony."

"No like Joseph Logan. He no like me. He want two sisters for squaws, not one. I go to sacred Salish Medicine Tree to pray for guidance. For four nights I share tepee with Spukani. On fifth day we have Salish wedding. Smoke pipe, beat drum, play my love song, dance all night."

"Congratulations."

"You understand?"

"Congratulations is the best I can do." She knew Spukani would be as compliant and faithful as a small dog, but she also knew that in hungry times, Schweeleh ate dog. And so she said nothing more.

"You friend always," he said.

"Always was, always will be."

"Friend to end of time."

"Yes."

"You visit us in village sometime."

"Maybe. And maybe I should have done that when you were still available. Don't mind me. All is good. I love my Three Boulder. I'll be sticking close to home for some time yet."

"I go. Pony tied up behind big rock. Must ride fast."

"Sure. Spukani wouldn't want you to stay here even one night."

"Wife big with child. I go."

She gasped. He didn't notice or else ignored it. He hitched up his leggings.

"Really?" she finally said. "How big?"

"Big enough."

"I understand that."

"I . . . I go then."

She nodded, and Schweeleh walked out of her tepee. She knew she must be further along than his wife, but some women showed more.

She made sure her eyes were dry and followed him out. He hurried behind the third boulder and a moment later reappeared mounted on a big-headed pony with an upright mane. As he rode past her, his eyes remained lowered, looking downward toward the valley. She half-waved to him as he disappeared into the darkness of what she knew must be the last warm night of the year.

"Congratulations," she called after him. "That's the best I can do."

CHAPTER TEN

The fires were gone. It wasn't the end of the Salish, but it looked like the end of happy campfires with Schweeleh. She listened to pony hoofbeats descending her mountain and continued to hear them long after the rider would have been back in the valley. Finally, she trudged into her tepee, feeling exhausted by what had happened and what hadn't happened and what the future might be like. She patted her slightly swollen belly, which had gone unnoticed by Schweeleh, and settled down fully clothed on the buffalo robe. She curled up and tucked her hands between her knees but still felt cold. She was not one to weep, but a single tear trickled down her right cheek and lodged in the tiny scar there that had marked her long ago when a Pawnee arrow grazed her face. She closed her eyes so hard she created a second tear. Her mood was such that when the Ignoble Incident flashed like lightning inside her head, she seized that horrible happening and lodged it in the front of her skull. But she still would not let it consume her. She told herself the fear that filled her when Sunshine forced himself on her was nothing compared to the fear felt during that first encounter with the Pawnees. Her life on the frontier had almost ended before it could begin. Yet she was alive still, and she had more reason than ever to live.

As Bet continued to lie there on her buffalo hide after Schweeleh's short visit on the last warm night of the year, her mood lightened, and she uncurled herself from her ball. A second tear never left her eye. Recollections of her excellent frontier education under the old Frenchman's tutelage had replaced her petrifying thoughts of the failed horse-stealing raid and the nearly completed Morning Star Sacrifice. Even the memory of Louis Pierre Coquerel's death couldn't make her melancholy the way it used to do. He had lived a full life of love and adventure and had died doing what he loved best. To her, his demise now felt more like a beginning than an end. Indeed, since she laid him to rest in that beaver-rich northern river, she had done four years of mostly satisfying roaming on her own terms and met her share of halfway decent men.

Some of their names she had forgotten, but others she remembered well, like the Nez Perce Yellow Bull who wanted to marry her and took her home for his mother's approval, and of course the Salish Schweeleh who so respected her wish to be independent that he stopped talking matrimony and finally settled on marrying another. His parting gift was not only this luxurious buffalo robe but also his expressed wish to be her best friend till the end of their time on this earth. There was that bad man, too, the one she called Sunshine who was anything but. Her mood, though, was too good now to allow memory of him to spoil it. She knew, at last, she could sleep soundly — that's what her body, especially her feet, told her she should do. But her mind loved to be contrary. She thought of her earlier swim in Beaverhead Lake. She didn't want that to be her last swim of the year. It was far from hot now, but she removed her breechclout and the rest of her clothes and ran naked to join the beavers.

Soon after Schweeleh's visit, the first real cold spell hit, what Louis Pierre Coquerel called the "willow killer," because it would knock off the last of the willow leaves — a

157

sure sign that winter had arrived. In the cold mornings that followed, symptoms surfaced. Bet would awaken to burning sensations, as if the lightning fires had returned but inside her. She had a need to get wet and liked to sit by Beaverhead Lake or Lost Trout Creek and dip her head in to guzzle the coldness or dab ice water on her hot head and splash some of it on her protruding belly as well. She craved grub worms, snails, and cotton-wood bark. No matter what she ate, nausea followed her to the base of Lonesome Pine, where she would retch to the amusement of Jay Talker. She had been through this before, at least the early stages. She would have had Red Elk's baby if not for the Arap-aho medicine woman's skullcap potion. And she would have had Yellow Bull's baby if she hadn't executed those three jarring leaps from a ledge after leaving Nez Perce coun-try. In neither instance was it the right time to become a mother. What about now?

She certainly had time to think about that question each day as she fetched firewood and water, made sure her tepee fire never lost its last spark, mended her clothing and moccasins, ate her peculiar fare, and danced with her unlit pipe tomahawk. Her nights were quiet except for the crackling fire and the howls of coyotes and wolves. In the middle of several nights, she awoke in a sweat thinking how Sunshine labeled her: *Crazy white bitch running around in the mountains.* Was he really that far off the mark? Why did those words haunt her? A white woman living alone in the wilderness by choice would be regarded in tame society as an aberration — one that filled men with mistrust, lust, and disgust, though sometimes clothed in sympathy. How dare a female of the species step far out of place into a land of savage men and beasts?

That she would get herself knocked up with not even a midwife within a thousand miles could only be expected and was proof that the West destroyed the fairer sex and promised only catastrophe for any children born alive. At all hours of the day, she heard from the good people of Boonville and points east — family, acquaintances, and strangers all voiced the same opinion inside her head: *By hook or by crook you have stayed alive. We suspect you have sold your soul to the devil. Taking care of yourself is one thing; bringing a helpless child into your self-imposed hell on earth is another. A lone wolf raising a fawn in a den makes better sense. Who is the father anyway? Do you know? The devil may keep you safe, but your bastard child shall be damned and doomed!*

"Damn you," she screamed when she heard their collective voice one solemn morning, the coldest so far. "The father was the bastard and counts for nothing. My baby hasn't been touched by him and never will be, 'cause he is as dead as yesterday. And I have *not* sold my soul or my body to the damned devil!" Never had a new human life advanced this far inside her. She bared her belly and stared at it, or rather, through it, seeing as true as life a fully formed, if naturally curled, being with arms, hands, fingers, feet, toes, and ears. She couldn't quite make out the sex, but that mattered little. She might be out of her mind, but she wanted this baby.

She decided she would celebrate Christmas this year. Her family used to do that in the backwoods of Kentucky, with Mama Hex heralding the birth of her Savior in song and prayer and having the children hang garlands of mountain laurel on the meetinghouse, while Pappy Hex got into the spirit of the occasion at the log cabin by smoking his corn pipe, drinking locally distilled corn whiskey, and laying out home-made wooden hatchets, slingshots, and yo-yos as gifts for his brood. The only other times Bet had celebrated the day was when Louis Pierre Coquerel served as her constant frontier tutor. He never went to sleep on the eve, carrying on like he was all possessed till dawn and right through until late afternoon. He discharged weapons every hour, drank brandy if he had any and grog if he didn't, sang songs about each of his dozen wives in at least three languages, danced vigorously with or without Bet, gave her gifts of tobacco and blackstrap molasses, shared his jolly stories about visits from St. Nicholas in more civilized lands, and asked all Indians to stay away from his camp on the white man's great medicine day.

She woke up before dawn on what she thought might be Christmas morning, and who would argue with her if it wasn't? A light snow had fallen overnight, and she ate some of it pure and then mixed in dried blueberries and ate some more. She drank water for she had nothing else and broke out her pipe tomahawk, inhaling just enough smoke to honor the memory of Louis Pierre without irritating the little one inside her. She had no husbands to sing songs about, and on this morning, she had no wish to sing about Schweeleh, Red Elk, Yellow Bull, or any other man, not even St. Nick. So, she sang about the three boulders, her lake, her creek, the snow, and the wind. When her voice tired, she squatted in front of

161

undecorated Lonesome Pine and wor-
shipped it as the tree of life. And then she
danced with herself or her partner within,
mostly the dances of native people who
might not have ever heard of Jesus Christ.
When Jay Talker showed up and watched
her curiously, she bid the bird a merry
Christmas and he left her the gift of a tail
feather as he flew off in search of his own
morning meal.

By late afternoon she had run out of
celebratory energy and had cocooned herself in her two buffalo hides — one old, one
new — close to her tepee fire. She whispered
reassuring words, not to herself but to the
one inside her who she was convinced had
large ears. "Celebrating Christmas will even
be more fun when you are on the outside,"
she said. "And we will celebrate each year
till I am as old as the mountains. You were
not intended as a gift — by man or by God,
if there is a God — but as sure as the sun
and the moon and the stars, you are *my* gift,
one I shall cherish more than the air I
breathe until the mountains crumble to the
sea." It sounded a little too serious and
roughly biblical, so she added one quick
"Amen" and laughed.

Over the next week, she forced herself to
walk circles around Three Boulder and up

and down Lost Trout Creek pointing to plants and animals and naming them. The little one would grow quiet in the womb as if listening to her every word. Bet could hear the child softly mouthing questions, and she gladly passed on her knowledge, practical or not. It beat talking to Jay Talker, who preferred to talk back rather than to listen.

"These are things to know later," she said, tapping her belly button. "But don't worry, little one, I'll repeat everything when you come out and see all the wonderful things for yourself."

She squashed all notions to speak of bad things. An aching head or a runny nose barely slowed her step, and when dizziness threatened to knock her flat, she rested only for a few moments. After their longest walk, practically to the valley and back, she sat in front of the tepee and pointed out how the jagged points of the mountains were poking holes in the big sky, causing it to bleed bright red, pink, and orange. Describing this glowing winter sunset pleased her and when it was over, she described the moon and the stars. "This is my world, little one," she said, and she meant more than the earth. "It will be your world, too. We are closer to the stars in the high country. I am the mountain woman, and you are my sweet mountain baby."

Come the New Year, Bet was exhausted and in far too much discomfort to want to celebrate anything. She had gained much weight and her lower back hurt when she sat or stood or bent to lift firewood. It helped to stretch out on her buffalo hide, where she had trouble keeping her eyes open any time of day. But then a new, deeper pain hit her on both sides of her waist and across her tailbone to the back of her thighs. Trudging anywhere through the snow made things worse, as did twisting or bending forward. Even resting didn't resolve this pain, and the activity in her brain aggravated her condition. Since old Louis Pierre Coquerel's death she had mostly lived alone on the edge, beyond the reach of civilized hands, dirty or clean, but now she questioned her right to live that way. It struck her as selfish.

She never had dwelled on her age, whatever it was, though no question she had *aged.* Not that she minded; it happened to the tamed ones, too, and drew far more attention in civilization. Still, her body had begun to confer with her mind even before the redheaded mountain man arrived at her old home like a ball of wildfire. The body feared becoming barren and shriveling to death, and the mind agreed that it happened to any woman who lived long enough. The mind reckoned it had lived with this body for nearly forty years.

At about the same age, Mama Hex had churned out her ninth child — that difficult candlelight arrival in backwoods Kentucky of a bald, big-headed female she named for her sister, since poor Betty would never have even one child let alone a husband. Mama Hex took sick during the move to what would become Missouri, and her tenth child was hollering in the womb by the time the Hex family reached Femme Osage. Mama Hex expected number ten to be a boy because of all the pushing and shoving inside her, and she planned to call him Daniel after Mr. Boone — or Daniela should a girl emerge. She died before the baby boy could be delivered, and he died the day he was born.

"Daniel is a good name," Papa Hex said while still in denial that the mother of his children was gone. "It belongs to our neighbor, a legend. Daniel Boone grew long in the tooth with much luck and good fortune, but he knows in his every fiber that life is a gamble."

Daniel Boone was still alive when Bet departed in *Western Engineer* with Manuel and Mary Lisa, and her father was, too . . . barely. During the War of 1812, Pappy Hex chose not to join the local militia, but he proved life was a gamble even when you didn't go to war. His gun failure during the Shawnee attack back in Kentucky was repeated during a hunting accident in Missouri. He was smoking his corn pipe at his favorite deer stand when a lingering spark set off a powder charge prematurely, causing the barrel of his muzzleloader to explode and send metal fragments into both eyes. He did not completely lose his sight, but after that accident he drank himself blind most nights and demanded that his two daughters still at home wait on him hand and foot. His oldest daughter had run off with the part owner of a New Orleans gambling house. Of the three sons who had survived childhood, one had been killed by the British and their Shawnee allies (who had also migrated west), one had hightailed it back to Kentucky to look for a lost love from his boyhood, and one had remained at home with the mental capacity of a child and the drinking capacity of the old man.

That's the way it happened sometimes. Bet would be contemplating something fresh and hopeful, like her coming baby, when suddenly her aches and pains would trigger morbid thoughts that attacked her brain like a pack of wolves. Roaming the Rockies as she did and encountering only Indians, wild beasts, and the occasional mountain man, she remained out of touch with not only her family but also most of civilized society. She had no doubt, however, that Pappy Hex was dead and little doubt that the slow-witted brother left at home had followed in his footsteps to the Boonville cemetery. As for her sisters, she imagined the one in New Orleans out on the streets after being abandoned by her gambler husband and the two in Boonville taking in wash and selling rhubarb pies to make ends meet while their husbands worked their plows from dawn to dusk.

Like most Americans, her sisters would consider the unexplored territory that was the West *uninhabitable* because it lacked order and institutions and plowed fields, and if they wondered about her at all, it would only be curiosity about what kind of horrible death she had suffered in the wilds. Bet wondered most about Aunt Betty, who had been more than a half-century old when left behind in Kentucky. If still alive she'd be pushing ninety. Bet remembered her as a tough but understanding bird, loaded with too much gumption and spewing too many assertions to suit Pappy Hex or, for that matter, any man. Bet pictured her aunt in some place like Lexington sitting straight-backed in a rocker, fanning her gaunt but still engaging face while sipping coltsfoot tea and mouthing hominy grits. Stranger things had happened, such as Bet herself surviving all these years in the Rocky Mountains.

"This is your Little Betty — your Betty II — speaking, Aunt Betty," she said from her tepee door one day when a wind swept down from the northwest and not even Jay Talker cared to make an appearance. The wind cut through her so hard Bet thought it might carry her message, if not her entire tepee, all the way to Lexington, Kentucky. "Hope you are weathering the storms. I'm trying to do the same. I got more reason than ever to put off dying. It's not just another new year in the mountains; this one promises new life. That's right, Aunt Betty, your favorite niece is in the family way and the little one is well on her way here. Maybe I'll call her Bess, sort of like you and me but different enough so she can be her own person. Of course, it could be a boy. I can live with that. I'll just have to be extra careful to raise him right — you know, to be kind to his mama and all around polite to female persons of all ages. I'll call him Daniel 'cause Mama Hex, your sister, lost one with that name, and I figure it would have been her best one. You might be wondering about who the father is of my Bess . . . or Daniel. Please don't, Aunt Betty. The father isn't anyone you'd know, not anyone I know either, and he plain wasn't worth knowing. Let me just say he is now stone-cold dead — actually, burned beyond a crisp — and that's a good thing. Take care of yourself. I miss you, Aunt Betty, especially when the wind is a-blowing like this."

Bet closed and secured the front flaps of her tepee, and when she bent over the pain in her pelvic region flared up something awful. She grimaced and steadied herself before waddling back to her buffalo hides to lie down. Having this baby would be a relief. She wanted to give birth today, though of course she must wait. All female creatures must wait — bears, beavers, squirrels, rabbits, buffalo, wolves, mice, and whales. Only the human kind might stop the waiting on purpose. Not this time. She'd wait as long as it took.

CHAPTER ELEVEN

The wilderness bristled with danger, perhaps even more so than when drought ruled the land and wildfires raged. Temperatures had plunged. The cold was so bitter that Bet shivered even when close to her lifesaving tepee fire, and the snow was so deep she could barely manage a path to her cache pit. She dug a waste pit out of the snowdrifts halfway there one day when the wind was spewing clouds of snow in the right direction. She had enough firewood stacked in her tepee to last her a few moons, and she ate enough snow with her dried berries, nuts, and pemmican to satisfy her hunger and thirst. Having enough warmth, food, and water wasn't her real problem. Having a baby was.

She berated herself for not thinking things through. Having a baby was hard enough, having a baby alone in the wilderness was harder, having a baby alone in the wilderness in late February was insanity. The Arapahos called it the Moon of Frost Sparkling on the Sun, but she hadn't seen the sun in days. Jay Talker had sounded alarms about snowstorms and snowy owls approaching, but she had stopped listening to him. And then one day he was gone; he'd abandoned Lonesome Pine and flown south to warmer climes. In the back of her mind, she had been thinking that when her time neared, she would go down to the Salish village and seek assistance from Otter Woman, the well-thought-of medicine woman. But she had kept putting it off. Part of the reason was that Schweeleh was down there with his pregnant wife, Spukani. It was their village, not hers. She had made herself believe she could do it alone at Three Boulder, to prove a point to them, to herself and to everyone else, including the dead redheaded mountain man. Now it was too late. Maybe she could slide or roll down the mountain, but that wouldn't do the little one much good.

Dying was one thing, but it would also mean killing the human seed that had grown in darkness and was now nearly developed enough to see the outside light. Would she be able to do enough to keep them both alive before, during, and after the arrival? The more it snowed, the more doubts filled her head. It began to seem like such a long shot that she asked the Salish, Arapaho, Lakota, and Nez Perce creator gods and animal spirits to show kindness and mercy. A couple of times she even ignored her cynicism and prayed to the God that Mama Hex once prayed to night and day. She couldn't help herself. All that prayer had worked for Mama Hex for many years; nine times she had given birth to healthy babies and survived. Of course, the tenth time neither mother nor child made it. That was the time that came to dominate Bet's thoughts.

On the morning that she figured her own time was less than a moon away, she forced herself outside and trudged toward the waste pit for a squat. A burst of tears ambushed her, and they flowed only a short way before forming tiny icicles on her cheekbones and nostrils. The little one kicked twice, as if to complain about the cold penetrating the thick womb walls.

"Sorry, so sorry, Bess . . . or Daniel," she said, wrapping the buffalo hide tighter against her big belly. "None of this is your fault. You must know that. I'll do my best, and I'll keep looking to the sky for help and guidance. You can bet on that. But, like my

Pappy Hex used to say, living is a gamble. I'm not going to whitewash anything. To be totally honest, little one, we might just have to get a little lucky to whip this thing."

She woke that afternoon to a thrashing in the bushes. She raised her head and quailed at the danger of an intruder. It was no animal. She heard the crunch of snow and creaking snowshoes. One human being approached. Considering her dire circumstances, she might have welcomed such a sound and felt her luck had taken a turn for the better. But it wasn't that way at all. She knew in her heart it wasn't Schweeleh or any other familiar face, and strangers always made her apprehensive. She shivered as if Death itself was snowshoeing to claim her. Hearing a man's voice set off further alarms because it was not only unfamiliar but also so deep it seemed to be coming from beneath frozen ground and ten feet of snow.

"Wagh!" the voice said. "This a woman's camp?"

Bet reached for her pipe tomahawk.

The snowshoes stopped creaking. He was right outside her tepee door, listening to her silence. She had heard such panting before.

"Can you hear me?" the man continued. "I'm iced over and wolfish. Hello inside.

I'm looking for the woman who went white Indian. I see your smoke. You must be in there. Hello, hello. This child come to palaver. Say something if you can. You haven't went under, have you? That would be a pure shame."

She couldn't very well tell him she was dead and nobody was at home. And she couldn't bring herself to welcome him in, either, no matter how much she needed help. But there was no need to say anything. He wasn't going to leave without looking inside. And when he did, she would play it by ear. If he could offer her any assistance at all she would take it. If he had anything else in mind, she figured she would bash him over the head with her last ounce of strength.

She listened to him slide his feet out of the rawhide thongs of his snowshoes and remove some kind of bundle from his back and then brush off his clothes as if had been invited into a fine Eastern home. He struggled with the tepee's tied-down front flaps. It gave her time to prepare a little longer. She stood behind the door, and when he entered, she pressed the pipe tomahawk into the small of his back. Without being asked, he dropped his bundle at his feet and then placed his rifle, hunting pouch, and powder horn on top. He was short but with a wide back and coarse sandy hair that stuck out of his fur hat to below the shoulders of his bearskin coat, which had stiffened and whitened with frost. He was no Indian.

"Reach," she said. He raised his hands, his fur mittens still on, and when she told him to keep them up, he did. "You want something, mister?"

"I could say I was just passing by or got lost in the storm, but that wouldn't be the truth. Mighty cold doin's out there."

"Well, you best tell me the truth or I'll . . ."

"Shoot?"

"Don't think I won't. I can't miss at this range."

"I don't doubt it, if that was a rifle barrel you were jabbing into me."

The pipe tomahawk wavered some, but only because her arms were shaky. "Whatever it is, it'll kill you just as dead if you make a sudden move."

"This child don't move sudden when it's cold enough to split a tree and I'm achin' in my middle from walking peculiar on all that snow. But if you want me to be truthful, you best be truthful your own self. I know that's no long arm of any kind."

"Well, it's not short."

"I believe that. You got pluck. Can I drop

175

my hands?"

"Not just yet. State your business."

"Right now, I'm lowering my arms and moving closer to your fire. My whiskers are iced over and I ain't felt much of anything in my feet and hands since setting out at dawn two days ago. It never hurts to be hospitable, you know."

"I do not. You're plumb wrong about that, mister."

"Maybe so. I'd rather get it in the back quick than freeze to death."

He stepped over his bundle and rifle, walked straight to the fire, flipped his mittens onto her buffalo hide, and began to alternately rub and clap his hands. He kept his back to her, and she knew she wouldn't have shot him even if she owned a firearm. She stepped forward to position herself between him and his rifle and kept her pipe tomahawk pointed at his lower back. She felt as silly as a little boy pretending to shoot a Redcoat with a hickory stick. Her arms grew heavy, and she lowered her weapon. He was out of range anyway. A sudden impulse to wipe the snow off his coat surprised her, because without question he was a mountain man. Maybe it was because he was so short, and his hair wasn't red. She wondered if it was a motherly urge.

"I don't hear any shooting," he said. "Only silence. A penny for your thoughts, not that coin will do you much good up here."

"Never mind my thoughts," she said, although she was flattered he would ask what she was thinking. Schweeleh was about the only man she ever knew who did that. "You better state your business, mister."

"Actually, I already did. My business, as mentioned outside, is with you, that is if you are the white Indian woman everybody is talking about, and I can't believe there could be more than one of you camped out up here where even Ol' Ephraim gets cold feet."

"Don't turn around," she told him, though he hadn't yet showed any indication to turn away from the fire. His feet, hands, and face were now practically in the fire. "Just who is talking about me?"

"Well, for starters, last summer some inhospitable Blackfeet I met up in Hell Gate goaded me by telling me how the White Woman Who Never Dies could walk through fire and was braver than any white man who came to hunt their buffalo or trap their beaver. I didn't take their bait, and they didn't take my scalp. I had reason to leave that country then. But I had reason to return in the fall. And here I am in winter.

You know something, White Woman Who Never Dies? I used to think you were just another Blackfeet legend."

"Everybody dies."

"Perhaps you prefer to be called Pale Woman Who Lives in Mountains Alone. They call you that, too."

"This isn't the land of the Blackfeet."

"Yes, I know. This is the Place of the Bitterroot, Flathead country. They talk of you, even more here, and they are far more hospitable than the Blackfeet."

"You had business in the Salish village?"

"Yes. And now this child's business is here."

"You want to talk to me. Why?"

"It's not every day a man gets to talk to a living legend. Actually, I came here to do more than talk."

"Oh? You'd better explain yourself, mister."

"A Flathead man asked me to bring you a few things — buffler meat, a wooden shovel, a wool blanket. You'll find them all ready to be unwrapped, Miss White Woman Who Never Dies/Pale Woman Who Lives in Mountains Alone. That's quite a handle."

The stranger tittered — nothing disdainful about his laugh. She let down her guard enough to glance back at the bundle on the ground.

"My name is Bet Hex," she said.

"Yes, Bet. He called you that . . . that Flathead man."

"Schweeleh?"

"Yes, Schweeleh. He was sorry he couldn't come himself. He is troubled by your situation, what with this heap of snow. His squaw spoke against it, didn't want her man leaving her side when she's feeling so poorly. She is heavy with child."

Bet sighed. "I know."

She was cold and needed to get off her feet. She asked him to move away from the fire so she could get to her buffalo hide. Instead, he turned around and stared at her, first at her face, then her belly. His bluish-gray eyes widened as he looked her clear through. She tried to stare back equally hard. His close-cropped sandy beard pleased her and his pencil-thin mustache amused her, but his large, sharp nose pointed like a nocked arrow between her eyes. Despite his bulky coat and broad shoulders, she could tell he was more spare than anything. He abruptly removed his fur cap and held it over his heart. That wasn't something most mountain men would do.

"Lord almighty!" he said, running a hand

through his hair. "Beg your pardon, ma'am. No wonder that Flathead fellow was so dern worried about you! These mountains ain't no place for a white woman, let alone one with child."

She motioned him to move away, but grew dizzy, lost her balance, and fell, twisting her body at the last instance to avoid landing on her big belly. The pipe tomahawk went flying. The side of her head struck something softer than the ground — the bundle the stranger brought. She wasn't sure if that was fortunate or not, for she was still conscious and he was moving toward her. Had he snowshoed all the way up to Three Boulder on a rescue mission simply because a Salish Indian he didn't even know was worried? She couldn't help wishing Schweeleh had come with him. It wasn't easy to trust a mountain man, even a short one who wondered what she was thinking. She felt about for her pipe tomahawk, but it was out of reach. Her hand touched instead the cold hammer of the stranger's rifle. She found the double trigger and without lifting the rifle she pulled twice.

The explosion and cloud of white smoke that followed surprised her; she hadn't really expected the gun to go off. The stranger yelped, jerked one foot in the air, hopped around on the other foot, and then toppled over onto his side.

"It was loaded," he said, stating the obvious as he shook his head in disbelief.

"I'm sorry," she said, and it was the truth. "I never even shot a squirrel before."

CHAPTER TWELVE

They were some pair of strangers in the tepee well into February, the Moon of Frost Sparkling on the Sun. They mumbled or moaned to themselves more than they talked to each other. It was as if they figured spending words on each other would cost too much of their vim. They slept on opposite sides of the fire. She only learned his name, Eldridge Hawkinson, after a week, but then promptly forgot it. Her belly grew, as did her discomfort. He noted that his only wife was a Crow woman who he had married last year and, as far as he knew, had yet to give birth. He said nothing more about her or Bet's condition.

His left foot was in shambles. The .50-caliber round ball from the Hawken rifle had gone right through the moccasin and the foot, leaving behind broken tendon, bone, skin, and nerves. She had cauterized the wound with a red-hot stick and killed some of his pain with a constant snow treatment. But he wasn't going anywhere. The best he could do even after several weeks was limp about the tepee using either his rifle or her pipe tomahawk for support.

His inactivity didn't hurt his appetite any. Fortunately, he had brought all that buffalo meat, which she wasn't much interested in except to please the little one within. He didn't bother with suspending the pieces of meat over the fire for a good roasting. Instead, he tossed them onto the fire and when he figured they were done, he yanked them out, dusted off the ashes, bit off a chunk or two for her, and then ate heartily. In between meals, he gnawed on morsels of raw meat like she'd seen Indian buffalo hunters do. It made her squeamish, and one day he noticed, so she made like she was having pregnancy pains — cramps, indigestion, shortness of breath, nausea, burning sensations. She didn't have to pretend too hard. Her signs of discomfort were enough to make him groan and crawl off to eat his meat in peace.

"We best dry the rest," he said one day when the meat didn't taste so good. Though they had been sharing the tepee for weeks, it was the first time he had said *we,* meaning the two of them. Whenever she said *we,* she meant her and the little one inside.

"Don't know if *we* feel up to it," she said, holding her belly. "I can't eat without my heart burning. I haven't slept. I'm as puffed up as a frog. My feet don't fit in my moccasins anymore. Look how fat they are."

She stretched out her legs, flexing her chubby feet and pointing her tiny toes at him. He chose not to look. He never looked unless he didn't think she was noticing. He hopped over to the tepee entrance and threw open the flaps. The refreshing sunlight poured in, and as it enveloped her body, she felt a glow from head to toe.

"I'll be damned if the snow ain't sparkling," he said, stepping outside.

"What?" she said. "Snow can't burn!" She was thinking of the fires of the summer. Her head had been more than muddled lately. Despite how badly she felt, she had looked at the wounded but otherwise extremely healthy man and had experienced certain stirrings that made her think she must have been picturing Schweeleh when he was free and unrestrained.

"Come see," he said.

"Too bad for you," she muttered to her feet. She got up and joined him.

The sun was out bright and proud, the sky cornflower blue. From the tepee to

Lonesome Pine, the blanket of snow glittered, each flat snowflake reflecting a portion of the sun's image, and she saw colors — many miniature grounded rainbows forming and dispersing at will. She was unaware of her bare feet until he took off his fur cap and laid it on the snow path so she could stand on it. He was putting all his weight on his one good foot, so she hooked her arm in his to help support him. He didn't say anything, but he didn't break away. The sun's intensity couldn't take away all the cold of the Moon of Frost Sparkling on the Sun, but she wasn't about to shiver. On the side where their hips touched, any movement by one was answered by the other — it was like rubbing two sticks together to make a fire.

"The snow falls harder up here, and the sun shines brighter," he said.

"I know . . . I mean . . ." Of course, she knew, but she liked hearing him say it. She waited for him to ask what she meant, but he didn't. "I . . . I love the high country," she continued. "I'm alive. I mean even when I'm cold and hungry, ache all over, and my resident jaybird deserts me, I am glad to be here."

"Amen, sister. I reckon I've neglected to say so . . . to you, that is."

"I don't blame you. I shot you."

"I reckon it was not your full intention."

"How's the foot?"

"Cold, but no colder than my good foot. How 'bout yours?"

"Both fat."

"I meant, are they cold?"

"Oh. Not really. Not inside your hat. Thanks."

His slight nod and twist of that little mustache was all it took to make her legs thaw from ankles to hips. It wasn't springtime yet, but she felt the world newly born. Mama Hex had on occasion brought up Eve and Adam in the Garden of Eden and, unlike most of her other biblical references, it must have stuck with Bet. *One simple, pure woman and one simple, pure man brought together by fate and now impatient to see, hear, smell, touch, and taste each other, never mind that a baby was already on the way.* Bet inhaled deeply and exhaled slowly. She wondered how close to the sky that old Garden of Eden actually was and whether patches of snow ever dappled its quiet apple orchard and shrubbery.

"You best get back to the fire soon," he said softly.

"Not yet. We needed fresh air. I mean both of us, you and me . . . not sure about this one." She patted her belly and this time he looked. "You're talking to me out here."

"Figured it was about time. I can't hold a grudge for more than a month, except against the Bug's Boys. You know, the Blackfeet."

"I do know them. Not intimately, of course."

"I imagine not. They're a rough bunch . . . at least to us who trap beaver and hunt buffalo."

"I've done those things . . . well, a little."

"This child been trapping and trading for a long, long time, a good decade. First left St. Louis and come out to the mouth of the Yellowstone with Andrew Henry's party back in '22."

"I left St. Louis with Manuel Lisa's in 1819 . . . eh . . . well, just a little longer than you."

"I wasn't suited to be a company man, that's for damn sure. Lasted only one year with Henry and Ashley at Fort Henry. Found me a partner and we took to free trapping."

"I didn't last that long at Fort Lisa. The Arapahos captured me."

"That must have been horrible."

"Not as bad as you might think."

"How'd you get free of them?"

"The Pawnees captured me."

"I see. At least they are friendlier toward us, you know, Americans."

"I was chosen to be a victim of their Morning Star Sacrifice ceremony."

"Queersome. I guess you never know with Indians. How'd you get free of that?"

"An old French trader named Louis Pierre Coquerel."

"He bought you. I understand. So, you became his captive?"

"It wasn't like that at all. Those years were good. I learned much."

"And once you had learned enough, you left him."

"He died. And then I was on my own."

"What about that Flathead fellow, the one who asked me to look in on you and bring you the supplies. He captured you?"

"Nothing like that. He never forced me to go with him or . . ."

"And you couldn't capture him, I take it?"

"Schweeleh and I have been great friends. We always will be."

"Even though he is married, and that little squaw will give him a full-blood baby?"

"I have my own baby."

"Schweeleh is the father?"

"When you talk, mister, you sure do talk."

"No reason for secrets. We've been living

together in that tepee for quite a spell."

"My feet are starting to get cold."

"Sure. I'll take you to the fire . . . or you can take me. My foot is burning."

"Burning?"

"It aches. Sometimes I just can't stand it. Just need to lie down."

"Me, too. We've had enough fresh air and sparkling snow."

She bent low to snatch his hat off her feet, and he bent with her. They straightened up together, turned together, and then moved toward the tepee — not so much like Eve and Adam, she thought, but like some mythical two headed, three-footed creature. He might be crippled, but she could feel the power in the arm she held and the thigh that repeatedly bumped against her leg and once or twice against her big belly.

"I got a confession to make," he said as she parted the tepee flaps for him. "Most every year I go downriver to St. Louis to sell furs and resupply, but I mostly go to lay my weary bones on a soft bed for a fortnight or two months."

"They got some high-flown women back there?"

"A few — some strumpets, too. One breed likes to tell me a man's pleasure is wrong or don't suit them, and the other tells me I got

189

to pay for my pleasure. I like my women more primitive. Anyway, I never favor St. Louis for long and once I have my fill, I make tracks west again. The mountains keep calling me back . . . the mountains and the beaver."

"And the primitive women."

"You're the first primitive white woman I ever met."

"You're the first mountain man I've met who wasn't *too primitive.*"

"We best change the subject."

She laughed and gave one end of his mustache a little twist because she couldn't help herself. "As for me, I haven't been back to St. Louis once since I left in 1819," she said, but it sounded too much like a boast. So, she touched his cheek real gentle like and tried to make amends. "Not that I blame you for wanting a soft bed and all. Fact is, loneliness isn't foreign to me. There've been times I contemplated heading east to see if I have any family left in Missouri. But then I sleep on it and, well . . . I'm just not suited for that . . . eh . . . kind of life."

"You plan to stay away from the settlements evermore?"

"It looks that way."

"Like I said, primitive."

Inside, he laid down on the buffalo hide Schweeleh had given her — on her side of the fire. She saw her pipe tomahawk right there beside him. She picked it up, used the sharp edge to scratch her back, and then tossed it well out of the way. When she lay down beside him, he didn't stir. After a while, when she decided to remove his clothes, he stirred just enough to be of some help. When she removed her own clothes, he stirred some more. His good foot rubbed against her quickly warming feet, and they did not feel nearly as fat. But his hands did not reach out for any of her nakedness.

"You said you have a Crow woman," she said.

"Yes."

"You love her very much?"

"Enough to make her my first wife."

"And your wedding was just last year?"

"No ceremony. No ritual. I gave her family a horse. The Crow have no marriage rules. Her parents and everybody else accepted her decision to form a marriage union with me — that is, everybody except for one young man who wished to marry her but wanted to count coup on an enemy first. Still learning how to count, I hear. We are living with her mother's clan."

"I see. And might you have another

woman?"

"Another woman or another wife?" The man laughed pleasantly, and his good foot deserted her feet and ran up one of her legs to the calf, then the knee and then higher yet.

"I think you catch my drift, mister."

"My foot isn't too cold, is it?"

"Hell, no. I'm betting your hands aren't either." She brought one of his hands to the thigh nearest him.

"Some Crow men have multiple wives, you know." His hand wasn't moving much.

"No, I didn't know, but it doesn't surprise me."

"There's a mountain man named Beckwourth so good at killing Blackfeet he become a Crow war chief with maybe ten squaws."

"Good for him. I was right, your hands are warm, too — at least this one is."

He began making a series of small circles with his warm fingertips. "Don't worry. I have no desire to be another Beckwourth."

"I'm not worried. I understand if you want just the one Crow wife."

"Yes, I believe so. But . . ."

She turned onto her side, trapping his hand between her thighs, and began to part the hair around each of his nipples.

"This is good, then?" she whispered into his right ear before blowing a little hot air into it.

"Could be."

"I mean I want it to happen, mister."

"Amen, sister."

"I think side to side is best, considering . . ."

"Yes, considering. Whatever you think best."

He was not full of talk once they had gotten off their sides. She was glad he didn't ask what made her want to become intimate with him well into the Ninth Moon of the Pregnancy, as she called it. He did not ask again who the father might be. Without even leaving Three Boulder, he shot three rabbits, two mule deer, and a porcupine, but he left the beavers alone. They worked together at drying the buffalo meat and some of the fresher meat over smoky coals. With the little shovel he'd brought, and mostly working on his knees, he cleared a path to a makeshift wooden rack in a sunny place next to the third boulder. On the rack they hung meat strips, short and long, to dry in the sun. After several days, the strips were leather dry. Some of this jerky they brought inside the tepee to eat at their leisure and the rest they put in her cache pit, which he also freed from snow. The mountain man worked hard, and she imagined how much more he could have done with two good feet.

They kept lying at night on the same side of the tepee fire. Sometimes he even asked her how she felt. Her answer was always the same: "Damn good." And when she asked him how he was doing, he'd inevitably reply, "I'm feeling right pert." It stopped snowing and the icicles that had formed on the three boulders began to melt. On the twelfth night, when she finally told him she no longer wished to feel him inside her, he took it philosophically.

"Life goes on," he said. "Night keeps lapsing into day. Mountains rise and valleys sink. I best punch the fire."

The next day was her time. Considering that his wife had never given birth, and Bet had never seen the process clear through, they worked well as a team. He had heard of the Crow way, which was done without medicine or interference and was done fast. He drove two stakes in the ground and then piled up robes, blankets, and clothes against them so that when Bet knelt and grabbed the stakes her arms rested on something soft. As she knelt, he hovered over her on one leg wringing his hands.

"That's all I know," he admitted. "Are you relaxed?"

"Reasonably. How 'bout you?"

"Me? I . . . What do I do next?"

"Wait for the little one to appear."

"Just like that? Won't I have to, you know, reach in and pull?"

"Don't go doing anything like that, mister. The same force that caused the seed to grow inside me will shoot the baby out."

"Magic?"

"Mama Hex called each birth a miracle, until the last one, which killed her."

"Man alive! I got to do something."

"No. I won't die. This is my first, and I aim to be a living mother."

Bet gritted her teeth but still let out a howl when the pain hit. Getting stabbed repeatedly in the stomach couldn't have been any worse. She thought the torment would flatten her but then she suddenly began to hum one of Mama Hex's long-forgotten spiritual songs — about "rejoicing in glorious hope" and the Lord "who has purged our stains" — and somehow stayed on her knees.

"So what do *you* do next, mother?" he asked, as if there were some secret cure for all this.

"I keep breathing and hang on to these

stakes for dear life."

Now the pain hit her in powerful surges — in her lower back as well as in the front. It was as if the paws of a bear were inside her, twisting, pulling and squeezing her bowels. When Bet screamed, he backed away, tripped, and fell on his backside. She kept screaming and so did the mountain man. When she first began to push it was as if her pelvis were made of broken glass, but she soon got the knack of it. She knew the worst was over. She stopped screaming and pushed diligently until the purple head crowned with only a brief burning sensation. The mountain man recovered in time to kneel beside her and stagger at the sight of the bloody head. The baby did not come out in a shot, but inch by inch, and in the end, he was there to loosen the cord and make the catch. The baby cried and began to breathe the mountain air. After Bet turned around and stretched out on her back, he placed the wet, slippery creature on the mother's belly and the pulsating blue cord held the baby there. He provided a clean, warm knife at Bet's request, and when the cord became thin and white, she cut it and then tied it with string. She knew more than she thought.

"It's a girl," he said.

"Very good, mister," she said. "We did it."

The newborn jerked her head and opened her eyes. Then she shrugged her shoulders.

"She's so little. Should I do anything now?"

"Bit knows what she's doing." The little one's mouth became active; sucking sounds came out.

"Bit?"

"Short for Bitterroot. I was going to call her Bess, but I changed my mind while I was kneeling there howling like a wolf. It just came to me. I'm Bet. She's Bit."

Everyone was quiet for a few minutes.

"Little Bit," he finally said.

"Yes, but look at her climb. Right up the mountain."

The baby was already making crawling motions toward Bet's breasts. And she made it with almost no assistance. Bit licked, latched on, and began to suck.

The trapper turned his head away as if it suddenly hit him that mother and child needed their own private time together. He fetched an armload of sticks from the pile. With his back to the two females, he fed sticks to the fire, one by one. He glanced back once while the suckling was going on but didn't turn to face them until all was quiet.

"Is something wrong?" he asked.

"Bit's sleeping," Bet said, closing her own eyes.

"Is that good?"

"It's natural. Even a mountain baby can't be climbing all the time."

"Sure. You look sleepy, Bet."

"We both need a little sleep. Get some rest yourself, mister."

"Sure. I'll just go lie over there. But isn't it time you stopped calling me *mister*? I mean I've stopped calling you *sister.*"

"Good. I'm not your sister, mister."

"Stop that, Bet. I mean please."

"You don't like being called mister, mister?"

"I've told you my name — Eldridge Hawkinson."

"Oh, yes, I almost forgot, mister. Sorry. Eldridge Hawkinson is quite a mouthful. Anyway, you just don't look like an Eldridge, Eldridge."

"True. But I got a nickname that fits, seeing as I spend so much time in the wild country and got a nose large enough to sniff out hidden beaver and hostile red men."

"Ridge?"

"Guess again."

"I can't. I'm too sleepy. Won't you let me sleep with my baby?"

"Sure. If you call me Hawk."

"What?"

"Hawk. That's my nickname."

"Really?" Bet's eyes popped open. She suddenly felt wide-awake and about as comfortable as when she was giving birth. "That's what your Crow wife calls you?"

"Sure. I call her Fallen Leaf and she calls me Hawk. But I was called Hawk long before I met her. My pard gave it to me when we first laid eyes on each other with Henry's Yellowstone expedition."

"Your pard?"

"That's right. My partner. Red."

"Red?"

"Rufus C. Dixon is his name. Everyone calls him Red. He's the reason this child left Fallen Leaf in her village and came back to the mountains so soon."

"I don't understand."

"You see, the last I saw of Red was last spring at Travelers' Rest. He —"

"Travelers' Rest! Where Lewis and Clark . . ."

"The same. He went off all huffed 'cause I was neglecting him and courtin' my Crow woman."

"Courtin'?"

"Not a whole lot of courtin' actually. A

good deal of amorous activity, you understand."

"I understand, all right."

"Well, Red didn't understand. That is to say, he understood to a degree, but it was all too much for him. He was overcome. It's hard to explain."

"No need. I get it."

"Anyway, we had words. Then I headed to the Yellowstone with Fallen Leaf, but I expected Red would come find me there in the Crow village. Never did. So, I come looking for him in the fall."

"And you didn't find him."

"That's right. Still missing. 'Course I got diverted here for the winter — not that I got any complaints, mind you. I'll keep looking for Red when the snows melt. Thing is, I'm a-feared the Bug's Boys got him, either that or he was snared by one of them wildfires that blazed through the mountains last summer. I like to think he found himself a good squaw like I done and settled down some. But I checked every peaceable Kootenai, Flathead, and Shoshone village for miles around. Nobody seen him, and he's hard to miss, what with his flaming red hair and red beard and his being near as large as one of your three boulders."

Bet shuddered and squeezed her eyes shut. She clutched her baby for dear life.

CHAPTER THIRTEEN

It was easy for Bet to keep her secrets because motherhood, peace, and security were what mattered to her now, and Little Bit did *not* have red hair. Her male guest became restless, but not so much to search for his missing trapping partner or to return to his Crow wife in her village. He said he hadn't been stuck in one place for so long since leaving the family home in Ohio. Plus, he wanted to test his wounded foot outdoors instead of babying it in the tepee. His solution was to go hunting. It made perfect sense to him. Game had grown mighty scarce around Three Boulder.

His limp might never go away, but it did temporarily vanish while snowshoeing with his Hawken rifle in hand for balance. He had success on all three of his hunting trips — shooting an elk slowed down by its thin legs cutting through the icy crust; a mule deer with an injured hind leg that caused it to limp; and a bighorn sheep that was feeling overly safe on a craggy ledge at the top of the mountain. On one of his hard cold treks, he had to race across a snowfield to avoid an avalanche that took a few trees with it as it swept past him. On another, he escaped a storm by spending the night in the same den as a sleeping bear that he couldn't bear to shoot, seeing as he was the beast's uninvited guest and all.

The baby only needed mother's milk and Bet would have been content with her stored nuts and dried meat, but still it pleased her to be provided for by such a capable hunter. He turned the elk hide-hair-side out and spread it on the ground for Little Bit and also gave the baby girl a deer-hide blanket. Never once did Bet have to remind him to fetch firewood, water, or fresh snow for cleaning the baby. When he was there at night, she never worried that she would be cold or that a pack of wolves would raid Three Boulder and carry off her baby. She had stopped calling him "mister." But Eldridge Hawkinson still didn't roll off her tongue, and she didn't like to call him Hawk even if the name fit. Instead, she called him "Eldy," which he said was all right as long as they were alone together and nobody else could hear it.

For most of her time in the mountains, Bet had been on high alert and busy as an untrapped beaver because nobody else was around to see that her needs were met. Now, with Eldy behaving the way Bet imagined a well-trained husband should act, she had become content to laze around. Her only job was to feed Little Bit every three hours, day or night, and whisper sweet words of affection into the closest tiny ear. The baby slept sixteen hours a day, and Bet nearly matched her, if not in full sleep, then at least in a semi-dream state. Lying around the warm fire, breastfeeding, dreaming, and whispering as much as she did, she stopped wearing her breechclout, belt, and shirt. Instead, she wore a straight tube dress made of a single elk hide folded in half or else nothing but her leggings. She had transformed from a mountain woman into a lady of leisure, but she felt she deserved this time of restfulness after so many years of hard living on the edge.

Eldy certainly never complained about her new softness and internal peace. He not only had killed another elk to provide her with the hide for the dress but also had worked the hide to the proper softness and sewn the two edges together. What's more, he held Little Bit, danced with her in his arms, cleaned her bottom, and did his own whispering to the little one. He would have breastfed her if he could. The baby clearly liked listening to the sound of his voice, and when he moved about the tepee, she tried to follow him with her little blue eyes. In return for all he did, Bet always made herself available to him, sometimes even when the babe was suckling. She didn't mind if Eldy woke her up; the baby had gotten her used to that, and anyway she always managed to get enough sleep in the course of twenty-four hours.

It was that way through most of the Moon of Buffalo Dropping Their Calves. Late in the month they had their first argument since the day she shot him in the foot. It all started with the month's name.

"That's Arapaho time, ain't it?" he asked one day when he woke up on the wrong side of the buffalo hide. "Call it what it is in American — March."

"I could, but I won't," Bet said, stroking the patchy yellow hair of her sleeping child. Bit had been born with a full head of hair, but she had been losing some of it. Bet figured it was temporary and of no great concern, though that didn't mean she had to like it. And something about the patchiness was irritating her this morning.

205

"You got something against March?"

"If you must know, I once lived with the Arapahos and I took to their moons."

"This is a long way from Arapaho country. Why do you keep calling it that, anyhow? There ain't no buffalo in the mountains. The only thing dropped up here was by you — that sweet little by-blow."

"By what?"

"Just a name this child heard somewhere along the line . . . no doubt back in society."

"It means bastard, mister."

"That right? I sure wouldn't call a little girl *that*. No need to start calling me *mister* again."

"You'd rather I call you *bastard*?"

"Well, I'll be a son of a bitch. No need for us to be calling each other names. This is your Hawk you're talking to . . . I mean Eldy."

"I know who I'm talking to — Hawk, partner of Red."

"Right, Red. You remembered?"

"I . . . I won't ever forget that bastard. I mean that name."

"You don't even know him. Why'd you call my old pard a bastard?"

"Red is as easy to remember as Sunshine."

"What does that mean?"

"Nothing! Stop shouting. You'll wake up

206

my baby."

"Me? I'm not the one shouting. What are we fighting over, anyhow? It was just some word I heard. I didn't mean nothing by it."

"*By-blow* isn't just some word. It was mean. Nobody calls my daughter that, to my face or hers."

"Look. I'm plumb sorry. I didn't sleep good last night."

He reached down and put his hand on top of hers as she gently stroked what yellow hair still clung to Little Bit's head. She stopped petting, but she let him keep his hand there and smiled at the man who shared her tepee. He was wrong to call her daughter that name. But even good people said the wrong thing sometimes. And he really was Eldy, the man who had done so much for her and for Little Bit, too. She owed him. And she was fond of him to boot. Just because he had been Red's associate didn't make him *like* Red. Maybe it had been weighing on the back of her mind that this man, as good and gentle as he was, had once been Red's fur trading partner. She wouldn't let such thoughts continue. He meant too much to her.

"I'm sorry, too," she said. "We've both said stupid things. We square?"

"Square."

"Good. You should sleep. Your snoring is no bother to me."

"It ain't that. Could be I'm getting restless again. It's been goading on me."

"You want to go out and shoot another animal or something?"

"No, not this time. We have plenty of dried meat in the cache. You have enough hides."

"You could shoot another deer . . . for the baby. She'll need clothes."

"Not for a while. Not out here."

"If you don't want to hunt, what do you want to do?"

She took hold of his hand, put it on her chest, and held it there so he could feel her heartbeat.

"Not that," he said, letting his hand slide off. "To tell you the plain truth."

"More sleep would help?"

"Maybe. But it won't happen now. My mind's been a-wandering places."

"Oh. Well, you tell me, Eldy. What do you want to do now?"

"I seen the last two days the snow's been melting in the warm sun."

"Really? I hadn't noticed. But it's still not spring in the high country. It isn't yet the Moon of Ice Breaking in the River."

"That would be Arapaho for April?"

"Yes, sorry. Isn't that how this whole silly

argument started?"

"No comment. Anyway, it's over."

But the Moon of Ice Breaking in the River arrived, the melting of snow and ice accelerated, and Lost Trout Creek overflowed its banks. The weather had abruptly stopped dancing back and forth between winter and spring. They did not argue again, but her Eldy became even more restless, with a week of sleepless nights. Watching him *not* sleep made her toss and turn, too. Once she even accidentally tossed Little Bit off her belly. When enough snow had melted, they took a walk to Beaverhead Lake, taking turns carrying the baby. A beaver appeared, carrying in its mouth roots and stems from its underwater food cache. It swam to its lodge but not before slapping its tail on the surface as if to say, *Not you again.* Bet was glad to see the animal had survived the winter, too, but she said nothing. After all, Eldy made his livelihood trapping beaver, and she didn't want to start an argument.

"You know I have to go," he said.

"Do I?" she said.

"I can go without snowshoes now. I'll leave them for you."

"I don't want you to go. You still limp."

"My foot is fine, as fine as it will ever be."

"I am still sorry about that, but the shooting accident did cause you to stay."

"Yes. And then other things did. I'll go to the village below. It will take me less than two days. Somebody will loan me a horse — maybe that Flathead fellow who still has a hankering for you even though he married one of his own kind. He owes me for taking good care of you and the baby all winter, even if Little Bit isn't *his* baby."

"Schweeleh doesn't even know I have a baby. You are the only one who knows."

"I'll tell him, and look in on his squaw's baby, too. Would you like that?"

"Suit yourself."

"I didn't think your baby was a secret, just the identity of the father."

"Don't start that again. I haven't forgotten that name you once called Little Bit."

"I don't want to start anything."

"I know. You want to end it. You want to return to your Crow wife and make your own baby."

"She is my squaw. Crow men have more than one squaw you know."

"So you told me. You aren't a Crow."

"Mountain men have more than one squaw. Take Beckwourth . . ."

"No. I don't want him. Or you. I'm nobody's squaw."

"You are sure enough complicated for a primitive woman. You did say you didn't want me to go, Bet. Anyway, I'm not going for good. I am not even going to see Fallen Leaf in the Crow village at this time. I have unfinished business."

"Trapping business?"

"No, but seeing that beaver getting active again did remind me of Red. I got to make one last large effort to find my partner."

"And if you don't?"

"I'll come back to get you. I'll take you to the Crow village. They'll be others there to help you care for your baby, and we can —"

"Like Fallen Leaf? No thank you. This is my home, our home."

"Not mine. I —"

"I didn't mean you, mister. I meant Little Bit and me."

"And so I'm a mister once more? I can't take you along with me when I look for Red. It won't be safe for you or the baby. I'm going to take a closer look in Bug's Boy country."

"An eye for an eye? I heard tell of that."

"Only thing can be done. Them are damned bad Injuns. Maybe you've gotten along with the Blackfeet so far, but I ain't at all sure how and you might be the only one. They're dangerous and you can't trust

211

a single one of them."

"Right. Not like mountain men."

"Is that fair? What have I done except care for you even though you shot me in the foot?"

"Something I'll just have to live with."

"You want me to get down on my knees and ask you to be my squaw . . . my wife?"

"No."

"Even if Fallen Leaf didn't exist, you would turn me down. Am I right?"

"I don't know. I just don't want you to go."

"I said I'll be back here, whether or not I find Red. Then I'll ask you again to come with me to the Crow village."

"You won't come back. Like you said, the Blackfeet don't like you."

"I will — this child don't aim to lose his scalp just yet. If they rubbed Red out, this child will take revenge. I owe it to him. We been partners for . . ."

"I know, but it's over."

"You mean me and you? I told you I'll . . ."

"I mean the partnership."

"Me and Red?"

"Yes, you and Red."

"That's not true. We quarreled over Fallen Leaf, but we've quarreled before. If I find the ol' feller alive and kicking, we'll patch things up as always."

"No, you won't, Eldy."

"What do you know about it? You never even met Red!"

"I did. Once. You won't find him."

"How can you be so sure?" He paused. "You know something, don't you?"

Little Bit began to cry. It was time for a feeding. The baby never forgot that. Bet slid a breast out of her elk-skin tube dress. She never denied the little one.

"Well?" Eldy said. "The babe can wait, damn it. Where did you see Red?"

"Up north, above Hell Gate, not too far from Blackfeet country. I had a tepee there by a creek."

"What creek?"

"I never gave it a name."

"When?"

"Last year. It was during the Moon When the Hot Weather Begins. Before the fire came."

"And? What was he doing?"

"You don't want to know."

"He's my partner, sister. Of course I want to know! Tell me."

When Little Bit found the nipple, Bet turned her back on the man who had been sharing her tepee but was now going away.

"Red is dead," she said.

CHAPTER FOURTEEN

Of course, she had to explain why Red was dead. After blurting out the news, she had no choice. Eldridge Hawkinson had shared her tepee, helped her give birth, provided for her, and protected her. No other man before had ever done all of that; she never before had wanted a man to do all of *that,* not even Schweeleh. Whether Eldy left her or not, whether he ever came back or not, she had needed to tell him the truth about his longtime trading partner and the violent demise.

It took her two days to explain it once and another two days to explain it a second and third time, with more explicit details each time. He believed her — why would she make up such a horrible story? — but at the same time didn't believe her. He had always thought of Red as being bold and boastful when it came to finding and trapping beaver, avoiding or shooting hostile

Indians (depending on how many there were), and consuming great quantities of whiskey, but he insisted when it came to females of any color Red had always acted awkward and timid.

"What he did to me was plenty awkward," Bet told Eldy on explanation day number five as they sat in the tepee, the sleeping Little Bit between them. "But he was no more timid than a dog with hydrophobia."

"So, you killed him just like that?" he said, tugging too hard on one end of his mustache as he had been doing frequently of late.

"As one would a mad dog."

"For doing what I've been doing here for months?"

"If you can't see the difference, then . . ." She couldn't finish; his attitude was too incredible to believe. Right before her eyes, despite all her difficult explaining, he had undergone a transformation. Five days ago, he had seen her as a tender lover and a doting mother. Now he saw her as an unfaithful squaw and a slaughterer of man.

"Red was my partner."

"So you've said ten thousand times."

"He stuck by me through thick and thin for a decade. He saved my life more than once from the Blackfeet. One time we was surrounded by . . . you wouldn't understand. You can't possibly understand how it is between a man and his pard out here."

"I'm getting a pretty good idea. I reckon I don't understand how it is between a man and his wife, either, not out here, not anywhere. I just know how it is — was — between you and me."

"You could have killed me, too, if you had aimed a little higher."

"You know I wasn't aiming. It was an accident. Anyway, a foot is a long way from any vital organ."

"Why didn't you just bash my head in one night while I was asleep?"

"Stop it, Eldy. That's all to pieces humbug. You think I make a practice of inviting mountain men into my tepee and murdering them?"

"I don't know. What do I really know about you? You choose to live in the mountains all alone, the only white woman for a thousand miles in any direction. It ain't natural. I know of white men who turned Injun and disappeared into the mountains, but never a white woman who give it a second thought let alone done it."

"I must be a crazy white bitch, just like Red said."

"Well, Red wasn't too delicate, but he had a point. The way you live ain't normal no matter how you slice it."

"Normal like Red? Whether you saw it or not, your partner was a bastard."

"He had his faults sure, like all of us, but . . ."

"A bastard is a bastard, Eldy. I'm sorry. But I'm *not* sorry I killed him. If he raised from the ashes this instant and tried to do me that way again, I'd kill him again. You can bet your life on that."

He snorted and then pinched his nostrils, twisting his hawklike nose. He glared at her. Words formed on his lips but didn't come out. It was just as well. All his words lately were hurtful. Finally, he looked down at Little Bit, and so did Bet. Little Bit had slept through it all and was still asleep but making a full range of whistling, gurgling, and snorting sounds. Bet lifted the naked baby into her arms, pressed her to her bosom, and patted her milk-white shoulders. Eldy stopped glaring, but he kept looking, his bluish-gray eyes becoming various shades of gray. It seemed to Bet to be a concerned look, and she forgot for a second that the man she had shared her tepee with had become downright aggravating.

"She'll be fine," Bet told him. "Sounds worse than it is. No need for worry. Now that the days are finally warming up, she has decided to be under the weather. Has a mind of her own."

"What?"

"I said she has a mind of her own."

"I don't doubt it considering who her mama is. I was just thinking — it was near eleven of your moons ago that my partner paid you a visit at your old camp."

"Sounds about right, but you make it sound like a social call. Damn it, Eldy. He came uninvited, a stranger, and put me through hell."

"So, you killed him in self-defense?"

"Something like that. Yes. Yes. What else! I feared for my life. Haven't I made that clear?"

Eldy nodded as his eyes widened. He looked clear through her again just like he did the day he first showed up at her tepee.

"And out of it came a new life," he said, twisting both ends of his mustache at the same time.

She squeezed Little Bit closer to feel more skin against skin.

Eldy reached out and tapped the baby on the bottom. He grinned and turned his gaze to the smoke hole overhead. "Good old Red," he said. "You got the jump on this child, ol' pard. So, tell me, how does it feel to be a papa, you crazy bastard?"

■ ■ ■ ■

With no chance of reuniting with his trapping partner on this earth, Eldridge Hawkinson had no reason to head out of the Bitterroot Place and set foot in the Blackfeet country northeast of the Hell Gate. No remains of Red would remain up there to bury, not with the fire and the wolves, and the bone-picking ravens. No revenge was necessary up there since the troublesome Bug's Boys were not responsible for Red's death. And even if he had wanted to pursue beaver pelts in the northern waterways right now, which he didn't, he wasn't set up for it and, in any case, had never set traps without his partner. Fallen Leaf would be waiting for him back at her Crow village near the Yellowstone, but he had only promised his squaw he would be back by the time of the cottonwood snows — and that wasn't until June.

The whole revenge thing did haunt him some, though, and caused considerable meditations, which he shared with Bet because he was sharing so much else with her and was opposed to resurrecting the silent treatment he had given her after she shot him in the foot. In the backwoods of

Ohio, his rawboned mama had raised him to be as honest as the day is long, and his Bible-thumping daddy had taught him to trust in the principle of "an eye for an eye" day or night. The mountain man code he readily took to called for looking out for one's partner, which he admitted he had done a poor job of, and also for exacting revenge when somebody did the partner wrong, which he said he couldn't do in this case because the somebody was a white American female who had become another kind of partner. Furthermore, she said his late partner had violated her (the baby was strong circumstantial evidence) and she had killed him in self-defense, which was justified in practically anybody's code. To top it all off, he was thoroughly enjoying their private high country life and in any case had no wish to share a tepee with a dead woman.

"It ain't easy to get that revenge notion out of my hard head," he confessed. "I'm going hunting. Be back in three days. Don't go away."

He was true to his word. He returned in three days dragging a carved-up moose carcass. He was offended when she said she wasn't hungry. But it was true. She had just eaten her fill of treasured eggs gathered with no small difficulty from the shoreline of Beaverhead Lake. With Little Bit in one hand and an egg in the other, she had needed to duck and run to avoid an aggressive male Canada goose that flew at her face. The experience had been frightening and it had put her child at some risk, but at least she had done something. She hardly listened when Eldy told her of his long-distance shot that downed the bull moose while it was migrating in the valley to its summer range. It was a hard drag up the mountainside, he said, and now he presented her with the head. She stared at the tongue hanging out, which the mountain man considered juicy and tender and would likely eat raw.

"All right, the meat doesn't interest you right now; it will later when I cook it," he said, throwing his bloodstained hands in the air. "It should interest you what I decided about the other matter."

"I thought the hunt was all that mattered."

"My revenge, remember?"

"You figure to kill me like you did this moose?" she asked as she tried to get Little Bit to suckle. Ever since the goose chase the little one had been wheezing.

"I had nothing against the moose; killed him for meat, not for —"

"Revenge, I know. Does your vengeance include my baby, too?"

"For you to ask such a thing sours my milk."

"It must — she'd die without a mother. Or do you plan to take her to Fallen Leaf since Little Bit was born of the seeds of your partner's death and . . ."

"Stop! I was just ribbing you 'bout revenge. My mistake. It's no ribbing matter. I see that now. You know I could never do nothing mean to you, let alone to Little Bit. You'll be happy to know — and maybe old Red would be turning over in his grave about now if there was any part of him left to turn over — I done got rid of that revenge notion while I was off hunting by myself."

Bet shushed him, as if nothing he or she said or did mattered. She listened hard to the whistling sound that the baby made each time she breathed out. He wasn't listening.

"Not only that," he continued. "But I also decided that you are *no* danger to me."

"What? I have no idea what you're talking about. Little Bit doesn't sound right. Her breathing isn't normal — all that whistling. Do you hear it?"

"Suspicious types might very well think

you'd be considering doing away with me to keep the killing of my partner a secret from law enforcers, seeing as I am the only other person who knows . . ."

"Law enforcers in the Bitterroot Place? Anyway, what I did was *no* crime."

"Don't worry. I haven't given a second thought myself to bringing you to justice in St. Louis. In fact, I've made a decision to stay here longer."

"What?"

"I said, *I'll stay!*"

She hadn't asked him to stay since telling him about Red. He made it sound as if he was doing her a favor, and maybe he was if she wanted to do nothing more than lay about being a mother and lover. It was easy to put off going back to the way things were — relying on herself for food and comfort and coming and going as she pleased — because she had a baby now and she had lost some of her hard edge. Her body belonged to the baby and to this mountain man. He would go eventually, though, for Fallen Leaf was waiting and trapping beaver was still in his blood, even though there were less beaver each season and he had never gone to trap them without his trusty partner.

"I almost forgot to tell you, Bet," Eldy

said, pausing to pull a thin slice of moose meat out of a pouch. He began talking again once his mouth was full. "Your friend, what's his name, gave you this." From out of his buckskin shirt, Eldy drew out a lumpy cloth doll dyed red and wearing a white dress.

"Schweeleh? You saw Schweeleh?" She waved the doll in front of Little Bit, but the baby only began crying, the whistling sound now coming between gigantic sobs.

"I reported to your friend. After all, he was the one who sent me to you last winter. I told him I was damned glad he did because . . . well, that was man-to-man talk. I also told him you survived the winter just fine and gave birth to a little blond girl who wasn't his."

"You said that?"

"Yes, but don't fret. I said I didn't know who the baby belonged to."

"She belongs to me . . . and herself. Did Schweeleh say anything?"

"He said he hoped your baby would like the doll."

Little Bit scrunched up her tear-stained face as if the doll might bite her on the nose.

"I'll save it for her," Bet said. "Back in Kentucky my Aunt Betty gave me a doll that I loved and called Dolly. This is Dolly II."

She was about to tuck the doll in the front of her buckskin shirt, but that only made Little Bit wail louder. Maybe the baby thought Dolly II was competition. "Anything else Schweeleh said?"

"He said he and the other tribal hunters had decided to go on a spring buffler hunt on the Plains."

"I mean about the baby and me?"

"He is happy for you of course, but he and his wife, what's her name, have their own concerns."

"Spukani had her baby, too?"

"Big bucking baby boy. They call him Wildfire. He was suffering from a barking cough during my visit. And she has another one on the way. She's getting round again already . . ."

"One is enough for some of us." She tried to hold the red doll against Little Bet's belly, but the baby thrashed her arms and legs until the doll fell to the ground.

"Their boy didn't want it either. The father gave him a rattlesnake rattle instead."

"I'm sure Little Bit will want the doll. She's not feeling well right now. That's all there is to it. Her breathing is labored. Listen, would you."

"Pretty smart baby," Eldy said. "She's whistling already."

CHAPTER FIFTEEN

Eldridge Hawkinson's extended stay was cut shorter than either he or Bet had anticipated. Whether Red's death was what stood between them or not, something did, and it spoiled their domestic bliss. They smoked together from her pipe tomahawk only once, and it was hardly relaxing. She had killed Red with a similar pipe — that fact seemed to hang in the air with every puff of smoke. Lovemaking fell by the wayside. She rejected his every effort to become intimate, and he, whether because of his own nature or because of her Red experience, never forced the issue.

She became all mother, and a constantly worried one at that. Little Bit kept coughing. Bet heard not only whistling wheezes and barking coughs but also rattling mucus. The baby's head felt hot at night, and she lost interest in her regular feedings. Rest didn't help. Cool baths in the creek and tin cups of water didn't help. A tincture Bet made by adding fresh arrowleaf balsamroot to warm water seemed to loosen the baby's phlegm and soothe her throat. But it wasn't enough. Jay Talker returned with the warmer weather and tried to chat with Bet, but she was preoccupied with the new little human being, and the large male newcomer had no use for a camp jay. When Jay Talker tried to make a new nest in Lonesome Pine, the human male hurled stones at the noisy bird.

On the last day of the Moon of Ice Breaking in the River, after the sick baby's noise-making had kept him awake all night, Eldy told Bet the time had come — he must leave Three Boulder immediately. The huge high country had narrowed considerably, and his foot had healed as much as it ever would. He had the itch to push on. His destination was the Crow country, which had everything a mountain man could want — Indians eager to trade instead of kill, beaver-filled creeks, buffalo herds, deer, antelope, fresh grass, good wood, clean water, and an enchanting squaw. His plan was to catch the Flathead buffalo hunters at the Salish village and travel east with them as it figured to make the long journey safer and he also wanted to come home with plenty of salubrious meat for Fallen Leaf.

"She loves to eat buffler, all the parts," he said twice to make sure Bet heard him. "She prefers the delicacies like the hump ribs, tongues, boudins, and, with the cows of course, the fetuses. But she does savor tail of beaver, too. Fallen Leaf has quite the appetite."

Bet said nothing, because her baby was bawling again. He apologized for the sudden announcement, explaining several times that while he didn't want to go now, he was afraid the Flathead hunters would leave their village without him. Her lack of response only made him more eager to go. He pecked her on the cheek and patted the crying baby on the bottom before heading to the tepee door with his bundle and his rifle.

"You'll be fine now," he called back to her. "The worst of the cold and snow is over. It's springtime, even up here."

"Wait," Bet said. "Fetch my cradleboard, would you?"

"Sure. You going somewhere?"

"*We* are going with you." She stood up with the baby in her arms. That seemed to lift Little Bit's spirits. She stopped crying and went for the nearest nipple. "Lay out my breechclout and my other old clothes. I

228

don't feel dressed for travel in this loose robe."

"Are you serious? I mean I'm glad if you are serious."

"Of course, I'm serious."

"Wonderful. It's just that I've asked you to come with me to my Crow village a dozen times. You've always said it was impossible, because of Fallen Leaf, your love for Three Boulder, and your wish to remain a . . . a — how did you put it? — *a free and independent mountain woman.* That does sound, especially with a child, a little . . . you know, *crazy.* I'm . . . I'm delighted you've had a change of heart and want to . . ."

"My heart has not changed. We are only going with you as far as the Salish village."

"Oh? I don't understand. Your friend, eh . . . Squealer, is married."

"Schweeleh."

"You think he is like me and is willing to take on a second squaw . . . eh . . . wife?"

"I'm not thinking of him or you. I'm thinking of my baby. She's sick."

"I can't help you there. I can get a baby out into the world, but . . ."

"I know. The Salish village is home to the healer Otter Woman. And if need be, I'll even turn to Joseph Logan and the other

229

God-fearing Iroquois who brought white man's medicine with them into the valley. I'll do anything."

"And if — when — your baby gets better?"

"We'll come back home. Three Boulder is our home."

"Just you and her?"

"That's right. And you'll be shooting buffalo for Fallen Leaf."

"I suppose I will. And then, in due time, I'll see about trapping again, that is if I can find me another partner."

"And can find the beaver."

"I know there's some right over there in your little lake. They done built a dam to make a swamp at the head. There'll always be beaver somewhere."

"Don't you come back and kill my beaver."

"Of course, I might like it so much in the Crow village I'll make myself a chief like Beckwourth . . . or at least an assistant chief. Sure, why not? I don't need to be wading in beaver dams and freezing or starving the rest of my born days. Instead, I'll hunt buffalo and fight my enemies and be the best dern Crow warrior I can be. Fallen Leaf would like that."

"Like you say, *wonderful.* We're wasting

time, Eldy. Let's go."

She got dressed in her old breechclout, tight belt, leggings, and shirt. Because of swollen feet, she had gone barefoot before the baby came and got used to it afterward while mostly lying around the tepee in her lingering winter stupor. Now when she slipped into her moccasins, they again fit just right. She had too much yellow hair to stuff every last strand into her coonskin cap. That was fine. She figured she would give some of her valued hair to Otter Woman once the healer made Little Bit well again. For the first time ever, Bet put a baby in her cradleboard, and Little Bit, having little wiggle room and having exhausted herself crying, immediately fell asleep. Bet still attached the pipe tomahawk to the side of the board. If everything went well in the village, she would be ready for some long celebratory smokes.

"Nothing else you want to take?" Eldy asked. "Not your buffalo hide? No food from your cache?"

"No need. I'll be among generous friends down there. Anyway, we'll be back here soon — me and my baby."

Even with Little Bit riding on her back and making a pother, they moved quickly with little talk and spent only two days and one night on the trail. The Salish welcomed Bet and her baby to their village. Some no doubt assumed Eldridge Hawkinson was the father, but nobody asked. Eldy was pleased the young men hadn't yet set out for the buffalo hunting grounds to the east. They had heard a report that the Blackfeet were already present for their own spring hunt, and the Salish wanted to avoid a confrontation. Runners were also sent out to see if the Nez Perces and Kootenais cared to join them on the hunt.

Schweeleh came out of his tepee to greet the visitors but managed only a nod to Eldy, a faint smile for Bet, and a glance at the whistling baby in her arms. Eldy acted altogether cheerful and started to speak of his wonderful winter at Three Boulder, but Schweeleh only stared at him with a long face and then slipped back inside.

"Maybe we interrupted something, you know, an intimate moment between him and his squaw," Eldy said. "You never know with these Indians. When they got a mind to copulate, they copulate."

"Unlike mountain men?"

"If you want to go there, you bet I will."

"And tell me all about you and your accommodating Fallen Leaf?"

"She makes a warm lodge, and she likes to do most any . . . But I was thinking 'bout you and me."

"Sure you were."

"Ah'll swar by hook."

"No need. Think anything you like. I'll do the same."

"But really I was thinking about . . ."

"Forget it."

"Whatever you say, but back to your Schweeleh."

"Spukani's Schweeleh."

"Appears that way, don't it? Still, him and me got reason to palaver seeing as we got so much in common, and we both got cause to thank each other." He gave Bet one of his penetrating glances, but she just shrugged and stroked her baby's brow. "But it'll keep," Eldy said. He patted her on the head and then did the same to Little Bit's bottom. "Maybe you got some things to tell him yourself. I am dry. You don't mind if I go off and see if one of these friendly villagers will offer me something stronger to drink than melted snow water."

Bet barely nodded before quickly bounding into the family tepee, niceties be damned. What she saw were two worried parents. Schweeleh had positioned himself with arms crossed in the back of the tepee next to Spukani, whose hands were twisting atop her large belly. In the front of the tepee knelt Otter Woman, who was tending to the big baby boy Wildfire with her specially prepared herbs and mysterious incantations to the animal spirits. Bet held back, not wanting to interrupt. But Otter Woman suddenly stood and turned in one motion and waved Bet forward. The healer listened to Little Bit breathe for just a few seconds before she signaled Bet to put the baby down on the same deerskin as Wildfire. Bet did so with care.

"Same for one, same for two," Otter Woman said, and she began to give the second baby the identical treatment. Her high-pitched shamanistic incantations filled the tepee and pained Bet's ears. Bet had heard mountain lions, either fighting or mating, make similar piercing screams. The unnerved mother took to pacing on her side of the tepee, at every turn taking a nervous glance at the two ill babies. She realized that the concerned couple on the opposite side were chanting prayers in Salish that were nearly drowned out by Otter Woman's shrieks. Bet finally walked over to them to find out who they were praying to — the Great Spirit Amotken or lesser animal spirits.

That wasn't made clear, but Schweeleh offered a translation. "For our son," he said, "we ask he get, with least amount of effort, all things needed to live long life, to kill much many animals and enemies, and to steal greatest number of horses. For your daughter, we ask she also live long life and make friend to Wildfire as you make friend to me."

Bet savored the translation, especially the last sweet words. But she had to whisper a question into Schweeleh's ear: "That is Spukani's prayer, too?"

"We pray together," he replied. "Not to white man's Creator. You must do that."

"*Must?* That's the kind of thing Mama Hex used to tell her nine children. I didn't listen so well."

"Must do only if you wish."

"I might wish later. Thank you."

Later, when Wildfire and Little Bit took a turn for the worse and Otter Woman had all but run out of steam, Joseph Logan the Iroquois and his wife, Spukani's sister Sakaam, arrived with a brown bottle of patent medicine, a silver cross, and a Bible brought to the Bitterroot by one of the Salish visitors to the Black Robes in St. Louis. Schweeleh and Spukani stopped their traditional prayers and stepped out of the tepee to allow Joseph Logan to pray in English while his wife and Bet knelt on each side of him. Next came small doses of the tonic for the little ones. Wildfire vomited first, and then Little Bit, and twice after that they vomited simultaneously. Schweeleh reentered the tepee on the run, smashed the medicine bottle with a tomahawk, and dismissed Joseph Logan. Sakaam stayed on her knees as if dazed until her sister escorted her out. Bet cleaned up the mess the babies had made on themselves and each other while Schweeleh picked up the broken glass.

"I did try," she said. "I was praying and wishing and hoping."

"Never mind."

"But there must be something more I can do . . . we can do."

"Salish babies much strong." Schweeleh took his son in his arms and proudly held him high overhead until the boy sounded ready to retch again.

"Mine isn't Salish, of course," Bet said. "Not even half." She picked up Little Bit and rocked her.

"Still good and strong. She have strong mother."

They lay the babies back down, elbow-to-elbow, and wrapped them in a clean deerskin blanket. Neither baby was crying now, but their breathing was irregular and loud.

"It's going to be a long night," Bet said. "Nothing more to do, I reckon."

"At dawn, we go to Medicine Tree," Schweeleh said. "It make good medicine."

She knew of the sacred Salish Medicine Tree, but she had never seen it. She closed her eyes and pictured a tree with little brown bottles growing from every branch. Next thing she knew, Schweeleh had wrapped his strong arms around her and pulled her in so close that her right ear and long yellow hair rested against his throbbing chest.

A large contingent from the village traveled south up the valley, the mounted young buffalo hunters leading the way, followed by women and children either walking or riding ponies that pulled the sick and elderly on travois. Bet insisted on carrying her baby on her back, and Spukani, at Schweeleh's insistence, walked next to her doing the same. Schweeleh stayed close behind them so he could look at the faces of the two babies in their cradleboards and also guard the rear in case of attack.

Eldridge Hawkinson did not come along. The night before, he had found only two villagers who possessed any whiskey, and only one of them was willing to share the strong medicine with the mountain man. That was enough. The brew of raw alcohol, molasses, tobacco, and dried camas root flattened them and neither could be stirred in the morning. Joseph Logan and his obedient wife Sakaam were also absent. He believed no tree, no matter how close its top was to the Creator, could serve as a shrine and that all spirits associated with the so-called Medicine Tree were created by men like Schweeleh whose inability to adapt to Christian religious practices threatened to doom the tribe.

The mountains pinched the valley into a narrow passage that the party followed until their path was all but blocked by an enormous three-hundred-year-old ponderosa pine tree. The Salish worshippers spread out around the massive trunk and left offerings of beads, ribbons, and other colorful things. Schweeleh cut off a lock of Bet's yellow hair and offered that. Bet said he'd better make that two offerings, so he cut off another lock.

Schweeleh explained the events that followed. The young hunters asked for protection on their upcoming travel to the buffalo country, for a successful hunt in which they killed many buffalo but no more than the tribe needed, and for a safe return. But then two ambitious brothers stepped forward and one asked that the protection extend to battle should the Blackfeet attack, and the other asked that many enemies should fall. Next, the sick and elderly were led or carried to the base of the tree and they prayed while gazing up the trunk toward a patch of blue sky. They told stories of a time when animals but no people were here. The evil Bighorn Sheep Ram would not allow people to come to the narrow valley where the Medicine Tree grew. But the Coyote, a true supporter of the human race, tricked the Ram into butting the tree, which caused its horn to become stuck. With the Ram immobilized, Coyote cut off the Ram's head and that allowed the Salish to visit the Medicine Tree and pray, which in turn allowed them the freedom to dig up all the bitterroot they needed to sustain themselves in the valley and to travel to the Great Plains to hunt bison.

"Nice story," Bet said. "But how does any of this help Little Bit and Wildfire? They're bawling louder than ever."

"Since Ram lost head, we worship here. We give thanks and pray for the well-being of all."

"You mean all Salish?"

"All people."

"Mountain men?"

"Yes."

"Women?"

"Yes.

"White babies?"

"Of course."

"Blackfeet?"

"Coyote killed Bighorn Sheep Ram, not all evil on earth."

Schweeleh was done answering her questions. He spun her around so he could remove Little Bit from the cradleboard and then, using only one hand, released Wildfire from Spukani's cradleboard. Being free of their confined places only made the babies cry with more abandon. The worshippers all turned their heads to look, some not hiding their annoyance at this unbecoming display on sacred ground.

The two mothers watched in amazement as Schweeleh stepped over or around the elderly tribesmen and pressed the noses of both babies against the furrowed and fire-scarred reddish-orange bark. Their tiny noses twitched as they sniffed the Medicine Tree's sweet aroma. Schweeleh pulled both babies away from the trunk and held them high in the air, one in each hand. Bet anxiously squeezed her fists to her chest as she and seemingly everyone else listened. No coughing or crying — but some sniveling. Schweeleh immediately lowered the babies and again let their noses brush against the bark. After a half minute of this treatment, Schweeleh once more raised the pair to face the crowd. The babies now breathed quietly and regularly as if their nasal passages and lungs were completely clear.

It might have been a coincidence or some higher power at work, but Bet saw no reason not to credit the tree.

"That's what I call good medicine," she said, smiling.

Spukani did the same, and then the two mothers received a great treat — Little Bit and Wildfire smiled back for the first time in their young lives.

CHAPTER SIXTEEN

The Salish men made preparations to "go to buffalo" before the Moon of Ice Breaking in the River had ended. The main hunt would still come in late summer when the bison were plump and had less hair, which made it easier to tan the hides. But it had been a hard winter, and the entire village was hungry for fresh buffalo meat. Some of the squaws were going to the Plains on this spring trip so they could spare the male hunters the chore of butchering the fallen beasts. Eldridge Hawkinson, both when drunk and sober, asked Bet to come along, not necessarily to hunt or to butcher but because from the hunting grounds it was only a short distance to the Crow village. Yes, he was certain Fallen Leaf waited for him with open arms and he wanted to be with his squaw again now that he was finished with his old partner business. Yet he insisted, and he seemed most sincere, that life would be so much better if Bet stopped roaming the mountains and came to live with Fallen Leaf and him as a threesome. On the morning of departure, he repeated his words.

"Better for you?" she asked.

"For all of us," he said, twisting one end of his mustache, "after a period of adjustment. Aren't you tired of roaming the mountains alone?"

"It would be a foursome, you know," she replied as she stroked the hair of her sleeping baby, breathing so quietly and peacefully now — the way it had been since the visit to the Medicine Tree. "And Fallen Leaf will want one of her own. That would make a *fifthsome.*"

"The possibilities are endless. I've told you mountain men, like Crow men, and Flathead men, are permitted to have multiple wives. You know I'm a good shot, a damn good provider, don't snore louder than your average bear, and don't bear no grudge."

"Thank you for your invitation and your kindness, Eldy," she said, but her mind drifted to the family tepee of Schweeleh, her dear Salish man who presently only had the one wife.

"But," he said. "I'm waiting for the *but.*"

243

"No but."

She knew Schweeleh was going on the hunt and that Spukani wasn't. That sounded inviting, and lately she had started to wonder if perhaps Schweeleh, with all his traditional Salish beliefs, ever thought about taking a second wife. Spukani's sister Sakaam wasn't available, of course; she had, for better or worse, married Joseph Logan.

"So," said Eldy, now twisting the other end of his mustache, "you might come with me on the hunt and see if . . ."

"No. I won't."

Spukani wasn't going to make the trip with the hunters because she was with child and because she wanted to keep watch on the health of her big baby boy, Wildfire. Bet decided she best be the same kind of mother at the moment. She would stay close to Little Bit, even though the baby's breathing was just fine. Bringing the baby along was out of the question — too dangerous. *I'm no Sacagawea,* she told herself. Anyway, there were other reasons for not going. If Mama and Pappy Hex had taught her anything, it was to respect the institution of marriage, no matter how mismatched the man and woman happened to be. Schweeleh had chosen Spukani, a traditional wife for a traditional Salish man — there was no changing that. Bet had no desire to kill or butcher a buffalo anymore, if she ever had, but that was purely secondary to the realization that she too much desired the tall hunter who hadn't asked her to come along.

When the hunters and their female helpers mounted their ponies, Bet let Eldridge kiss her goodbye full on the lips. Even as he did so, she looked past him to where Schweeleh was saying a long goodbye to his family. He held Wildfire high so that they were face to face. "One day, my son, you will go to buffalo," he told the boy. Wildfire nodded his head as if he understood and began kicking his chubby little legs as if he was raring to go. Schweeleh then gently bumped his flat belly against his wife's belly, and as he handed the boy to her, he said something that Bet translated as, "Now go to Mama." Once Spukani was clutching the boy to her chest, Schweeleh gave them both a big squeeze, and Spukani finally spoke. Bet came up with a rough translation: "Be good. Be safe. Come home with much meat."

Bet finally caught Schweeleh's eye. Their long silent stare was stronger than any vocal goodbye. When he finally blinked, she blinked back. It was like a private wave.

"Last chance, Pale Woman Who Lives in

Mountains Alone," said Eldy, who was nothing if not tenacious. "I'm like all these Flathead boys, feeling brave as a buffler bull in spring."

"Good luck to all of you," she said, without looking at the mountain man.

"Come on now. You really don't want to roam these mountains forever. Little Bit will be plenty safe. Soon as we cross the divide, I'll shoot the first buffler I see, we'll carve it up fast, say a quick goodbye to your Flathead friends, and head straight for the Crow village. Fallen Leaf will be eating hump ribs that very night. It will please her."

She looked at him now. "And she will be pleased to see me and my baby come share her tepee?"

"It's my tepee, too. I'm the hunter man. She's my squaw and . . ."

"Forget it, Eldy. That's your dream, not mine. If I went, I'd only come back here. I mean to the mountains. Three Boulder in the Bitterroot is my home, not some crowded Crow village on the Yellowstone."

"The Crows believe their country to be paradise on earth."

"Good for them. The talking jay and I prefer the Bitterroot."

"You have spent many years roaming. So why not roam with me to the Plains? And

246

perhaps settle down with me there for a while? How do you know you wouldn't like it playing with your child in a family tepee and having a man provide for your every need all the time?"

"Oh, and Crow women just sit around doing nothing all day?"

"Certainly not. Fallen Leaf will do the women's work and . . ."

"And I'll just lay about with my baby?"

"And with me. That wouldn't sound so bad to plenty of women. Easy living."

"Look, I'm not leaving Little Bit and I'm not going to take her. For all anyone here knows, the Blackfeet are still out there on the hunting grounds."

"Damn it, woman. They must be gone by now, and I'm not afraid of them Bug's Boys anyway. I got a rifle that'll shoot center and I ain't a-feared of fighting if need be. You'll see."

"So you've said, and I believe you, Eldy. Little Bit doesn't need to see any of that. The Blackfeet are good shots, too, with bows and arrows or white man's guns, and there are many more of them. The Salish have been losing battles with the Blackfeet for a hundred years. Just ask Schweeleh."

"A sad truth," said Schweeleh, who sat a pony that looked too short for his long legs.

"One day we win, maybe with help of Nez Perce and Kootenai, but we win. And win or not, we keep fighting our enemy, because we love buffalo."

"Be careful, Schweeleh," Bet said. "You are a family man now." She quickly turned her back to him and to Eldridge Hawkinson. Little Bit wanted to suckle. It mattered not what else was going on in her mother's world. Suckling was all that mattered. She caught the eye of Spukani, whose own baby was already suckling vigorously as if there might not be any milk tomorrow. Wildfire was a good name for him. Bet then thought of her mutual stare with Schweeleh. A certain understanding had seemed to pass between them. They might have only one thing in common right now, but it was the most important thing — young children. Bet would not turn around to watch the hunters ride off into the sunrise.

As much as Bet loved Three Boulder, she did not rush back there with her baby. The elderly gentleman Left Hand invited her to stay, saying that the Pale Woman Who Lives in Mountains Alone was like a daughter to him and should not *always* be alone. He said it was all right that she share his tepee, since he had vowed never to remarry after losing four wives — one to another man, one to white man's smallpox, one to a difficult childbirth, and one to ambushing Blackfeet in Hell Gate canyon — and since all three of his children were also long gone to the spirit world. Why he kept cheating the Place of the Bitterroot of his old bones, he had no idea — it was out of his hands and in the hands of the Great Spirit Chief.

To her, he was like the kindly grandfather she never had, or at least had never known. He respected her wish to raise a child alone in the mountains — at least he never told her she was crazy or foolish. And he never touched her, except her hair, which she allowed him to stroke whenever his right hand grew shaky. His left hand was steadier, but he held it in reserve in case he was required to hunt or go to war again. Sometimes his right hand gently touched Little Bit's hair, too, but only when he was in one of his trances brought on from remembering too much.

"Her hair is your hair," the old man kept repeating. "Yellow like sunflower."

"I am glad," she told him. "I would hate for it to be red like the sun."

"That beaver man with the nose of a hawk like your hair very much?"

"I suppose so. But not as much as you do."

"He want you for his squaw?"

"For number two squaw. He already has one, like . . . like most men do who are not young."

"I had four wives when young, never more than two at same time."

"I'm sure the ladies found you irresistible."

"They find me. First wife also find Nuu-chah-nulth, the Wolf. They run off to the Salish Sea."

"Love is curious."

"Peculiar, too."

The God-fearing Catholic Joseph Logan was proof of that. Only three days after the hunters departed, Sakkam took sick enough to forgo her husband's patent medicine bottle and turn to the herbs of her sister and Otter Woman. This disappointed the former Iroquois warrior who then turned to Bet and tried to convert her to his way of thinking through spirited evangelism. He took a hands-on approach in a secluded spot behind the long ceremonial lodge. When she slapped his hands away, he only looked to the sky and said he would pray for her. He proceeded to do so on the spot, asking the Lord to forgive this white woman for turning heathen.

"You figure whatever god you're praying to will give you permission to do what you please with me," she said to him point-blank. She noticed for the first time how his eyebrows ran together like two caterpillars banging heads.

"I can save your soul," he said. "I aim to marry you proper next year."

"You know that sick woman you left in the house with the white cross is your wife."

"Indian marriage. I'll marry you proper when the time is right."

"Over my dead body. If I don't kill you first."

"You talk like a heathen even with a baby in your arms. Put your baby down and I'll teach you how to act like an English lady."

"You?"

"I was a Hudson's Bay man. I was educated in the King's country. I can win you over to my side soon enough. Put the baby down."

"The hell I will."

"Mind your tongue. We have time . . . until next year. Then the time will be right. We must have faith."

"How do you figure next year, mister?"

"I know it is hard to wait. Patience is a virtue."

"Oh, I'm very virtuous. I can wait forever."

"Only till next year, pretty lady. You know we sent a four-man delegation to St. Louis to convince the Black Robes to come here and teach us the word of God. Those men met with our friend William Clark, but . . ."

"The William Clark of the Lewis and Clark Expedition?"

"You know of another friend named William Clark? The Salish were nice to him in this place long ago, and he was nice to our delegation in St. Louis. But all of Clark's sympathy could not convince the Black Robes the Salish were worthy. Our four men showed too much of their savage natures and spoke too much of their false gods. One returned empty-handed and ashamed; a second with a Bible but nothing more; the other two died on the way home. The failure was complete. But God will not forsake us. Next year I will lead a second delegation to St. Louis. Chief Tjolzhitsay, Big Face, has agreed to this. We are of the same heart on this matter. Unless we embrace the superior religion of the Black Robes, the Salish people will be lost. Our prayers will be answered. I will succeed in my mission. I will bring back at least one of the Black Robes."

"To save the Salish, who really aren't even

your people?"

"Yes, to save them. And this Black Robe, this Jesuit priest, that comes here shall marry us in proper fashion."

"Land's sake!"

"It shall be so. God gave me a sign last year — a burning bush."

"You mean during that horrible dry spell when the wildfires were burning many trees and bushes?"

"It was not simply a burning bush I saw. It was a miracle. It was a word from God — a Holy Spirit fire. You have heard of the Holy Spirit?"

"Mama Hex might have mentioned it a time or two. My Aunt Betty always said her sister was filled with the Holy Spirit. It was especially noticeable when she was cooking. All us children burned ourselves in the fireplace and on the stove. It was a family tradition back in Kentucky. Pappy Hex burned himself more trying to fire up his pipe. He did do a lot of bush and tree burning back there, too, trying to clear land for planting I suppose. And then one day the Shawnees — you know the Shawnees? Well, they burned down our house. It wasn't much of a house, but —"

"You are changing the subject."

"I am? I thought the subject was about

fire and burning things."

"The subject is how I am spiritually connected to you and how the master plan is for us to wed next year."

"Master plan? I have no master."

"God in heaven . . ."

"Stop that. You don't talk like an Indian. No god or spirit would sanction such a marriage, not even the trickster Coyote."

"That baby in your arms doesn't have a father, does she — I mean one whose name you know or can mention?"

"That is no business of yours or God's or anyone else."

"A proper marriage by a priest would right things for you and . . ."

"Wrong. Go home to your wife, you sick bastard."

CHAPTER SEVENTEEN

The easiest way to get away from Joseph Logan would have been to leave the village and return to Three Boulder. But Bet found reasons to stay. Left Hand was a gracious host. He provided food and shelter and made friendly, if repetitive, talk. The way he stroked her hair was soothing, and she liked how he never complained about Little Bit. He told her the baby cried less than a Salish child, and anyway a baby's cry now and then was a nice reminder that life goes on no matter how many lives are lost to fighting, smallpox, and tired, aching bones. While Left Hand hadn't gambled since the time smallpox killed his second wife and many friends during a hot streak with the dice, he encouraged her to gamble with the other old men of the village. They were eager as usual, and they liked her to win, at least enough to keep playing with them, while Little Bit slept soundly in a basket made of paper birch. This time, Bet didn't need their help. She started kissing the beaver-tooth dice each time before she tossed them, and she went on a roll for three nights that won her a bone-handle knife, tobacco, a digging stick, wild strawberries, two belts, an elk-teeth necklace, and a fan made of eagle feathers.

Joseph Logan found his moments to approach her for private palavers about God, the Black Robes, mankind, womankind, and marriage, but not a word about children. He acted as if Little Bit never was born. He told Bet that among the Iroquois, women had "trial marriages" with many men, not so subtly suggesting that he and she should stand trial somewhere. He saw fit to object to her manly attire, especially her breechclout; all proper Iroquois women wore long skirts, he insisted. He even mentioned a blue wedding dress he had seen worn by a princess in London that he thought would be the perfect costume for Bet to wear during next year's marriage ceremony that only he was planning. She delivered enough hand slaps and one solid face slap to convince him to keep his hands to himself, even if, as he claimed, his hands had been blessed by God.

At first, she had little contact with any of

the Salish women, although one morning she ran into Spukani when they happened to both go to the river at the same time to wash their babies. Schweeleh's wife could only remain standoffish for so long before she reached out and touched Little Bit's amazing head of yellow hair and then proudly showed off Wildfire's left foot, which had six toes. With sign language she indicated that this was a gift from the Great Spirit, a lucky charm that would serve her son well as he grew into manhood and became a hunter and warrior and perhaps even a shaman.

As Bet prepared to put her river-washed baby back in the cradleboard, Spukani ran to them wagging a finger and shouting *no* in English. With her own baby she demonstrated a better way. First, Spukani covered Wildfire with tallow to protect his skin and then she wrapped him up to the waist and placed him in his cradleboard. Next, she pounded buffalo chips into a powder, which she poured into the wrappings. With graphic sign language, she explained that the powder absorbed urine and feces and thus lessened the chance of diaper rash. Whenever Wildfire had a bowel movement, she threw away the old powder and replaced it. When Spukani held up two fingers and wiggled them, Bet understood — that was the average number of times a day that Spukani changed her Wildfire.

They walked back to the center of the village together. Spukani supplied Bet with enough cow chips from a four-foot-high pile to last for two moons of changing. In thanks, Bet gave her the recently won elk-teeth necklace. Bet pointed to the other woman's rounded belly and turned both palms up. Spukani understood and smiled, holding up four fingers — the number of moons to go before she gave birth to Schweeleh's second child. After putting the necklace around her neck, Spukani pulled back her black hair and showed off earrings made of abalone shell that her husband had obtained in a trade with the Nez Perces and given her as a reward for presenting him with a healthy son.

"When you go, Schweeleh have me," Spukani said.

"You mean a year ago? That's right. I found a home in the mountains and Schweeleh found you in his own village . . . or rediscovered you or whatever he did. Congratulations."

"You first." Spukani pointed to Little Bit, who had fallen asleep in her cradleboard.

"Yes. The seed that became my baby was

growing inside me when I came here last year. Too small to notice."

"Father not Schweeleh."

"Right again."

"Pale face?"

"Very pale."

"Father know?"

"Never knew. Very dead."

"Make sad?"

"No. Him very bad." She smiled. "I am glad to have my little one. Like you."

"Schweeleh!"

"Wildfire's pappy. He is glad, too. I can tell."

"You miss?"

"Schweeleh? He hasn't been gone hunting that long . . . oh, that's not what you mean. I miss many people, and no one. It's hard to explain when we don't speak the same language. It would be hard to explain even if we did. Do not worry."

"Schweeleh like."

"I suppose he does like me. And I like Schweeleh. He is good friend."

"Miss Schweeleh. Good wife."

"I'm sure you are. Please don't worry. No need."

"You go soon?"

"Oh, you *are* worried. Look, it's just like last year, Spukani. I left the village before he returned from the hunt then. It will be the same again. If anyone has cause to worry, it's your sister Sakaam. I wouldn't trust that husband of hers, Joseph Logan, as far as a mountain man can spit tobacco juice."

Spukani knitted her brow. "Joseph Logan? He here. No hunt."

"Right. Not for buffalo. He is here to watch over the women and children. That's a laugh."

"You laugh ha-ha?"

"Not exactly. He thinks I'm a heathen, a terrible sinner in the eyes of God. Still wants to . . . wants me . . . Oh, never mind. Sakaam deserves better, though. Joseph Logan is a two-headed snake."

"You know Snake Monster? Coyote kill him."

"Not sure we're talking about the same snake. But watch out for the one who watches over you."

Spukani nodded as if she understood all about Joseph Logan. Possibly she did. Anyway, the big worry wouldn't come until next year — if and when he brought a Black Robe back from St. Louis who would give weight to his tradition-crushing spiritual beliefs and could also perform a holy marriage ceremony.

In the warmer days after that, shoots, greens, and bulbs emerged with vigor. Bet figured there would hardly be a trace of snow in the high country. She grew restless. The woman known for roaming the mountains wanted to roam once more — but not too far, only back to her home, back to Three Boulder. She packed up her gambling winnings and her cow chips and began saying her general goodbyes to the elderly men of the village. It was not easy leaving Left Hand's tepee. He shed a tear because he had lost so many wives and daughters through the years and she had filled in for all of them. It helped him deal with departure day when she used her new bone-handled knife to cut off a lock of yellow hair and presented it to him — so he could keep his right hand stroking peacefully in her absence.

"Wait," he said, calling her back to the tepee. "Not yet. Hold your horses, Pale Woman Who Lives in the Mountains Alone. That name is like the winter nights — too long. I call you Yellow Hair."

"Call me whatever you like. Did I forget this, grandfather?" she asked, kissing him on his creviced forehead.

"And this," he said, reaching toward her cradleboard. She thought he wanted to touch Little Bit's head one last time, but instead he took hold of her pipe tomahawk.

"You promise me last smoke," he reminded her.

And so she had. They sat down facing each other. She crossed her legs, but his tired and aching bones wouldn't allow him to do the same anymore. He kept his legs out in front of him — extended but bent — as he pulled on the pipe with the vigor of a young brave.

Spukani and Sakaam showed up in good health and smiling, but not to smoke. At first it wasn't clear what they wanted. Left Hand had to translate.

"The sisters don't want you to go yet either," the old man said.

"Really?" Bet said. "I thought . . ."

"Stay," said Sakaam, dropping to her knees and looking everything like a child who knew she must say prayers but hadn't learned the words to use.

"No need to beg me," Bet said. "What are you doing?"

Sakaam was clawing at the ground like a dog looking for a buried bone.

"Yes, stay," said Spukani as she also went to her knees and scratched at the earth.

"I don't understand," Bet said. "They want to bury me here?"

Left Hand laughed so hard that his whole body shook like a gnarled tree in the wind. The sisters spoke to each other in Salish and cackled like prairie chickens. Little Bit woke up and started thrashing about in the cradleboard. Bet grew impatient waiting for Left Hand to explain. She stamped her foot and demanded to know what the big joke was about. It brought to mind those childhood times when she got more and more red-faced standing among her older brothers and sisters while they laughed at her expense at something beyond her comprehension. She had nothing against laughter per se, but when she was the only one *not* laughing, it was like being slapped in the face.

"I'm going," she said.

"Stay," the sisters repeated.

Spukani located the digging stick attached to the side of Bet's cradleboard. She loosened the rawhide, raised the stick, and wiggled it in Bet's face.

"I won that fair and square," Bet insisted.

"You dig?" Sakaam asked.

"Dig?"

"With us."

"Huh?" Her mind had gone soft. Of course, they didn't want her to help build her own grave. But what?

Left Hand stopped laughing about the time Bet finally realized what was going on. She felt silly and it stung her face to suppress it from breaking out in laughter — at herself. It was the root-gathering season; it happened naturally about this time every year.

"The sisters want you to stay and celebrate with them, Yellow Hair," the old man said. "The bitterroot is ready."

The Salish women walked north with their digging sticks to the best bitterroot grounds in the Bitterroot Place, and Bet walked alongside them with her baby on her back. She was as familiar as they were with the bitterroot plant and Schweeleh had once showed her this very location, but she had never been with the Salish people at the right time for the first harvest. And Spukani did tell her something valuable about the bitterroot she hadn't known before — that an infusion of the root would increase the milk in a breastfeeding mother. The young men were still off hunting buffalo on the eastern Plains. But that was fine; the women of the village had always done the root gathering. Self-designated watchdog Joseph Logan walked among them, keeping a close eye on certain swaying backsides. He carried no stick, but a Bible in one hand and his made-in-London Hudson's Bay flintlock rifle in the other. Several older men brought up the rear, walking with their bows and arrows and in some cases their walking sticks. Left Hand wanted to protect all the women, particularly Yellow Hair, so he gathered up his bent bow and a few arrows, but he was too old to make the long walk. With help he mounted an old pony that moved slower than the women.

By the time Left Hand finally reached the digging grounds, many of the women had already worked their paddle-shaped wooden sticks vigorously. Their baskets were half full with the large, fleshy taproots that they all knew were most tender and nutritious before the flowers bloomed in another moon; then, the roots became too bitter to enjoy. They all also knew to break off a piece of each root and rebury it, because after replanting, the bitterroot would develop a new root system and flower again. All digging stopped when Left Hand dismounted without any help and leaned against a splendid boulder that had a hump like a buffalo. The great stone had long been a monument to ancestral Salish root gatherers and, as Left Hand told the gathering, would honor their memory for generations to come. Left Hand did not talk long. He called upon the respected healer Otter Woman, who had been leading the first-roots ceremony for half a dozen years and was expected to hold the position for life. Sometimes the young men were not off hunting buffalo at the opening of the bitter-root season, but even then they stayed in the background and allowed Otter Woman to run the show.

Looking as nimble as a mountain goat, Otter Woman scampered to the top of the boulder and, peering into the darkening clouds, thanked the Great Spirit and other Salish spirits for this essential food gift. Then she leaped from the boulder, landing gracefully on all fours like a mountain lion. The other women, including Bet, brought their baskets of roots and set them down in a circle around her as she bowed repeatedly to the ground, or perhaps to the under-ground where the roots spirit must have resided. Otter Woman then rose to her feet and seemingly off the ground, defying grav-ity for a few moments. After that, the women went back to their digging, while the few men present watched. Bet leaned her cradleboard against the sacred boulder and worked hard and efficiently. She would spot buds and then dig a small trench around a plant, making it easier to extract the entire root. Spukani stopped her own work to watch her.

"Never see white woman dig," Schweeleh's wife said. "You dig good."

It felt good, Bet decided, or rather re-minded herself. It had been a while. Living a life of leisure, whether lying around in a hide tepee or a log cabin or a city mansion, was not for her. It was fine to work in a group now in the valley, but she knew how well she could work alone in the mountains later. Little Bit would watch her work, and play, too. There was time enough for both in the Bitterroot Place. She paused in her happy labors three times — twice only long enough to check on her content child and once just a little longer to admire the dirt under her fingernails.

It grew dark earlier than expected because the clouds turned black. The crash of lightning over the jagged mountains caused some of the women to drop their sticks and stare. It was the first storm of the season. Thunder followed. And then, for the second time in her life, Bet saw the Thunderbird come out of the West, beating its prodigious wings, shooting lightning bolts like arrows and shrieking to high heaven. Maybe it would generate rain — maybe not. Much snow had fallen in the mountains during the winter when the Thunderbird was dormant, but that did not mean the drought was over. Otter Woman wasn't taking any chances with the weather, though. She bowed to the power of the Thunderbird and declared the first harvest over. The creature opened its giant beak, causing a collective gasp below, but only a drop or two of rain came out before the beak closed and the bird turned and vanished into the clouds.

Only the closing ceremony remained. The women quickly regained their composure and placed the first roots of the season in a pile that stood taller than everyone there. The women encircled the pile and the old men, including Left Hand, joined the circle. Only Joseph Logan stayed out of it, but he was kneeling behind the boulder praying away, no doubt to the real God he thought responsible for the good root harvest and all the other bounties of life. Those in the circle, knowing the ritual well, turned their backs on the roots and faced the sun, or at least where they had last seen it before the clouds covered it. They all raised their right hands in a salute to the Great Spirit or the sun, neither of which were visible, and then Otter Woman led them in chants of acknowledgment that they were a blessed people and thankful to be fed.

The chants continued as rain fell, soaking the people and the roots. The Thunderbird's fiery form appeared for a moment between two mountain peaks, but after three flaps of its mighty wings, it disappeared into the very storm it had created. The rumbling in the mountains grew louder, and lightning continued to flash. Nobody could remember such a strong spring storm in the valley. Nobody complained, though. The bitterroot ceremony was an occasion for happiness.

"Rain is good," said Left Hand.

Those were his last words. His tired, aching legs gave way and he fell to the ground. Some thought a sudden bolt of lightning had struck him down. Others thought the old man had drowned standing up, or his ancient heart had finally given out. Bet, though, heard the whir of an arrow and could have sworn she saw him lower his right arm and raise his warlike left one seconds before the end came.

What Joseph Logan thought was uncertain. He was still on his knees praying in the rain when he toppled over and cracked open his skull on the boulder. He was probably dead before his head hit. He had three Blackfeet arrows lodged in his back. It later became clear that the one arrow to Left

Hand's throat had been enough to silence the oldest of the Salish men.

CHAPTER EIGHTEEN

The Blackfeet were champion ambushers and raiders. This had been known by generations of Salish. Trouble from these hostile neighbors to the north was always on their minds, but when violence actually occurred it still caused shock, especially in the women, who did not always understand such matters. The root gatherers had been worried about their hunting men and the few bison-butchering females who accompanied them because most of the bloodshed between the tribes occurred at the hunting grounds or on the road to and from buffalo country. When Otter Woman led the women north to the best place for bitterroots in their valley, they had given little thought to any immediate danger for themselves. For one thing, the warlike young Blackfeet bucks were known to be off on their own spring buffalo hunt, either on the Upper Yellowstone or near the Three Forks of the

Big River. Their collective mind was on meat, which the Blackfeet called *natapi wak-sin,* or "real food," rather than on edible plants and other *kistapi waksin,* or "nothing foods." For another, when Blackfeet made war for reasons other than to protect their right to as many buffalo as they wanted, it was usually to capture as many horses as possible from their weaker neighbors. The women root gatherers were all afoot, the only horse among them belonging to old Left Hand and hardly worth stealing. And while the Blackfeet sometimes took scalps as well as horses, they usually didn't go out of their way to take the scalps of women or children. The Place of the Bitterroot was out of their way . . . *usually.*

Left Hand would have known, though probably not Joseph Logan, that harvest was the most likely time for a Blackfeet raiding party to ride deep into the valley. As much as the Blackfeet savored their meat, buffalo or otherwise, some of them also had a taste for precious bitterroot. Where they lived to the north and east, bitterroot was relatively rare, so they had to travel over passes to gather it (which the men who made these trips had no interest in doing), trade for it (which often seemed a waste of time and too costly since in their hearts, roots were "nothing food" that could not keep up a man's strength), or raid for it (usually accomplished without much fuss since women — either Salish or Kootenai — were the ones who dug the roots, peeled off the outer covering, and removed the red "hearts," the source of the bitter taste).

Making sense of this last Blackfeet raid into the valley wasn't so easy. While the Salish women had built up an impressive pile on the rainy first day of the harvest, the raiders took less than one-quarter of the roots. The rest they tried to quickly set on fire, a futile effort in the downpour. Most of the roots were simply scattered as the whooping Blackfeet rode roughshod back and forth over the pile. While the raiders had killed the oldest (Left Hand) and youngest (Joseph Logan) of the armed men present, they allowed the few other men to drop their bows and arrows and run or crawl through the mud puddles to safety — once out of sight, these men were out of mind. One Blackfeet lifted the considerable scalp of Joseph Logan and won the approval of his fellow tribesmen. But the raiders left Left Hand's head untouched — perhaps out of respect for his many years as an enemy warrior but possibly because his hair was so thin and gray on top. The raiders were not intent on annihilating the female root gatherers, though two women fell to arrows while making a run for it, and a third was trampled to death by the hooves of Blackfeet ponies.

For the most part the raiders were satisfied to humiliate the enemy women by counting coup on their heads and bodies. Bet was able to grab her cradleboard and bring Little Bit out of the line of fire. While shielding her baby with her body, Bet watched many of the horrors unfold. Otter Woman lost consciousness when a pony's flank smacked against her head. One warrior, his face smeared in black war paint, saw her stretched out on the ground and with scalping knife drawn approached her with deadly intent. But something made him abruptly change his mind. He shoved the knife back in the beaded sheath attached to his belt, climbed the nearby humped boulder, pulled his penis out of his breechclout, and emptied his bladder on the medicine woman. The fellow raiders around him laughed and punched their fists in the air; this was surely a feat that would be talked about in Blackfeet villages for years to come.

Bet saw Spukani, carrying Wildfire, and Sakaam, with hands free, run past the

boulder and successfully leap over the lifeless body of Joseph Logan. Immediately
afterward, Spukani tripped over a root and
went flying forward. Before she hit the
ground, she managed to hand Wildfire off
to her sister, who, without breaking stride,
squeezed her nephew tight and kept going.
The Blackfeet simply ignored her. Spukani
was not so lucky. A knife-wielding raider,
who looked even more ferocious because of
a jagged scar that ran across his forehead
from ear to ear, sprang toward her as she
picked herself off the ground. Scar Face
stopped short when Spukani suddenly
turned to face him with her nose coated in
mud and blood dripping from her chin.
They both froze — the Salish woman out of
fear, the Blackfeet man out of apparent
indecision about what to do next. He might
very well have cut her open and ripped out
her unborn baby. Instead, he lowered his
knife, picked up a digging stick one of the
fleeing women had dropped, and poked her
belly once, almost gently. That must have
counted as a coup, because when Spukani
finally turned and bolted, he dismissed her
with a hand gesture and began to leisurely
scratch his back with the digging stick.

And then Little Bit woke up and began to
cry. Bet took her out of the cradleboard,

but it was hardly the place for a breastfeeding, so she clasped a hand over the baby's drooling mouth to muffle the sound. Little Bit didn't like that; she repeatedly bit down on the palm until Bet cried out and withdrew her hand. The incessant little one had already grown a couple teeth.

Scar Face stopped scratching his back. He walked slowly to the boulder, cocked his head to one side, and fixed his eyes on the pair. Bet tried to cover Little Bit's mouth again in case the crying angered the warrior. But Little Bit spit as if she had tasted sour milk and then again tried to bite the hand that fed her. Scar Face looked amused. Briefly. Then he tossed aside the digging stick and reached down.

If Bet had not left her recently won knife back at Left Hand's tepee, she would have drawn it. Her precious pipe tomahawk was back there, too. She had no weapon. She shielded her baby as best she could because she knew of Indians on both sides of the Mississippi River who lifted captured enemy babies off the ground by the heels and bashed their brains out against rocks or trees. But Scar Face didn't touch the baby. He placed both hands on Bet's head and ruffled her hair — not quite affectionately but without evil intent. She knew she would not be scalped. His eyes flashed with a combination of curiosity and gentleness. He wore no feathers and only a trace of war paint. He had a topknot and three thin braids. She stared long enough at his forehead through the hard rain to grow comfortable with the long, jagged scar whose outline mimicked the Bitterroot peaks.

"Oki," he said. "Hello."

She was in no mood to return his greeting. She lowered her eyes. Little Bit was swallowing rainwater, so she pressed the baby's face to her ribs.

Scar Face raised one foot and then the other right under her nose, showing her his black-dyed moccasins.

"I know who you are," she said. "I know you are thirsty for blood. I didn't know you made war with women, children, and old men."

He shook his head so hard that two of his braids repeatedly slapped his face. He then made a fist and pounded his chest. "White Buffalo."

"All right. What's on your mind, White Buffalo?"

He grinned, and his grin was as wide as his scar. His teeth weren't quite white, but they were straight and strong. "Know you," he said, pointing a finger between her eyes.

"See in *nitawashin-nanni* — our land."

"I once made my home north of the Hell Gate. I never bothered your people and they never bothered me. Now I live in the Bitterroot Place. I thought it was safer."

He frowned and shook his head again.

"Right," she said. "Not very safe."

"No talk," he said, making one of his hands open and close like a beak.

He pulled her by one arm to her feet while she held onto Little Bit for dear life with the other. Maybe he wasn't so gentle after all. She doubted him even more when he pulled out his knife. But he only pushed her away and then spun around to confront a tribesman who wore a beaded war shirt and waved a war club. The two warriors exchanged loud words in their language, and it looked like it would soon be war club against knife. But White Buffalo blurted out something that made the other man suddenly lower the club, take a step back, and wipe his face. His war paint was running in the rain. When White Buffalo flicked his wrist as if shooing away a fly, the other warrior whooped, raised his club, and ran off in search of other prey.

Bet was stunned but relieved. "What just happened?" she asked. "He wanted to kill me and my baby, didn't he? What did you say to make him go?"

White Buffalo didn't respond and kept his back to her. She spoke louder, repeating her questions. Nothing. She thought maybe she could slip behind the boulder with her baby and make a run for the mountains. But then he turned suddenly, and the extraordinary ear-to-ear grin was back on his face. For some reason, with danger still all around, she thought of past Indian lovers — Schweeleh, the Arapaho Red Elk, and the Nez Perce Yellow Bull. They were men with color. Even in the heat of passion or in the afterglow, none had smiled this way. And this unusual Blackfeet warrior, quite handsome even with the eye-catching scar, had just saved her life to boot. His grin somehow found room to widen ever further. It almost seemed like he was reading her mind.

"Thank you," she said. "He would have . . . you know."

White Buffalo stopped grinning so he could compress his lips and then generate a jarring thud, perhaps the sound of a war club crushing a human skull.

It made her shiver and smile at the same time.

"But what made him run?" she asked, and then she pumped her legs like a man running so that he would understand the question.

"Know you," he said, tapping his finger against her forehead. "Tell him who."

"Who I am?"

"You White Woman Who Never Dies."

The jaded horse of the late Left Hand never ran off during the attack on the root gatherers and easily fell into the hands of a raider who wanted to trade it for the yellow-haired woman White Buffalo had captured. No deal. White Buffalo wanted the horse to more easily transport his human spoils of war. He wasn't about to give her up. The other warrior, Morning Moon, indicated that they should immediately share both the woman and the horse, but White Buffalo waved him away. The other man refused to go, and the two argued until White Buffalo revealed the identity of the captive. Morning Moon looked duly impressed; it seemed all of these wide-ranging Blackfeet knew of the woman who survived on her own in the mountains. He wanted to touch her to make sure she wasn't a trickster spirit. White Buffalo said no, but the two Blackfeet did work out a mutually agreeable trade. Bet was not consulted. White Buffalo kept the woman of legend and got the horse, but he gave up his strong juniper bow and every one of his arrows — since he hadn't shot a single one during the raid — plus two luxurious locks of his captive's yellow hair that he gently removed with his knife. Bet did not protest, figuring she would be getting off easy if a little hair was all she lost.

Morning Moon tied her locks of yellow hair to his topknot and strutted about in the rain like a sage grouse. White Buffalo just stood there watching, his arms folded tight against his thick chest. Bet didn't know whether to be amused or frightened, so she pretended to be tending to Little Bit while watching both Blackfeet men out of the corner of her eye. Other raiders called out to them as they rode past, the successful raid completed. Morning Moon found his horse, leaped onto its back, waved his new bow in the air, and galloped away. She walked with her baby to the other side of the boulder, and White Buffalo didn't try to stop her. The rain stopped abruptly, as if the Thunderbird had grown tired of trying to wash away human blood and misery. She visited each of the five lifeless bodies left in the mud. She didn't recognize the three dead women but didn't look too closely; they had lost their hair and most of their clothes. So had Joseph Logan. When she last saw him, three arrows were lodged in his back. Now she counted more than a dozen, piercing him everywhere from his mutilated scalp to his bloody bare feet. His white man pants were missing.

"Now he can join *his* God," she said. "Maybe that is for the best." She hoped Sakaam wouldn't mourn him too much. Maybe Schweeleh would take her into his tepee to join her sister as his second wife.

"*Netukka?*" asked White Buffalo, who now sat on the humped boulder watching her. "*Netukka?* Friend?"

She didn't bother to reply. She hurried over to where old Left Hand lay on his side.

"Left Hand wanted to protect us," Bet whispered to her daughter. "I wish I could have protected him. He was good to me. He was *my grandfather.*"

"Him *napi*?" said White Buffalo.

"No nap," she said distractedly. "Long sleep."

"Him *napi*? Old man?"

"Yes. My old man."

Left Hand's face looked peaceful, as if he was just taking a nap, and he might have been if not for the large-feathered arrow in his throat. She knelt beside him but didn't pray or cry. She closed her eyes and yanked at the shaft until she had pulled out the arrow, head and all. Her own strength surprised her. But she didn't have the strength to look at the fatal wound. She wasn't even sure why it was important to get that arrow out. Did she think it would help guide his spirit's ascent or perhaps allow him to keep talking in the afterlife? Or was she just *not* thinking.

With only one eye open, she stroked his thin hair, which the Blackfeet had left in place. All around her were digging sticks that the fleeing Salish women had dropped. She kissed the top of Left Hand's head and moved on her knees to the nearest stick. She placed Little Bit on a spot with more grass than mud and seized the stick. Without getting off her knees, she chipped away at the rain-softened earth.

"Bitterroot?" White Buffalo asked.

"Bury," Bet said. "Dig grave."

"Huh?"

"Can't leave him just lying here."

White Buffalo climbed off the boulder and tried to get her to stop digging. But his words and his hard hands on her shoulder had no effect. Even a firm kick to the backside didn't work. She was obsessed with making a better place for Left Hand. Finally, he scooped Little Bit off the ground and walked away. She didn't notice at first, but as soon as she did, her stick immediately cracked in two and she began to holler for him to come back.

But he kept going, and she had no choice but to follow.

"If you hurt one hair on her head, I'll kill you," Bet shouted. "I have killed before."

If he had any idea what she was saying, he didn't acknowledge it, nor did he seem the slightest affected by her tone. He fetched his striking black-and-white spotted horse and the late Left Hand's plodding mare. She picked up another digging stick and considered where she could plunge it to cause the most damage. But then he surprised her by carefully putting Little Bit back in the cradleboard. As he lifted the cradleboard onto her back, she dropped the stick. He helped her onto the mare and handed her the reins, and she thought about bolting, but she knew he could easily catch her on his horse, if not on foot. Besides, she didn't want to endanger her baby by making a break for it.

White Buffalo mounted in no particular hurry and casually signaled her to come along. She rode ten feet, then pulled on the single rein and looked back at the ghastly scene she knew she would never forget. The sun had come out again, and she could clearly see each of the five bodies.

White Buffalo stopped his horse and looked back at her.

"White Woman Who Never Dies, you come," he said.

"Why?" she said. "Why did this happen?"

"Huh?"

"Why did you do that? Why did you kill innocent people?"

"Kill?" He made a slashing motion across his throat.

"Yes. That's kill."

He pounded his chest. "No kill."

"Maybe not you personally, but your people killed for no reason. They killed women and old men who could do no harm. These harmless Salish people were gathering bitterroot. That's all."

"Bitterroot Salish bury. That's all."

He took her mare's rein and led her away. But he was right. When she looked back again, she saw some of the surviving root gatherers come out of hiding to take care of the dead.

CHAPTER NINETEEN

They rode north out of the Place of the Bitterroot. They were in no particular rush, which was good because her horse could only maintain a walk. It was dusk by the time they reached the Clark Fork. While fording the river on their mounts, the old mare stumbled, her legs and heart seeming to give out at the same time. Thrown clear, Bet began flailing away in water flowing too fast for comfort. Out of the corner of her eye she saw the poor dead horse go under. *Never mind the damn horse,* she scolded herself. She had a baby to save.

She tried to stand but couldn't touch the bottom with her toes. She could swim, but it wasn't easy with a cradleboard, and she soon tired herself out trying to reach a sandbar that wasn't as close as it looked. Little Bit must have gotten a mouthful of river because she began to choke. Floating on her back would mean drowning her immobilized baby. There was no resting now. Bet forced herself to keep going on her belly, her arms slapping at the water like a beaver's tail. She cursed her feet for not kicking hard enough.

"Hang on, little one," she yelled. "I won't let you go under."

White Buffalo didn't let either of them go under. He turned his horse midstream and rode to their rescue, yanking her onto the hindquarters of his spotted mount with such ease that she wondered how many times he had done it before. He didn't stop on the opposite shore even though they were wet and chilled, darkness was setting in, and the baby was crying. He rode hard into Hell Gate canyon and then up a well-worn side trail until it grew too steep to ride the horse. He helped her dismount and quickly checked on the baby. By pressing his palms together, laying his head on his hands and breathing deeply, he indicated that Little Bet was fast asleep.

He led the horse up a winding, rocky foot trail in the dark. She followed, keeping a close eye on the horse's blond tail. Halfway up the small mountain, he let the horse loose on a grassy clearing and then climbed for another fifty feet to a broad ledge with two bent birch trees whose roots clung to cracks in the rock. He stood near the edge and pointed — at the multitude of stars, she thought at first, but then she realized he was indicating something far below in the darkness, perhaps the winding path of the Clark Fork. She shook her head, not wanting to bring her baby any closer. A strange mingling of fear, hostility, gratitude, and warmth ran through her like a wind that couldn't make up its mind whether it wanted to be a chilling blast or a Chinook.

He shrugged and came at her. She backed away and turned to her side, thinking she was about to run her baby right into a rock face. Instead, she found herself right next to an entrance to a cave. He motioned for her to go inside and she did, barely having to duck. Then he motioned her to remove her cradleboard. She did. Little Bit was still asleep and remarkably dry. Bet sat down and gently rocked the baby anyway. But her backside was sore from the riding, so she lay down, curled up on her side with Little Bit in the crook of her arm.

White Buffalo busied himself, making a torch with a roll of peeled birch bark attached to a stick and then striking two hard pieces of stone together to create a spark that caught on the bark and made a flame. After that he made a fire far enough inside the cave to be out of the wind. The fire was for warmth, not for cooking. He pulled from his buckskin shirt two pieces of bitterroot, handing her the longest one. He gnawed at his portion raw. She had only eaten the root after it was boiled, which caused it to soften, swell, and exude a tasty syrup. But she gnawed away, and it quelled her appetite for the night.

They slept on opposite sides of the fire, but sometime during the night he moved over to her, wearing nothing but his black moccasins. He curled on his side behind her, applying only slight pressure. But it was enough to make her backside even warmer than her front, which faced the fire. At some point he grew bolder, pressing harder and then working to separate her, at least in part, from her clothing. She lay as still as she could even though she felt a spark catch inside her. She knew he was not a killer, at least not of women and children. His manners might be primitive, but in the daylight hours he had been gentlemanlike. What's more, he had been heroic — saving her life and her baby's, not once but twice — first back at the bitterroot grounds from one of his tribesmen with evil intent, and then when she was flailing in the Clark Fork River. He was strong and darkly handsome, and that long jagged scar on his forehead somehow made him appear susceptible to human kindness if not a victim himself, even though he was a Blackfeet. She let him do as he wished, and when it was over, she finally opened her eyes and felt none the worse.

During the night, she fed Little Bit twice while White Buffalo slept on his back, the leftovers of a wide grin on his face. After the second feeding she slept well. By the time she awakened, the sun was high in the clear big sky, and White Buffalo had already shot and butchered a deer. The meat was cooking over a merry fire. He served her venison for breakfast. As they ate in silence, he avoided looking her in the eye, as if he were a terribly shy man, something she never would have imagined a warrior of his tribe could be.

The new day seemed gentle. She decided she loved this spot. Maybe she didn't need a tepee at all, maybe this cave would do. Leaving Little Bit fast asleep, Bet dared walk far out on the ledge to get a sweeping view of what lay below — the long line of noiseless, sparkling river and straight, sun-splashed road passing through Hell Gate canyon. White Buffalo emerged from the cave wiping his mouth and patting his belly. He stood next to her and while they took in the view together, he took a deep breath. It made her want to breathe deeply, too.

"You brought me to an extraordinary place," she said. "It's beautiful."

He pointed at something in the canyon and said words in his language she couldn't understand. She couldn't see what he was seeing, either. But he kept pointing and talking.

"*Anima, anima,*" he cried out in frustration. "See, see."

She pointed to her own eyes and shook her head. "No *anima,* no see," she said. "My eyes are good, but you have better eyes. Is it something good, White Buffalo? I do want to see it."

He tapped her shoulder and then acted out a scene. First, he raised a hand on his forehead to shield his eyes as he scanned the horizon. Then he began to fire imaginary arrows with an invisible bow. Finally, he made slashing motions across this throat.

"Kill here!" he said, finally finding a couple of English words he knew.

She caught on, and her stomach went sour as if the undigested deer meat had spoiled inside her. On this spot, Blackfeet lookouts would spot their enemies — which was almost everyone outside of their tribal confederation — going through the narrow canyon and would signal to their fellow warriors who hid behind rocks and trees below, in position to execute an ambush. Suddenly nothing about the sweeping view looked beautiful. And then she finally saw movement — many men on horseback heading west through the canyon. She wished her eyes were sharper, but she could make out feathers on their heads and bright colors on their near-naked bodies and on their ponies, too. She saw rifles and bows and no saddles. Some kind of war party, she thought, a large war party — the line of mounted men showed no immediate end. But then she noticed that a few in the party were not wearing paint or carrying weapons — women.

"Nez Perces," White Buffalo said.

"You can tell that from here?"

"Kootenais," he said.

"Which is it? Oh, you mean both are down there?"

"Flatheads," he continued.

"What?" She went right to the end of the ledge to peer. "The Salish are there, too? But they went to the Plains to hunt . . ."

Iniksii," he said, finishing her sentence. "Buffalo."

She spotted a man riding taller and straighter than most of the others. After a small gap in the line, he was the first rider in the last group, and he seemed to be leading two extra riderless horses.

"Schweeleh!" she said, but of course she had no idea if it was really him.

"Netukka?"

"Yes, my friend . . . I think. That is, I think it's him. I know he is a friend."

"Enemy."

"Schweeleh?"

"All."

Bet nodded. The Salish buffalo hunters and butchers must have gone on their spring hunt on the Plains with their friends the Nez Perces and the Kootenais, and now they were all returning together. She knew that these tribes — and sometimes the Pend d'Oreilles, Shoshones, Spokanes, and Coeur d'Alenes, too — had been going to hunt buffalo in force lately to deter attacks by the powerful Blackfeet, who, unless outnumbered, would fight rather than share the common hunting grounds near the Three Forks of the Big River.

White Buffalo pursed his lips and again pretended to shoot arrows and slash throats. When it came to killing enemy warriors, perhaps he wasn't so shy. She was glad to see all the friendly Indians go past — far too many for any Blackfeet party to attack here or back where the buffalo roamed. But then she quickly turned sad, thinking of the Salish party returning to the Place of the Bitterroot and finding at least five fresh graves — those of the three female root gatherers, the God-fearing Joseph Logan, and eldest tribal member Left Hand. She snapped out of it; she had other things to worry about.

"I think I hear the baby crying," she said, as if speaking to a husband, one who knew English. "See you back in the cave?" She backed away from the precipice.

"See *Nitisitapi ponokamitta,*" White Buffalo said, shaking a fist.

"What's that? Isn't *Nitisitapi* what you call your people?"

"Real people."

"And *ponokamitta,* could that mean pony?"

He held up three fingers. "Running Wolf pony. Lean Coyote pony. Fat Horse pony."

"I don't understand. Are you talking about horses or people?"

"Ponies live. *Nitisitapi* die."

"Three Blackfeet have died?"

"Killed." He shook his fist again, then abruptly turned his back on the distant riders in Hell Gate. "By enemy."

When they were back in the cave, he devoured more hunks of venison while she breastfed Little Bit. He didn't say a word. He was fretting and eating as if the meat would fill up the emptiness inside him. She was worried herself about what would happen next. And she was also curious about the three dead Blackfeet warriors. There must have been a fight of some kind back at the common hunting grounds, and maybe, for a change, the Blackfeet got the worst of it.

When he finally finished his food, he was still in no mood for talking. He lay down on his back and didn't move for an hour. She nibbled at what was left of the venison, waiting for him to close his eyes. Not that she imagined she could slip away without him noticing. She wasn't sure she wanted to do that even if it were possible. In any case, though he stayed perfectly still, his eyes never shut. She wasn't sure where his primary home was, probably somewhere in the foothills on the other side of the Rockies. She hadn't lived that far east since the days she had traveled the frontier with the old Frenchman, Louis Pierre Coquerel. She could do it if she had no choice in the matter, but she wasn't clear whether or not he considered her his captive.

At the very least, she would make herself heard about what she wanted for herself and her baby. The truth was, even after last night's amorous congress, she no more wished to live with him among the Blackfeet than she did Eldridge Hawkinson among the Crows. She missed Three Boulder. She could always ask White Buffalo to come there and live in her tepee, but she wasn't sure she wanted even a temporary "provider" again. And if she ever strayed from the tepee, he was liable to cut off her nose — Blackfeet husbands demanded complete obedience. Besides, it would be wrong for him — that wasn't Blackfeet country. It was her high country, and too bloody close to his Salish enemies.

White Buffalo stood abruptly and rushed out to the ledge. He soon returned and reported that the enemy was all gone. Then he threw dirt on the fire and motioned her to come along. Bet stayed seated, playing with Little Bit, whose little hands had become active, grabbing at her mother's clothing and hair and earlobes. She had also figured out how to roll from her stomach to her back and liked to show off her new trick. White Buffalo grew impatient and stamped his foot. He also made fists, but she wasn't afraid of him anymore.

"We'll go when we're ready," she said. "Right now, we're playing."

"You come," he said. He raised a black moccasin as if he intended to plant it on her nose, but then merely stamped the cave floor once more.

"What happened at the hunting grounds?" she asked him. "Men were killed along with the buffalo?"

He squatted beside her and held up three fingers. "Running Wolf, Lean Coyote, Fat Horse," he said.

"I know. But did you — that is to say, your people — kill any Salish or Nez Perces or Kootenais?"

He hung his head and shook it.

She exhaled, like wind blowing through a narrow canyon. "I reckon even you Blackfeet have to lose sometimes."

"Enemy too many."

"So, they chased you away and killed the buffalo?"

"Running Wolf, Lean Coyote, Fat Horse."

"Yes, I know. Three Blackfeet were killed. The rest of you fled the field?"

"Huh?"

"The Salish and the others ran you off?"

"They kill. We kill."

"But you said you didn't kill any of your

297

enemies." She freed her right hand from the surprisingly strong grasp of Little Bit and formed a zero with her thumb and first finger.

"Enemy kill there. We kill here." He pointed south.

"You mean . . ."

She held her tongue. She didn't need to ask him what he meant. She saw the picture clearly now. The defeated Blackfeet had run, all right, all the way to the Place of the Bitterroot, where they had exacted revenge by attacking the Salish root-gathering party and killing five of their inoffensive enemies. Four victims had been scalped, at best, maybe mutilated in other ways, and the three women most likely had been violated. She clutched her baby a little too hard and stood up, disgusted at something, perhaps herself. Shouldn't she hate this man who had captured her and taken advantage of her in a dark cave and now was squatting beside her as if she belonged to him? The thing was, she still didn't feel quite like a captive and wasn't sure he had done anything that she didn't want, at least in part, for him to do. He had been kind and gentle when there was no need to be. He had saved her and her baby from drowning. She couldn't forget that any more than she could forget pulling the arrow out of Left Hand's throat.

"Damn you," she said. "Damn it all!"

"Dam? *Ksisk-staki* make."

"No, not the kind of dam a beaver makes. A human *damn*!"

"Huh?

"Your hunger for revenge is never satisfied, is it, White Buffalo?"

He pounded his chest. "White Buffalo. Yes."

"If Schweeleh were here right now you would want to take his scalp, cut off his private parts, and stuff them in his mouth."

"Huh?"

"I know Schweeleh to be a kind, gentle man, but perhaps he would want to do the same to you. Warrior deeds, you call them. I call it bad medicine. With you it is war first and killing buffalo second. Buffalo *only* give you food and clothing. War gives you renown."

"Talk much. Ready?"

"To go?"

"Yes. Go."

"We go. Little Bit and I go that direction — south. You go that direction — east." She did all the necessary pointing to make sure she was understood.

"You come." He reached out to touch her

arm or her yellow hair or something. She withdrew.

"I know you could make me go with you or kill me, but I don't think you want to do either of those things."

"No kill. Come."

"I'll walk down to the bottom with you — to Hell Gate. That's as far as I'll go with you. You're nice but I don't want to be Blackfeet property. I don't want to be anybody's property. I know you don't understand. It will keep till the bottom. Thank you for showing me the cave. We go."

They went. His spotted horse waited for him in the grassy spot. He offered her a seat on the horse, but she declined. They both walked, and he let her walk first. Behind her, she thought she heard him making funny animal sounds to Little Bit in the cradleboard, but she wasn't sure and didn't want to turn around and embarrass him. At a turn in the trail, he showed her a spring, and they drank their fill. Once more he offered her a seat on her horse. Gentlemen in St. Louis or New Orleans would have had more words, but she couldn't imagine them being any politer than this Blackfeet warrior. Of course, nobody else from his tribe was there to see him behave this way.

In Hell Gate she found a stick that she

snapped in half. She weighed the two halves and chose the one with the sharpest end to be her drawing instrument. She dropped to her knees, swept away some pebbles and hoofprints, and drew him a map in the dirt. He squatted again to watch. She had him move back to give her more room to work. She made wavy lines for the Clark Fork, Bitterroot, Yellowstone, and Missouri Rivers and upside-down V's for the Bitterroot and other mountains. Where she thought his Blackfeet village was located on the Plains she put a huge X, but he nudged her hand until she redrew the X closer to the mountains. At Three Boulder she created three adjoining circles that were totally out of scale; it was as if she had put New York, Boston, and Philadelphia in the Bitterroot Range. She decided to leave the Salish village in the valley off her map, as if that might somehow keep his Blackfeet raiders from finding it again.

"You go here," she said, poking her stick at the X. "Your home," she added, turning the stick toward him and accidentally poking the long scar on his forehead. "Sorry," she quickly added. "Understand?"

White Buffalo held out his hand until she gave him the stick. He tapped the stick against her chest, accidentally poking her right nipple, and then he drew three more X's right over her X. "White Woman Who Never Dies, White Buffalo, white baby," he said.

"It can't be," she said, taking the stick back. "That would kill the White Woman Who Never Dies."

"No kill."

"No, you wouldn't kill me. Nevertheless, I would die there. Here is my home." She drove the stick as if it were a spear into the middle circle, and it stuck in the ground.

"Home?"

"Yes, in the mountains of the Bitterroot Place — my home, Little Bit's home, not White Buffalo's home."

"White Woman Who Never Dies, you come."

She stood up and pounded her chest with a fist the same way she had seen him do. "You know I am also called Woman Who Roams the Mountains?"

He nodded without looking at her. His eyes were still on the dirt map or the stick in the ground. He had suddenly turned shy again and perhaps sad. It wasn't always so easy to tell about sadness, especially when it came to Indian men.

"I am a legend to your people, am I not?" she said. "And do you know why they spin stories about me? I'll tell you, White Buffalo. I have yellow hair, I am female, I go where I please, I choose to roam alone in the high country, lightning never strikes me, cold moons don't freeze me, fire doesn't burn me, white man's diseases don't eat at my flesh, ferocious wild beasts don't devour me, bad men don't kill me, Gods don't destroy me, I can live on nuts and berries but slay animals when starving, I can love men but kill them when necessary, I can give birth in a tepee, I can raise a daughter in my image, I survive in a world not supposed to be mine but *is* mine — I claim it for myself."

He finally looked up at her, but only to see if she had finished. She hadn't.

"You want to destroy your enemies but not your legend," she continued. "It's good you can't understand me because I'm probably not making any sense. I once was Little Bet Hex in the East. I became Big Bet in the West. I've been captured before. I like being free better. I like to roam alone. I talk to animals, especially one particular jaybird. He might understand me better than you do. Yes, I have been called a crazy bitch. That's not kind, but who am I to say there is no truth to it? Maybe all legends are deranged. You don't need me, White Buffalo. I am a legend; I am mountain woman. You can find a flesh and blood woman — a Blackfeet woman. Schweeleh found a Salish woman. Hawk found a Crow woman. So, go home, White Buffalo. You *must* go home."

"Home?"

"Yes. So long, White Buffalo."

She turned away from him and walked south toward the Clark Fork. This time she would cross the river without him. Maybe she would find the Salish bullboat hidden in the willow tree grove. If not, she would build a raft. But she would get across. Then she would walk deep into the valley once more, no matter how much her feet protested. She would stop at the mourning Salish village, but only long enough to offer a little sympathy to Schweeleh and her other surviving friends and to pick up a few of her things from the late Left Hand's tepee. If nothing else, she wanted her pipe tomahawk for a good smoke and her own protection. She would get a second wind and head out and soon go up the mountainside, following Lost Trout Creek past Beaverhead Lake to Three Boulder, where Jay Talker, she was certain, would welcome her back from his safe perch in Lonesome Pine.

She walked slowly but as steadily as she ever had. She inhaled the clean tang of the river and the warm, damp earthiness of the ground beyond. She also felt something deep inside her, another seed growing in her belly perhaps? *No point giving that a second thought, not yet.* White Buffalo didn't call out to her in English or Blackfeet. She could feel his doleful eyes on her back, on her fully occupied cradleboard. She imagined Little Bit smiling at him and waving goodbye with her powerful little fingers. She imagined *this* would make him grin.

CHAPTER TWENTY

Bet Hex did what she needed to do at the mourning Salish village, but did not linger. Nobody was celebrating the fine buffalo hunt on the Plains or the way the Salish hunters and their allies had driven off the outmanned Blackfeet hunters. The five dead in the valley had already been buried dressed in skins and robes. Had Left Hand and Joseph Logan, the two male victims of what became known as "the Blackfeet Bitterroot Butchery," been alive, they might have — for quite different reasons — tried to convince her to stay. The mourning feast held after Left Hand's funeral had included the disposal of the dead gentleman's possessions, but Schweeleh had saved the pipe tomahawk, realizing it belonged not to Left Hand but to Bet. A Salish woman's mourning period for a dead husband was known to last as long as a year but Bet made a friendly wager with Schweeleh that Sakaam would not mourn Logan for more than two moons.

Spukani seemed less sad than anyone, perhaps even joyful, because *her* man, Schweeleh, had not only distinguished himself against the Blackfeet but also had come home to her unscathed. She suggested, just in case Bet had other ideas, that if Schweeleh ever took a second wife it would be her widowed sister. Schweeleh admitted it could happen. He was pleased, of course, that Bet had escaped the cave where the evil Blackfeet kidnapper had imprisoned her. He didn't ask questions, for whatever happened had been out of her hands and there was nothing either of them could do about it. She saw no reason to tell her old lover about the nature of her relationship with White Buffalo during her "captivity" any more than she had the nature of her encounter with the truly evil redheaded fur trapper nicknamed Sunshine or her bittersweet time in the tepee with the partner called Hawk.

"You ready to go?" he asked her.

"Ready."

"Then go, if that be your wish. May the guardian spirits protect you."

She shook his hand the way white people did, and she watched him kiss Little Bit on the forehead and then on each cheek. Wildfire managed a wave of the hand at Little Bit with some fatherly assistance. Schweeleh was a good man, a good friend, but Bet didn't shed a tear. After he insisted on giving her much good buffalo meat and she insisted she didn't have too much weight to carry alone, she was off for Three Boulder. She hummed happily most of the way there but intermittently told her balky feet to behave.

Jay Talker whistled when she appeared and began chattering as if reprimanding her for staying away too long. She found her tepee undisturbed and when she cried out to give thanks, it was not to the white God or Amotken or one of those five daughter-mothers of his, but to a guardian spirit. For the first time in her life, she decided on her own guardian spirit; it could not be the Water Snake, because that spirit had enough trouble guarding Schweeleh, and in any case she had no great love of snakes. She chose the Beaver, in part because of how much she loved the family of beavers in nearby Beaverhead Lake but also because that furry creature had learned to be wary of mountain men with traps and worked incredibly hard to support a family, yet knew when it was time to play.

"I salute you, Beaver, my guardian spirit," she said, her head lifted toward the sky but in the direction of Beaverhead Lake. "I know you will provide protection, not only for me but also for my dear daughter, at least until she finds her own guardian spirit."

That got Jay Talker squawking his feathered head off.

"I'm sorry, I didn't mean to offend you" she told him. "But it's done. Beaver it is. If it's any consolation to you, Steller's Jay was my second choice."

Bet did not dwell on the bitterness of the Bitterroot Month, which had seen a handful of violent deaths in the valley, her separation from a fur trapper who had been nothing like his late partner the rapist, her parting from a Blackfeet warrior who had been gentler than she could have imagined, and another difficult goodbye from her best friend and onetime lover who had given himself over to traditional Salish married life. She and her baby had survived and now it was up to her and her alone to make sure the two of them lived on in peace and harmony, which she knew would take planning and hard work.

She ate only a small portion of the bison meat Schweeleh had given her. She laid out some of the rest, exposing it to the smoke of a smoldering fire for two days so it would keep longer. For the remainder, she removed the fat, cut it into strips, and, after drying it, pounded it into a powder before mixing in the fat and berries to create a pemmican that could last well into winter. She would largely forgo the bitterroot, not only because bad memories lingered in her head but also because she had waited too long to go gathering again. The plants were flowering, which meant the root was now too bitter to eat. But she found wild carrots, nodding onions, and pine cone nuts to munch on and used her bone-handled knife to debark trees and scrape off the gummy edible inside layer. The nodding onions had a dual purpose. She rubbed some of the bulbs and long grass-like leaves over her own body and Little Bit's to repel mosquitoes.

When the hot weather came, the fun berry-picking began — serviceberries, huckleberries, wild strawberries, chokecherries, and black haw berries. Food gathering, especially of fruit, was a necessary but enriching thing and a cause for celebration. Bet took particular delight in pounding the chokecherries until they formed thick cakes that she laid out on the three boulders to dry. Little Bit never tired of breast milk and her sucking power remained strong, but she didn't grow as quickly as expected, so Bet introduced mashed berries to her little one's diet. The sweet taste of huckleberries made the child smile. Still, she seemed determined to grow at her own rate, not wanting to rush anything. Bet assumed that Schweeleh's boy, Wildfire, was growing much faster in the village, but she stopped thinking about size, because Little Bit's coughing fits did not return, nor did she suffer from fevers, rashes, colds, or watery stools. Good health was the most important thing. The Beaver guardian spirit was watching over them.

The fire season was no doubt going on as usual, but somewhere else. She had no idea if her old home campsite to the north of the valley was burning the way it had the previous year. She didn't care. She saw no trees ablaze where she was and only got an occasional whiff of smoke blowing over the mountains and into the valley. Memories of the redheaded mountain man would forever burn inside her brain, but they were lodged too deep at the moment to spoil her untroubled day-to-day routines and small joys. She felt so good and Little Bit was such a joy that not until the weather got cold did the mother have a second thought about possibly being with child again. During Moon

When the Rivers Start to Freeze, November, she knew it must be true and immediately worried. It wasn't that she saw a second child as a burden, for she knew what it took to be a mother alone and knew there was no limit to her motherly love. She also believed Little Bit would be happy to have a playmate in the tepee. And she wasn't concerned that the father was the Blackfeet White Buffalo, for he would have no more influence on the living baby than the red-headed mountain man had on the life of Little Bit.

What worried her was the actual childbirth — not so much the pain involved, though that was real enough. *Women were destined to suffer during childbirth as the Bible decrees. It's the price women must pay for original sin.* That's what Mama Hex had preached. Of course, Mama Hex never believed that a laboring woman was destined to die if she kept giving birth, but that's what happened to her the tenth time. Bet knew it could happen to her this second time, especially if she lacked any kind of assistance. The first time, Hawk had been there, and even his inexperienced hand had helped.

The danger involved was what concerned Bet the most, and it wasn't so much the danger for the child. After all, she had already intentionally aborted twice in her life. While she would never do that a third time, she was convinced that pregnancy did not make a child — birthing did. It would be sadder should a child die at birth, but she knew that even when under a doctor's supervision, some babies were in the wrong position (feet first or sideways) and could not be successfully turned even with instruments. Their deaths from such difficulties were in a way part of life, and a woman could only throw up her hands and carry on with her own life — that is, unless the mother died, too. That was the greatest danger Bet feared, and not because she was selfish. If she should die giving birth to a second child, what would become of Little Bit, who already had a taste of life and knew how to smile?

As it grew closer to her time, her concern grew for her children — one nearly a year old, the other near birth — even though early wintertime on the mountainside was relatively mild. One day in the middle of January, which she had learned from the Arapahos was the Moon When Snow Blows Like Spirits in the Wind, the tepee flaps began flailing like fish out of water as the wind howled like a pack of wolves. Snow blowing out of the west pelted the hide cover of her home. Little Bit had begun to walk, but on this day, she reverted to crawling and never strayed too far from her mother. It was as if she feared bad spirits were trying to get inside. Bet offered reassuring words, as much for herself as for her little girl. Her own fear had rubbed off on Little Bit. Whenever the snow and wind stopped, she decided, she would put Little Bit on her back and make her way down to the Salish village. There would be some risk because of the icy slope, but she now felt staying put would be worse. That night, with the relentless wind keeping her half-awake, she had a horrible vision — the unborn baby dying on the way out, she herself dying of overexertion and heartache, and the little girl crawling in circles inside the tepee until she died of starvation and helplessness.

By morning the wind had stopped, and the snow stopped in the afternoon. Two days later, the sun shone bright and temperatures rose above freezing. Bet was ready to roll or slide down the mountainside. Her plan once she reached the village was to slip into Otter Woman's lodge and have the medicine woman quietly oversee the birth. Neither Schweeleh nor anyone else would need to know she was there. After a few weeks, when the time was right, Bet Hex and her two children — the newborn in the cradleboard, Little Bit already walking steady — would start for home without having created a stir in the other lodges.

As she would later admit, she wasn't thinking straight, and too far ahead as it turned out. On the way down the mountain, she kept her footing well, moving from tree to tree with knees bent and taking short steps to keep from losing her balance. In the cradleboard Little Bit, clearly delighted at not having to walk or crawl, made gurgling happy sounds. Bet was near the valley floor and seemingly safe when she leaned against a cottonwood to rest up from her tricky descent. As if directed by an evil spirit, two giant icicles dropped from an overhead branch. The largest one speared her in the belly, while the other crashed against the back of her head, sending bits of ice flying against the cradleboard. Bet fell to the ground, her bruised belly landing on a snow-covered boulder. She was knocked out, and Little Bit, after realizing she was no longer moving, began to bawl her head off. That could have been the end for both of them, and the unborn babe as well, except for two Salish boys carrying bows and arrows who were tracking a bull elk up the valley that day. One after the other, they nearly tripped over the fallen woman.

The smaller boy suggested the woman was dead, and not one of their people.

The other boy said it could not be. He detected life in her left pinky. And then, in English, he identified her: "White Woman Who Never Dies."

They both agreed the child in the cradle-board was alive, since she was crying. The smaller of the two poked her stomach none too gently. *"Aaieee, booo, ahhh!"* Little Bit said, and the boy laughed and poked her again. The taller of the two pushed his friend away, dropped his bow, and lifted the little girl up to his face.

"Who?" he asked her, shaking her slightly as if that could make her understand.

She looked him straight in the eye. "Pa-pa," she said.

Bet didn't hear that brief conversation, of course. Later, Spukani told her what was said that day, but Bet refused to believe Schweeleh's wife. "Impossible," she insisted. "Boys lie. Little Bit has only a mama!"

The boys had left Bet lying where she'd been struck down by the double icicle attack. Whether she was dead or alive hadn't mattered, since they could do nothing more for her either way. They brought the little girl back to the village, taking turns carrying her and dropping her only once — into a snowbank, no harm done, she hadn't even cried. It had taken some time for the boys to make it clear to their questioning elders that the baby hadn't been found alone. Once they revealed that the apparent mother was a white woman lying completely still on the cold ground up the valley, Otter Woman had taken hold of the taller boy and ordered him to show her the way. Half the village had rushed after them, also on foot, to see for themselves if the White Woman Who Lives in Mountains with Small Daughter could really be dead. It was Schweeleh, on his spotted pony, who reached Bet first and wrapped himself around her to provide warmth and restore life.

CHAPTER TWENTY-ONE

In the medicine lodge, Otter Woman worked hard before and after Bet Hex regained her senses. The medicine woman mashed roots, twigs, leaves, and bark and then boiled them to extract the healing oils that she applied liberally to Bet's head, belly, and chest while shrieking her incantations to the animal spirits. She did not try to summon the Great Spirit Amotken because she had never found him helpful in matters of childbirth, nor did she try to contact his five Mother-Daughters, whom Amotken had created from strands of his hair instead of relying on messy and painfully slow human-style reproduction. Otter Woman believed it was indeed Mother of Wickedness and Cruelty who was in immediate charge of the Salish world, and how could a spirit like that be kind to a human female and the life forming inside her?

Yet Otter Woman was full of hope, even

after years of births gone wrong, sickness, drought, wildfire, and Blackfeet attacks and degradations, including last year's first bitterroot harvest when the feared blackmoccasin warriors from the north not only killed five of her people but also rendered her unconscious and urinated on her from atop the sacred humped boulder. She knew well Coyote the trickster and his many faults — such as greed, jealousy, lust, and anger — but these vices served as a way Coyote taught the Salish how to live through similar vices and become better human beings. Coyote cared and she cared. She believed that the earth provided all the roots and herbs necessary to help people to overcome any illness that might overcome them. The Salish, like all people, needed guidance and an occasional helping hand.

Nothing needed to be done about Little Bit, who was out of the hands of both the mother and the healer. Schweeleh had brought Little Bit into his family tepee and insisted that his wife Spukani and her widowed sister Sakaam, who was now living with them, look out for the little girl as they would for his son Wildfire. Meanwhile, Schweeleh wore a path between his own tepee and Otter Woman's medicine lodge. Knowing he could do little himself to help

Bet and unaware that she had adopted a Beaver Spirit, he asked his own guardian Water Snake Spirit to protect his Pretty Pale Face.

Otter Woman finally emerged from the medicine lodge, and Schweeleh stopped in his moccasin tracks. One look into her glassy eyes made him wish he was confronting a she-bear rather than a human bearer of bad news. "Dead," she said, first in Salish and then in English, as if that somehow made it more official.

This was no time for acting like a stoic warrior. Schweeleh shrieked for ten seconds and then he muttered, "Bet Hex . . . Bet Hex . . . Bet Hex . . ." for half a minute, though he had rarely called her by that name. Finally, he slowly mouthed the three words *Pretty Pale Face* and sat down in his own worn tracks in the snow. He later admitted that he could not bear to go inside and see just how pale his beloved mountain woman had become in death. When Otter Woman put her herb-stained fingers on his head it was as if she were pronouncing his own death sentence. Yes, he had a loving wife who had recently given birth to their second child, a healthy boy, and enough food to get them all through the coldest moons. But at that moment he felt as if the

Water Snake Spirit had let him down and he would, if ever again capable of movement, stand up, run to the Bitterroot River, and drown himself.

It wasn't the end of the world, Otter Woman told him, but Schweeleh seemed inconsolable, so she went back inside the medicine lodge. When she returned a half hour or more later, he still sat there like a stone that could not feel the cold, only the pain of existing when all around him was dead or dying. She bid him come inside now. He asked her why he should bother. She said the patient was asking to see him. He shrieked louder than before. He did not believe communication with the dead was possible, at least not so soon after death.

Otter Woman called him a foolish man and reminded him that the name of her patient was White Woman Who Never Dies. He thought Otter Woman, who could speak in strange tongues and out-shriek him for no apparent reason, had finally gone over the edge. He told her flat out that she must have lost her mind or that trickster Coyote had taken control of it. She was not offended, but she laughed in his face.

It was then he heard another woman's voice. It came from inside and was familiar but had never sounded so piercing. "Damn it, Schweeleh. I'm not gone. Tote your carcass in here!"

He rushed inside the medicine lodge to make sense of it. Bet was sitting cross-legged on a bed of blankets, clutching her empty cradleboard to her chest. He reached out with some trepidation to touch her yellow hair, thinking he might feel only air. But the hair was real, so he laid a hand on her forehead and then rested the tips of two fingers against her neck as if checking her pulse.

"Alive!" he called out.

"On the outside," she replied.

"Huh?"

"Baby is dead."

"No, no. She with Spukani and Wildfire. In tepee home. Safe."

"I know that. Otter Woman told me. I meant my *baby* baby. Dead inside."

She cast aside the cradleboard and patted her belly, then grabbed her crotch and didn't let go. Schweeleh was too stunned to say anything in English or even his own language. All he could do was stand there and try not to gawk.

"Otter Woman had the power to relieve the pains of childbirth, but the child had to be sacrificed," Bet said. "She ended my suffering but tried to do more than her guardian spirt allowed and that always ends in tragedy. As for my own guardian spirit, Beaver, looking after me was task enough. Yes, it was to be a boy. I was going to call him either Louis or Pierre after Monsieur Coquerel, the good man who long ago saved me from the Pawnee Morning Star Sacrifice. I thought of naming him Schweeleh, but I think such a name would be a burden for a boy who was not a full-blood Indian. Besides, Spukani wouldn't like that, would she? Don't bother to answer. It doesn't matter. It's over now. I want Little Bit. She is mine."

"Yes. I not know you were with child again."

"How could you? I didn't want you or anyone else to know. Not that I was ashamed. I just thought it was nobody's business but my own. I would have loved this boy as much as Little Bit. Maybe if I had come to see Otter Woman sooner . . . maybe not. I don't know. Spiritual intervention is sometimes not enough in such cases. Humans are helpless. I don't blame myself. I don't blame Otter Woman. I don't even blame the father. He wanted me with him."

"Father?"

"Never mind. You don't know him. Now fetch my little girl."

■ ■ ■ ■

Otter Woman attributed the giant icicles that befell Bet Hex to Bet's less than benevolent Beaver Spirit. It was the medicine woman's opinion that Bet had incurred the wrath of her guardian by being audacious enough to try bringing a half-Blackfeet child into the world. Bet hadn't intentionally told Otter Woman that the Blackfeet warrior White Buffalo was the father, but in a state of semiconsciousness, she had mentioned his name.

Bet begged Otter Woman not to tell anyone, but it was too late. Spukani knew Bet's secret, having badgered the old shaman to learn the truth. And when Schweeleh brought Bet to his tepee to complete her recovery from her head and belly wounds, Spukani saw fit to reveal the terrible truth to him, for though she was the one he had married, she still saw the White Woman Who Refused to Die as her rival. Spukani knew that Schweeleh, like any good Salish fellow, had both fought fiercely and traded reluctantly with Blackfeet and did not consider a single one of them a friend. What use could her man have for a woman who shared blankets with one of the killer Blackfeet who had invaded the Bitterroot Valley at last year's bitterroot harvest time?

But Spukani's effort to disgrace Bet backfired in the eyes of her husband. Schweeleh never questioned Bet about what had happened during her short time in the hands of White Buffalo. To him it didn't matter whether or not she had been forced to submit to a Blackfeet's understandable if misguided passion. A rough translation of what he said to his wife: *Warfare is hell and sometimes love is, too. Bet and Little Bit went through hell to get here and they lost their son-brother. I will protect them from the Blackfeet and let them heal as long as they wish. Our tepee is their tepee. We made room for your widowed sister Sakaam and now we make room for my longtime friend and her living child, who Wildfire accepts as his own sister, and who Esel will also come to love.*

Esel, which meant "two," was Schweeleh and Spukani's second child, a baby boy who had just started to wave his arms and legs. Bet stayed on in Schweeleh's family tepee far longer than she expected and far, far longer than Spukani and Sakaam wanted. The three children were in good spirits. Little Bit liked to watch Wildfire play with his rattles and miniature coup sticks, and she tried to brush his already long black

325

hair when he was in range. Her hair had come in golden, like her mother's, and Wildfire liked to tug it, though he otherwise paid little attention to her. Little Bit enjoyed tickling Esel's tiny toes, while Wildfire devilishly relished pulling those same toes. Bet was involved in the year's bitterroot harvest, and this time it was done in peace with Schweeleh and the other men standing nearby to protect them rather than going on their spring buffalo hunt just yet. Before the female diggers went to work, Chief Big Face paid tribute to the late Left Hand, Otter Woman gave thanks to the Great Spirit Amotken, the people prayed and danced, and the men sang individually, though Schweeleh preferred to only hum.

Bet was still with the people at the start of June, the Moon when the Hot Weather Begins. The bitterroot plants were about to bloom and could no longer be easily peeled. Men and women went north out of the valley to where the blossoming camas shimmered like a blue lake. Bet had developed a strange fear about venturing outside the Bitterroot Place, but she kept it to herself and went along with Schweeleh and the others. The Kootenais went to the same camas prairie, but it was a time for sharing in the bounty. The spirits were consulted again before the massive digging of the deeply buried bulbs began, followed by the baking in pits that lasted three days and transformed inedible bulbs into delicious treats that were sweet, devoid of any bitterness.

"I still like bitterroot better," Bet told Schweeleh, who wasn't much of a digger but was good at finding rocks to line the traditional pits and building fires over them.

"Why so?" Schweeleh asked.

"Life isn't always sweet," she said. "Sometimes we must accept the bitter."

"Ugh."

"It's true and you know it. You married Spukani, didn't you, and her sister came with her. And not you, my Salish man — nor the young Arapaho man, nor the old Frenchman, and probably no mountain man either — ever officially wanted to be my husband. What's more, I have four times been with child in my life but, as fate would have it, only one of them has seen the light of day."

"Little Bit see. She good."

"Oh, yes, very good. Sometimes a little camas can sweeten up the bitterroot."

The peaceful bitterroot collecting followed by the camas gathering did Bet good. She temporarily forgot about the baby boy she had lost and the bad men, white or red, she

had known. But she could not forget Spukani, who never stopped resenting her presence, even when Bet did more than her
share of the women's work and helped with
baby Esel, or Sakaam, who was under the
false impression that her late husband, Joseph Logan, had shared blankets with Bet.

At the start of Moon When the Chokecherries Begin to Ripen, late July, the Salish
decided to move their entire village down
the valley, which meant following the Bitterroot River north. They did so because
their campgrounds had become tired and
because for the second year in a row no
wildfires were burning out of control to the
north. The abnormally early fire season of
three years ago, during which only the fire-
resistant larch and ponderosa pine seemed
safe, was still in the collective memory, but
the present was what mattered. The people
called upon Amotken and their personal
guardian spirits for protection (if not from
fire, than from drought and the Blackfeet),
Big Face gave his blessing, and they moved.

Bet Hex did not go with them. She went
in the opposite direction with Little Bit and
plenty of dried bitterroot and camas in her
cradleboard. She was eager to get back to
her Three Boulder mountainside home for
the start of her favorite time — the berry-

picking season. Little Bit wouldn't be able to help with that fun chore yet, but the mother looked forward to that day. During her time in the village, all the reasons she cared so much for Schweeleh were renewed, except, of course, for his ability to give physical pleasure to her. He was kind, understanding, supportive, and not too nosy. But it wasn't hard to leave, since Spukani and Sakaam were none of those things. On one occasion, when the sisters teamed up to quote passages from the late Joseph Logan's Bible and questioned her morals, she came close to rapping each of them on the knuckles with her pipe tomahawk.

"In a fix, come back," Schweeleh said to her the morning she set out for home.

"Don't plan on getting into any fixes," she replied, but she chose not to look at him directly because she didn't want to show tears, not with Spukani watching closely with arms crossed and showing the fervid gaze of a cougar sizing up its prey.

"In cold, come back."

"I don't think so. I shall stock up and be well prepared for the winter."

"Get sick, come back. Little Bit get sick, come back."

"I think at this point I can handle any sickness that might come up as well as Otter Woman can. I don't like to say it, but she's getting old, maybe losing her touch. Living can be hard, but I haven't lost my faith in my Beaver Spirit or my love for Three Boulder. We'll be fine."

"New baby, come back."

"No more babies for me, if I can help it. All I have to do is stay away from mountain men and Indian braves. Yes, that includes you, I'm afraid."

"If fine, come back. For visit."

"I'm sure we will . . . someday. Until we meet again, Schweeleh."

He nodded. "Amen," he said, as if he had heard a prayer.

CHAPTER TWENTY-TWO

She began preparing for winter as soon as she returned home: chopping and gathering wood, collecting berries and nuts, smoking and drying fish caught in Beaverhead Lake, building a better cache pit for stored food, cutting up a fur blanket to make warm clothes for Little Bit, getting daily weather reports of sorts from Jay Talker, and dealing directly each evening with her guardian Beaver Spirit while stargazing with her daughter. Since she didn't own any firearm, there would be a shortage of meat, but she had done without it before. She didn't bother the wild animals and they didn't bother her. In fact, when the first truly cold day arrived, a deer seemed to sacrifice itself for her.

The buck limped up to her tepee on three good legs, lay on the ground in front of her door, and didn't move when she came out to investigate. She left it alone, knowing if it got up and ran before morning, it would survive. But it was still there at dawn and in agony, with one of its hind legs shattered. She put the beast out of its misery by knocking it out with her pipe tomahawk and then slitting its throat. She thanked the deer before gutting it, slicing the pieces of meat into thin strips and hanging them on branches in direct sunlight to dry them and keep them out of the reach of hungry bears. Louis Pierre Coquerel had taught her all that long ago, although she had rarely put it into practice seeing as how various men had often been around just long enough to do such things, and when they weren't, she had no trouble doing without the flesh of animals.

"Well, now, Little Bit, would you look at that," she said, pointing at the meat hanging in Lonesome Pine. "You know what that is?"

"Birdie," said her precocious child, who Bet believed was full of mental promise and would one day possess more than ordinary beauty to boot.

"What? Oh, yes, I see him now, but I don't mean Jay Talker. Do you see the food?"

But Little Bit had stopped looking up. The little girl had taken hold of her feet and was sucking on her toes.

"Never mind. The point is there will be venison. Your mama can do it all, girl. Who needs to hunt a hunting man!"

The winter was harsh, as harsh as any she could remember in the Place of the Bitterroot. The west wind swept down the mountainside and through the campsite, carrying with it not only the cold and snow but also bad memories from other seasons — particularly the stillbirth of her baby boy, an event she now realized would keep coming back to haunt her for as long as she lived. What the redheaded mountain man had done to her wasn't something she dwelled on anymore. After all, as was becoming clearer every day, something extraordinarily good had come of it — a healthy, toe-sucking girl full of promise. As for her killing Sunshine, or Red, as his trapping partner Eldridge Hawkinson called him, thoughts of that act had stopped being any kind of bother to her. She had been in a state of outrage and self-preservation when she silenced him with the pipe tomahawk. It had been easier than killing the injured buck.

Not the elements of nature nor elements of mind could bring Bet Hex down for long. She believed in Beaver Spirit but even more so in herself. That is to say, she believed she had as much power at her command now as any Salish person, whether it be the old shaman Otter Woman or her former lover Schweeleh. She assumed her power would be readily available whether she was in the valley, on the Plains, following an Indian path west, and even back in Missouri or Kentucky. But she was absolutely certain her power existed at full steam in this particular place — Three Boulder in the Bitterroots. It was with pride that she stuck it out at home for many moons, even if the only ones she could boast to were Little Bit and Jay Talker. They had stuck it out too, though Little Bit had no choice in the matter, of course, and the blue-and-black male bird didn't seem to want to be outdone by a white woman. That's how Bet saw it, anyway. There was nobody else around to argue the point except Jay Talker, and the opinionated bird remained noncommittal for a change.

It wasn't until the Moon of Ice Breaking in the River, April, that Bet and Little Bit, now walking on her own at least half the time, slowly and safely made their way down to the valley floor. They hadn't needed to leave home — all was right at Three Boulder — but Bet had stayed there long enough and in the worst weather to prove her point that the two of them could survive and even thrive without any outside help. She thought Little Bit would benefit from being with someone her own age, namely Wildfire, and Bet admitted that perhaps she could do with a little socializing. Even mountain men *needed* that at least once a year.

She reluctantly also admitted to herself she wanted to see Schweeleh, but only to talk to, of course, for he was a married man. She had plenty of time *not* to think of him, because she and Little Bit had to go far down the valley to find the Salish village at its new location. It was only when she quite by chance came face to face with a shirtless Schweeleh as he stepped out of a red willow-frame sweat lodge that she remembered that while the ice was indeed breaking on the Bitterroot River, April was known to the Salish as the Lovemaking Month.

"Hot," he said, fanning his red face.

She hugged him. He felt warm, and as they hugged, he reached down to give Little Bit's head a pat. Spukani and Sakaam weren't inside the sweat lodge, he told her, even though she hadn't asked. They were back at the tepee using their combined skills to make Wildfire his first pair of beaded moccasins and Esel a new blanket out of woven plant fibers. Schweeleh said he had been sweating and singing in the dark lodge with four old people, including Otter Woman and a cousin of Left Hand, and they all had been praising *Tupia,* the spirit in the sweathouse. Suddenly, he broke away from her and stepped backward as if overcome by an ancient shyness. His face was redder.

"You . . ." he said, but he didn't finish his thought.

"You look good," she said.

He tapped himself on the chest over his heart and then patted his own head. "All good," he said. "You?"

"All good with me and Little Bit. It was a fierce but uneventful winter, just wonderful. We survived!"

"No other?"

"We didn't see a living soul up there, if that's what you mean — no unwanted visitors or anything like that."

"Sad alone?"

"I had Little Bit. Anyway, a woman alone is actually not alone. Her guardian spirit, in my case Beaver, is there to help when needed. Isn't that what you believe, too, I mean for a man as well as a woman?"

Schweeleh scratched his head and then his chest, which he stuck out. *"Skaltamix,"* he said, pounding his chest. "Man," he translated, in case she had forgotten that word.

"Ah, you mean sad because I had no man around? Absolutely not. No man, no chance of getting big belly." She boldly raised her shirt to pat her bare stomach but then felt bad about it. The baby boy she had never actually seen alive flashed before her eyes. She frowned and let out a long sigh that also caused him to sigh.

"Little Bit happy? Little Esel happy. Wildfire happy. Strong, too."

"As I would expect. And is your wife in good health?"

He nodded and softly said, "Good." But he quickly added, "Not so strong."

"Well, she is a little woman. Sakaam still sharing your tepee home?"

"Marry Sakaam."

"Oh, hell. I suspected you would, her being a widow and your wife's sister and so deprived and needful. I suppose it's the best for the two of them and . . . I think I better change the subject. Were you really actually singing inside the sweat lodge?"

Schweeleh began to hum as if he was hearing distant drums. "No sing," he said, laughing.

Bet decided to laugh, too, though she now genuinely felt sad and she wasn't alone.

Schweeleh's two wives did not pretend to

be glad to see Bet Hex's return to the village, but they didn't seem threatened by her presence. They merely accepted her as a guest who, while not wanted, was still treated hospitably. They also liked the way Wildfire played with Little Bit, as if she were a doll he could either hit or push aside, and the way Little Bit seemed to like keeping Wildfire entertained. At least she didn't cry. Bet didn't cry either, but she couldn't stand being there seeing the two wives talk about the two white female guests behind her back, or the way Schweeleh was often so close yet out of reach.

After several weeks, Bet carried her reluctant daughter out and moved to the other side of the village to share Otter Woman's tepee. Otter Woman was constantly burning herbs and would chant or shriek at any hour of the day or night, even when she wasn't trying to heal a sick Salish patient. It was not a good place to sleep or find any kind of rest, but Bet decided she must at least last through the annual first bitterroot harvest. Some days she left Little Bit with Wildfire and Esel and their two mothers and walked to the Bitterroot River to nap among the cottonwood trees.

On the day before the harvest was to begin, she was lying on the riverbank dreaming of a Blackfeet raid when she felt a hand on her shoulder and screamed. She was relieved to see Schweeleh hovering over her. His face was painted with red, yellow, and black stripes. He wore only his moccasins, breechclout, and a headdress. He had followed her partly out of curiosity but also because he had something to say that had nothing to do with past intimacies or rekindled romance. He quickly took his hand away and did not touch her again.

"I fight," he said.

She sat up. "What? With one of your wives?"

"Blackfeet."

"What? Oh, you mean you're going to fight. Why?"

"Revenge."

"Because of the Blackfeet Bitterroot Butchery, right?"

He nodded. "Kill Left Hand."

"I remember. That happened some time ago."

"No forget."

"Me neither. Did a war party form while I was napping?"

"Few go. Three."

"Just three? And you happen to be one of them. What can three do?"

"Revenge."

"I know that. But how can just three of you attack a Blackfeet village?"

"Be quiet."

"What? Oh, I see. You sneak in, assassinate a Blackfeet warrior or two, and then dash back to the Bitterroot. It sounds dangerous. Does it have to be you going? Can't they send younger men. I mean, you look to be in fine form, but . . ."

"Go now."

He hesitated only long enough to watch a duck fly down and land on the smooth river with a splash and two loud quacks.

"Be careful," she called out to him. "Come back."

He kept walking away. He was dressed for his hit-and-run attack but needed his weapons. She knew that much about how all men, white or red, fought.

The next day she went ahead with the women and their male guards to the best bitterroot field and found herself working next to Spukani, while Sakaam stayed back at the home tepee watching over Wildfire, Esel, and Little Bit. Schweeleh's first wife stayed physically close to Bet throughout the digging, and when Bet's antler-handled digging stick split in half, Spukani gave her a replacement. Somehow, they were closer now, and not just physically, what with them

340

both distraught over the possibility that Schweeleh might never return.

It was a successful first day and Bet was able to load her cradleboard with roots. She wanted to leave, especially after Wildfire accidentally poked Little Bit in the left eye with his miniature coup stick. But Otter Woman treated the little girl's eye with an oil wash from purple coneflowers and black-eyed Susans and said Little Bit should not travel for two days. After two days, their departure was delayed again, this time by Bet's churning thoughts. She could not bear to go back to Three Boulder without first learning Schweeleh's fate.

Spukani seemed to understand. She had begun pulling out strands of her black hair. Sakaam chose to imitate her sister. Bet did not doubt her anxiety was their equal, but she left her yellow hair undisturbed because in the middle of the night in Otter Woman's tepee, the only white woman in the village got a sign from her Beaver Spirit that she put into words: *Leave Your Golden Hair Alone and He Shall Stroke It Again.*

Three days later, Schweeleh and the other two Salish raiders rode into the village. They had eluded the dozen Blackfeet warriors who chased them through the Hell Gate and across the Clark Fork River. The trio had let their ponies loose in the mountains before squeezing into a hidden Bitterroot cave that Bet believed was the very same shallow cave she had taken shelter in when fleeing the wildfires and smoke in the year of the early fire season. They had remained in the cave overnight to be sure the pursuing Blackfeet had given up the chase and gone back to their home in the north. The next day, the trio had rounded up their ponies, which the Blackfeet had also failed to capture, and made their triumphant ride back to the Salish village.

The revenge killing raid was a success. One raider had been grazed in the back by a Blackfeet arrow, but Schweeleh and the other had come home unscathed. Schweeleh told everyone that his guardian Water Snake Spirit was guiding him the entire way. In all, the raiders had counted coup on a half dozen Blackfeet men, wounding or killing all but one and bringing home three scalps. Chief Big Face called for the people to assemble the next day for a scalp dance, and immediately ordered one scalp be hung on a pole and planted in front of the wounded Salish raider's lodge and the other two hung on separate poles at the door of Schweeleh's tepee. Those were the two owners of the scalps.

Bet was unable to get close enough to Schweeleh to let him know how much his safe return meant to her. The people swarmed into his tepee to hail the greatest hero of the moment while his two wives clung to their husband's strong arms, Wildfire clutched his father's sturdy right leg, and Little Bit, following the boy's example, held on with all her might to Schweeleh's left leg. It was a wonder the little girl wasn't trampled. Finally, Bet forced her way inside the tepee and carried Little Bit off to Otter Woman's lodge. But there was no peace there either. Otter Woman kept singing a victory song while tossing into the air a special powder that she claimed affected the fortunes of war. Little Bit dropped off to sleep soon enough, but Bet stayed awake half the night reflecting on the two scalps dangling in front of Schweeleh's tepee. She couldn't be certain, of course, but she kept thinking that the larger and bloodier of the scalps belonged to White Buffalo, her onetime captor and the father of her never-born baby boy.

In the morning Bet awoke late, and she and Little Bit had a leisurely breakfast of bison pemmican and a cottonwood mushroom broth prepared by their host as a farewell meal. They were going home. She did not feel victorious, only sensible. Society was not necessarily satisfying or safe. Human scalps were still on her mind. She would go without another visit to the tepee of Schweeleh, the honored warrior, and his wives, the unbecoming extensions of him. But their host would not let them go easy. Otter Woman insisted they wait for the procession to go by so as not to anger the Great Spirit Amotken. Like a sulking child with no alternative but to obey her parents if she wanted to avoid getting the strap or the switch, Bet waited, rocking Little Bit in her arms as if holding a doll instead of a living girl.

It was worse than Bet expected. Three women carried the scalps on poles in the front of the all-female dance procession. Bet didn't recognize the third woman, but the first two stood out like the claws of a grizzly bear — Spukani and Sakaam, those strutting sycophants spliced together to serve the double-scalp owner. Less than spitting distance from Otter Woman's lodge, the women formed a circle. Chief Big Face stepped into the middle of it and spoke about the heroism of the three raiders, who then entered the circle one by one as the women roared their approval. When the chief was finished praising the tribal heroes, the women danced and sang to the rhythm of beating drums. Spukani was dancing more exuberantly than anyone, and Sakaam, though hardly swaying at all, was singing at the top of her lungs. Bet wasn't sure what the wives had done with the scalp poles, but she was disgusted anyway.

"How long does this go on?" she asked Otter Woman.

She got no answer because inside the tepee the old lady was dancing and shrieking to her own beat. Next to her, Little Bit was spinning circles and whooping like a little Indian. Bet put on her cradleboard, which was loaded with dried roots, and then seized her daughter by the hand.

"Dance, dance?" Little Bit asked as her mother pulled her out the tepee door.

"No, no."

"Sing, sing?"

"No, no. We walk, walk!"

They left the village hand in hand, the mother yanking hard, the little girl dragging her feet. It would take them three days to get home to Three Boulder, and they would not return to the Salish village for the next year's first bitterroot harvest or the one after that either. It was as if the onetime Pale Woman Who Lives in Mountains Alone, and who had become Pale Woman Who Lives in

Mountains with Pale Daughter, wanted nothing more to do with Indian society, let alone the white society she had turned her back on long ago.

CHAPTER TWENTY-THREE

While Bet Hex and Little Bet were living at Three Boulder like a mother-daughter team of hermits untouched by both the evil and good in society, the Blackfeet made incursions into the Bitterroot Valley out of revenge and something deeper. Warfare was in their nature, but whether that made them so different from people all around the world is debatable. Usually, the invaders were satisfied with stealing horses, for the Salish had more and better horses than their northern rivals. Some Salish died. No doubt some Blackfeet died, too. Word didn't reach Three Boulder, where peace reigned and so did a kind of fulfillment that brought quiet happiness and sometimes led to smiles and laughter. The struggle for survival wasn't always such a struggle. It took hard work and sometimes a little luck, but it terrified neither resident. It was simply living — the only way Little Bit knew how, and the only way Bet Hex wanted.

The Three Boulder pair received no Salish visitors and no visits from white trappers either. At Beaverhead Lake, a family of beavers, most active in the darkness, still chewed the willow trees along shore and whacked their tails in the untroubled waters. Throughout the Bitterroot range, and the entire West really, the once abundant beaver had become scarce due to large-scale trapping. Bet had her beavers and her Beaver Spirit, though, and if she never saw another mountain man again in her lifetime that was fine with her.

While it is true that Three Boulder was close to being an idyllic place, or at least was remembered as such, it is also true that even peaceful and picturesque places are invaded by flying and crawling insects. *It was mosquito bites that drove us back down to the world of others.* That's what Bet said later, and there is truth in that statement. One day while bathing in Lost Trout Creek, mother and daughter were swarmed by what must have been a new species of those blood-sucking insects. The bites resulted in more than just reddish bumps and itching. They both suffered swelling of joints, red streaks all over their bodies, fever, faintness, and wheezing. Little Bit also developed hives that kept growing larger, changing shape and spreading. When they reached her throat and tongue, she had trouble breathing to the extent that Bet feared for her daughter's life. Bears and wolves and cougars and mountain men had all kept their distance for one reason or another, but not so those pesky mosquitoes that now seemed deadly. It was time to visit Otter Woman without delay. The old shaman might not be as effective as she once was, but Bet saw no alternative. In the middle of a rainstorm mother and daughter headed down the mountainside, only to find that the Salish had moved their village again, back south in the hope that the greater distance from Blackfeet country would at least partially discourage their increasingly aggressive enemy.

Otter Woman was moving much slower now, using a walking stick even inside her lodge. But she came through, making a poultice of Western yarrow to treat the infected mosquito bites and giving Bet and Little Bit cups of hot catnip tea that made them sweat and broke their fevers in twenty minutes. Schweeleh came around to greet them and was apologetic about not visiting Bet at Three Boulder. He had been busy, what with all the horse-related warfare in the valley and on the buffalo plains and with his duties as a father. Wildfire was a handful and Esel was a quiet, needy little boy. Second wife Sakaam's first child was called Mary to honor the Christian-like values of her late husband Joseph Logan, and Sakaam had heard even more wonderful things about the Black Robes from the other Iroquois now living among the Salish. Schweeleh remained a traditionalist, believing in Amotken, Coyote, and the Water Snake Spirit among others. Bet figured out that the not always complementing beliefs led to many arguments between him and his second wife. Spukani stayed loyal to her husband on the surface, but Bet suspected she was highly receptive to Catholic concepts and did a good job of not letting it show.

Bet was still happy with her guardian Beaver Spirit despite the mosquito attack that had nearly done her in and, more importantly, had put her precious daughter at death's door. She did not go around promoting any religion, or even talking about it with villagers. God was a mystery, of course, and at times it was easier to believe in Amotken, the Salish god of creation, rather than the mighty white Creator. Bet remembered how her mother had prayed like the dickens and believed in God despite everything that went wrong in her life, but she also remembered how Aunt Betty had spoken out against a wrathful God that she declared must have resembled a male far more than a female, at least in temperament. The only thing Bet told Little Bit, who had no interest yet in gods, angels, or spirits, was that the little girl would determine on her own in time just who was her guardian.

What Little Bit wanted to do was play. Wildfire, who claimed to have already shot a baby duck with his bow and arrow, was no longer interested and was none too polite about dismissing her. Esel and Mary were too young to play with, but Little Bit, once she was fully recovered from her mosquito sickness, still hovered over the littler ones, tickling their toes, touching their noses, rubbing their bellies, and telling them tales in English that she had heard from her mother about queens and princesses, dragons and bears, talking birds and powerful beavers. Bet stayed away from Schweeleh's family tepee as much as possible. She spent her time helping Otter Woman prepare meals and herbal concoctions and also to get around the village without falling on her head. She owed the old female shaman.

When Otter Woman picked up the whooping cough, she had no cure for herself and went through a long illness that lasted three moons. She would cough over and over until the air was gone from her lungs. When inhaling, she made a whooping sound that was in truth not so different than the sounds she used to make while going about the healing business. While that was somewhat amusing, it was no fun when her violent coughing caused her to fracture two ribs. Bet worried about catching the sickness and giving it to Little Bit and Schweeleh's three children, but the Beaver Sprit didn't let that happen. As soon as the old woman was out of bed and back to whooping in healthier ways while at work, Bet took Little Bit back to Three Boulder. Little Bit put up more of a fuss than the last time they'd left the village. Bet didn't want to use force, so she promised they would start coming to the village every third moon, and also got Schweeleh to promise he would soon visit Three Boulder and perhaps bring along Wildfire for the boy's first real hunt. It worked, for silly Little Bit had taken a shine to Wildfire even though he acted so mean.

Over the next few years, the mother-daughter team at Three Boulder broke out of their daily and seasonal routines a half dozen times to venture down to the valley. Little Bit loved each trip for the principal reason that there were other children there, Wildfire foremost among them, but she also took to exchanging funny faces with Esel and "mothering" the nervous and fearful Mary. The trips were always shorter than Little Bit wanted and too long for Bet, whose hopeless and helpless longing for Schweeleh seemed to grow no matter how little attention he paid to her. She still believed in her heart that they were kindred spirits, but his spirit had wandered in another place where it was smothered by his two wives and misdirected by a warrior's bloodlust.

It wasn't until 1839 during the Moon of the Falling Leaves, October, that Schweeleh finally made good his promise and brought his son to Three Boulder to hunt whatever mountain beasts they could locate. They did not share the tepee of Bet and Little Bit. The great Salish warrior-hunter and his young hunter son spent three nights under the open sky at Beaverhead Lake and another three nights in higher country. They left the beaver family alone. Schweeleh shot a bear with his trade rifle and an eight-point buck with a bow and arrow. Wildfire, now eight years old like Little Bit, wounded a doe with his little bow and arrow. Although Schweeleh needed to follow a blood trail and then use his sharp knife to silence the doe's high-pitched cries, father and son both declared it the boy's first real kill, not counting a duckling, a ground squirrel, and a sparrow.

It was hard to say which of the two was prouder over Wildfire's accomplishment, but Little Bit may have been prouder than both of them since she didn't have to witness the bloody event, didn't remember the time when her mother used her pipe tomahawk to finish off an injured deer, and didn't doubt that she was in love. Wildfire accepted her adoration. When done telling her what an excellent shot he had made, he further boasted that one not-too-distant day he would become the best buffalo hunter under the Salish sun. Then he permitted Little Bit to kiss his cheek. That wasn't the end of it. At Beaverhead Lake on the day before he returned with his father to the valley, Wildfire insisted that he intended to be a champion Blackfeet killer like his father and offered his other cheek for Little Bit to kiss. She readily obliged. They were just young children, of course, but their behavior disturbed Bet, who didn't want her daughter to grow up too fast or to be so adoring of an Indian boy too full of himself and lacking in manners.

"Good boy, good girl, good visit," said the amused Schweeleh as the four of them watched the large wedge-shaped heads of two beavers who were swimming leisurely past at twilight.

"Maybe good," said Bet, but she had stopped thinking of the children. She was longing to plant kisses on Schweeleh's cheeks and forehead and nose and mouth and entire body. But nothing happened. He had to get back to his wives and other children, all of whom would want a good supply of meat and firewood for winter. He would not leave her with fresh memories of his touch, gentle and powerful at the same time, or the feel and scent of his body when she touched him. But at least she and Little Bit would have enough bear and deer meat to last many moons.

"I am as sad as a beaver without teeth or tail," Little Bit said the next morning as soon as Wildfire and his father could no longer be seen winding down the mountainside.

"That's pretty sad, all right," Bet said. "All our beavers have their teeth and tails."

"Schweeleh said it, and Wildfire repeated

it and I'm saying it again to you."

"I suppose those two are sad, and we are sad — all of us are sad. None of us can escape a certain amount of sadness no matter who or where we are. We try to balance it with happy times. You understand that, don't you, little one?"

"Oh, yes, Mama. But if we were with them in the valley, we wouldn't be so sad."

"With Wildfire, you mean?"

"And you with Schweeleh, Mama."

"You are talking nonsense, little one. You are too young for such talk and Schweeleh is too married."

It was not all sadness that winter for the Three Boulder residents. The cache pit was well stocked, the west winds were almost gentle much of the time, the snow stayed outside the tepee, and a warm fire burned steadily within. They told each other stories, mostly tales of talking wild animals, the guardian spirits — including the Beaver Spirit and the "Little Beaver Spirit" (a creation of Little Bit) — and exotic characters from lands where neither of them had ever been. The only rule Bet had was no stories about real people, for Little Bit's thoughts were too much on what was happening in the Salish village and Bet figured pure imagination wouldn't be as sad or as harmful as reality.

Other things besides made-up stories continued to bounce around in Little Bit's head, of course, and even before the snow melted on the three boulders, the child was pleading for the next trip to what she began to call "The Place of People" and "The Promised Land Below." Bet put her off as long as possible, but the annual first bitterroot harvest did have a lasting allure and served a useful purpose.

"We'll go for the roots," she finally told her daughter.

"Good," her eight-year-old replied. "People have roots."

As it turned out, the first harvest in the spring of 1840 was overshadowed by a monumental buffalo hunt, and Bet could say little more than hello and goodbye to Schweeleh. He and more than four hundred other horsemen, including Nez Perces and Pend d'Oreilles as well as Salish, convened at Three Forks of the Missouri, where they killed five hundred buffalo in three hours without any interference from the Blackfeet. The trip was about more than just the hunt. It was also about religion. Jesuit Father Pierre-Jean De Smet had come west in no small part because of the fourth Salish-Iroquois delegation's 1839 pleading in

Council Bluffs, Iowa Territory, that missionaries come teach their people "Black Robe medicine" — in other words, how to live as good and fervent Christians.

Father De Smet elected to witness the big buffalo hunt. Lying on a high bluff at Three Forks, he marveled at the browsing buffalo that filled the valley below for as much as twelve miles around. Even as he thanked God for this serene scene, however, the picture changed — the herd took flight as the mounted Indians gave chase, bullets and arrows flying and the panicked beasts dropping right and left like brown sacks of potatoes. De Smet knew the savages needed to eat as much as they needed salvation, but he turned away, unable to watch the butchering that came next. That July at Pierre's Hole near the Green River, the zealous Jesuit held the first Catholic mass and performed many baptisms in what would become Wyoming. In late August he returned to the States to raise funds and make all the arrangements for an extended stay in the Bitterroot Valley the following spring.

Indeed, in April 1841 De Smet and a contingent of other Black Robes arrived in the valley and almost immediately began to construct the Church of St. Mary's on the east side of the Bitterroot River, some thirty miles south of Hell Gate. By coincidence Bet and Little Bit came down from Three Boulder at that same time, a month before the first bitterroot harvest because Little Bit wished to see "in the worst way" not only handsome Wildfire but also sweet Mary. Bet was somewhat reluctant to head to the valley that early in the new year, but she reasoned there was value in it. Besides running off at the mouth about her loneliness away from her friends, Little Bit also was suffering from diarrhea, and Bet knew that the elderly Otter Woman could still cure something like that. What's more, Bet knew Schweeleh would provide her with whatever bison and deer meat he could spare. She even knew what he would say to her: *It's the least I can do.*

The village had moved again, this time farther north, making the walk the longest yet for Bet and Little Bit. Most of the way they complained to each other about their aching feet — all four of them — and as soon as they reached Otter Woman's lodge, they collapsed on her bed of buffalo skins and put their heads on the rolled woven mats that served as pillows. They hadn't been invited, and Bet apologized for taking over the bed. Otter Woman immediately shuffled to the side of the bed and sat with a loud grunt. She touched their full heads of hair and beamed.

"Ah," she said. "Yellow."

"Yes, it is us," said Bet.

"I see," said Otter Woman, but she clearly was relying more on touch than her poor eyes.

"It was a long journey down the valley."

Otter Woman gave a sympathetic grunt, and with a few English words, many Salish words, and animated hand gestures explained that the chiefs believed the Black Robe religion was stronger than the old religion and would better protect the people from Blackfeet encroachment.

"You don't believe it," said Bet. "Well, neither do I. I didn't know the Jesuits had arrived already."

"Ugh," Otter Woman said.

"I'm not here for them. Little Bit is having some trouble at the bottom. Diarrhea — you know, loose, watery discharges from the bowels." Bet turned to her side and patted her own backside.

The old woman struggled to stand. She had become much feebler since Bet last saw her, but once she was up, she showed spring in her step. She rushed to the door, which she had no trouble finding, stepped outside, and spat twice. When she came back inside, she went right to work preparing two teas — one from the roots of the licorice plant, which Little Bit found pleasantly sweet, the other from sagebrush, which the patient found too bitter. Otter Woman insisted Little Bit drink both for the fastest cure. And it worked. No more diarrhea.

Although she could no longer make her rounds in the village, Otter Woman knew all about Father De Smet, who she called "De Smelt," after the fish, for being a follower of the "fisher of men." That was her name for Jesus Christ. Apparently, something to that effect was in the Bible an Iroquois had brought into Salish country many moons ago, but it made no sense to Bet. She thought the ancient female healer was losing her mind as fast as her eyesight. Otter Woman spent the next couple days advising Amotken to take direct action because the intruder *De Smelt* was trying to replace him with a white man's God and also was substituting angels for Salish spirits. "Black Robes more bad than Blackfeet," she blurted out to Bet in English amid much gibberish that didn't even sound like Salish. "Blackfeet kill body, Black Robes kill soul."

Of course, that was being contrary or plain crazy, Bet figured. Father De Smet and company were trying to save Salish souls. In the weeks to come, Bet learned that he was fairly successful in getting the old men to stop gambling and the young men, at least the ones he converted, to stop taking more than one wife. Schweeleh, as much a traditionalist as Otter Woman, naturally opposed these and other so-called moral reforms that the top Black Robe was trying to impose on the people, though Bet suspected her old lover must have realized that taking on Sakaam as a second wife had been a huge mistake.

Sakaam became more unloving toward Schweeleh the more she adopted Christian ways of thinking and behaving. She had a head start on most of the village converts because she had already named her daughter Mary, for the mother of Christ, and was already wearing a cross that her late first husband Joseph Logan had bequeathed her. She even came to agree with Father De Smet that her marriage to Schweeleh was not only invalid but also immoral. Still, she did not walk out of the comfortable home tepee for she adored the children, loved her sister, and heralded her husband for being an outstanding provider who never beat his wives. Meanwhile, Spukani was content to be the first wife and made a point of exhibiting no religious convictions one way or the other.

It wasn't until two weeks after her arrival in the village that Bet finally went to see for herself what Father De Smet was all about, leaving Little Bit behind at the girl's favorite place — the Schweeleh family tepee. There, Little Bit got occasional glimpses of Wildfire, though the boy spent most of his time outdoors fishing, swimming, and shooting his bow and arrow. When he wasn't present in the tepee, Little Bit still enjoyed teaching serious little Mary how to play games and teasing the shy and ever-ticklish Esel until he burst out laughing. Spukani and Sakaam approved, for Little Bit was so polite, so good at entertaining their small children, and so much easier to be around than her mother.

Bet located De Smet at the busy church-construction site, where he was taking notes in a journal and nodding his approval as the carpenters and other workers, as he put it, "engaged in raising the house of prayer." Occasionally he would look beyond them to the large wooden cross, the first thing the missionaries had built upon entering the valley, and his head would bob so severely that Bet thought it might break free from his neck and float all the way up to Heaven.

He didn't seem to notice Bet as she approached him from behind even though she twice cleared her throat and walked with heavy steps.

"A big change for the village," she finally said, instead of offering praise. She had no interest in change or progress, if this was genuinely that, and wondered if the man in black truly knew more about the spiritual life than Otter Woman or Schweeleh.

"The church and cross are at the center of our mission," he said without looking at her. "The land is fertile, and the Indians will learn to cultivate the soil and raise livestock."

"They do all right gathering their bitterroot and camas, tending their horses, and going to the Plains a couple of times a year to hunt buffalo."

"Of course, the Flatheads can continue to hunt. I'm not going to let them starve."

"That's nice of you. By the way, the Salish don't like to be called Flatheads. And I'm *not* a Salish — can't help who my parents were."

"I know who you are; you are the only white woman for hundreds of miles around."

"You have something against white women?"

"I must be frank with you, Bet Hex. I don't believe you belong here. Converting the Indians requires that they be isolated from contaminating influences, not only from the corruption of the age but also from what the gospel calls the world. I caution them against all immediate intercourse with the whites, especially if they are female."

"I don't believe I'm contaminating anyone. Anyway, I don't live here in the valley. I'm visiting with my daughter. We live in the mountains."

"So I have heard. You have never had a husband and you live as a wild Indian does instead of as a Christian. You come to the Flathead village to gamble with the old Indian men, to fornicate with the young men, to steal husbands, to call upon female shamans, to worship false idols, to steal whatever you can from these scrupulously honest people."

Bet backed away, too shocked to protest or deny anything. Father De Smet finally tilted his head to look directly at her. His face was red, perhaps from the sun, perhaps not. She needed to cross her arms and hug herself to keep from shaking. Neither of them spoke for several minutes.

"That's not all, Father," she said, abruptly breaking the silence. "I must confess to killing several unborn babies and one bad man, but don't worry, he wasn't one of your Indians and not at all God fearing."

Now, it was Father De Smet's turn to look shocked. His lips trembled but no words came out. She looked past him to the giant wooden cross, then crossed herself as she had seen her mother do back in Kentucky and Missouri. Not sure why she did it and feeling flustered, she turned away from him and ran back to Schweeleh's tepee to reclaim her unchristian daughter.

CHAPTER TWENTY-FOUR

No doubt Father De Smet was a great missionary full of good intentions but Bet Hex would never forget the hurtful things he said to her during their first encounter, and for the rest of 1841 she avoided making the trip to the Salish village that grew up around the mission. Ten-year-old Little Bit complained constantly about the isolated life at Three Boulder, and during the berry-picking season she tried to run away from home with nothing more on her person than a rawhide pouch half full of huckleberries. She was headed for the valley, of course, but Bet caught up with her partway down Lost Trout Creek, where Little Bit stood in the modest flow paralyzed with fear in the face of a she-bear and three cubs.

Bet diverted the black bears' attention by yelling, whistling, and waving her pipe tomahawk high in the air. After the bear family hightailed it downstream, Bet brought her daughter back to Three Boulder without a fight, but the winter seemed longer and darker than ever what with several ice storms crashing through, one whose gale winds nearly carried off the tepee, and with an endlessly pouting little girl.

Bet's hardline stance against travel to the valley didn't start to crack until the ice began to break up on Beaverhead Lake. A delighted Little Bit was immediately welcomed back into the Schweeleh family tepee, but Otter Woman was not in her lodge to greet Bet. Schweeleh explained that the old healer had wandered outside for no apparent reason during the fierce windstorm that felled trees, blew away tents, and broke the church windows. She had made it all the way to the church and apparently collapsed in the snow after throwing an ice ball at one of the church windows that was still whole. After that, she had managed to crawl as far as the wooden cross, perhaps to spit on it, before freezing to death. By her request, she had *not* been given a Christian burial. Father De Smet called it an act of God, for the old lady had surely brought on the wrath of the Supreme Being for showing such a lack of respect on holy ground.

"Life among Black Robes no good for Otter Woman," Schweeleh told Bet when he found her wandering about the village in a dazed state of mourning. "She go to sky, teach Coyote the trickster new tricks."

"She won't be forgotten," Bet said. "She healed even when enfeebled and blind."

"She say Lord's Prayer, the Hail Mary, Ten Commandments no good. She anger the priests."

"She called their leader Father De Smelt. Nobody could tell her what to believe."

"I believe like her. People divide. Some like him, want Christ, grow potatoes. Some like me, want Coyote, hunt buffalo."

"I know." She wasn't one to cry, but she rested her head on his shoulder and closed her eyes. When she felt his hand on her back, she knew she wanted him, forever, in sadness or in joy and health, but she had known that for a long time.

"Come to my tepee. Little Bit happy there. You be happy." He gently pushed her away from him and held her at arm's length. "You happy, make me happy."

"I better not. Otter Woman's lodge is empty. I'll sleep there. I'm certain Spukani and Sakaam won't mind keeping Little Bit overnight, and I know Little Bit will love it. How are things going in your tepee anyway? Family all good?"

"Good. Wildfire big, strong. Hunt good. Hunt buffalo soon. Esel little, makes big laugh. Mary like Sakaam. Sweet and sour."

"You didn't mention your first wife. What about Spukani?"

"Good. Big with child. Tsele — Number Three! Spukani want girl."

"That is good, for you, for her. I'll be good, too, and say goodnight."

Bet learned that at the time Otter Woman died, Schweeleh and other Salish hunters were on the Plains looking for buffalo and Father Nicolas Point had accompanied them, perhaps to give his blessing to the winter hunt. It was the policy of the Black Robes, as established by Pierre-Jean De Smet, to allow the Salish to go a-hunting as long as the buffalo remained, but the ultimate goal was to convert these heathen hunters and gatherers to Christian farmers. The Salish and Point were not on the Plains long before they were confronted by Black-feet hunters, and the inevitable happened — a fight. Nobody died, but several on both sides were wounded, including Schweeleh, who had a Blackfeet arrow glance off his right hip.

The Salish also captured one of the wounded Blackfeet warriors, but instead of torturing him, they released him after he appealed to Father Point for mercy. The Salish hunters protested, saying the Blackfeet never showed any mercy to their enemies. When Schweeleh told this story to Bet she remembered how White Buffalo had shown her mercy during and after the Blackfeet's bitterroot harvest attack that cost Left Hand his life. But she said nothing to the worked-up Schweeleh, who kept talking and gesturing to tell her how, after the hunters' return, Father Point had repeated his meddling by insisting they set free a Blackfeet man found spying on the activity at the mission.

"Point think we barbarous to torture enemy and scalp," Schweeleh grumbled as he talked to Bet in the back of Otter Woman's old lodge. He was putting most of his weight on his left leg because his right hip was still bothered by the arrow wound.

"You never were in favor of those things, were you? I mean, you have proved yourself to be an outstanding warrior without doing those kinds of things."

"Not the point. Why we must change? We don't displease Amotken."

"I don't necessarily disagree with you but clearly even some of your chiefs do. They have welcomed the Christian words of De

Smet and Point and the others."

"Pointless!" Schweeleh shouted, but when Bet laughed at his unintentional wordplay, he laughed, too. "Anyway, De Smet not here. Go to Fort Vancouver to see other missionaries."

"Wonderful. That might convince me to extend our visit. Little Bit is so happy here spending time with your children, and you know how much I like to see you. I only hope I won't be contaminating you and your people too much."

"Huh?"

"Never mind. It's just something *De Smelt* said to me a while back. But like you said, he's not here. So why should I worry."

Every week, Bet kept extending their stay in the Salish village, which kept growing around the mission. The main reason was because Little Bit didn't want to leave. She was growing up fast physically and Wildfire had started to take an interest in her. Their budding young romance included her taking long valley walks with him, fishing and swimming with him in the Bitterroot River, eating beside him the meals prepared mostly by Spukani, and gazing from the top of a hill at the moon and the stars. After all, they would both soon be eleven. Bet made Otter Woman's old lodge her home away from home. At first, she insisted Little Bit spend every night there, but that fell by the wayside soon enough. Spukani said she never tired of having Little Bit as a tepee guest, and assured Bet that Wildfire, though already starting to look like a warrior, would never do anything that violated honorable Salish customs toward the opposite sex.

It dawned on Bet that if she took Little Bit back to Three Boulder it would have to be as a prisoner, and the girl would soon try to escape. She had already attempted to run away once, and Bet remembered how as a girl herself back East she had tried to run away many times before succeeding. It made Bet sad that her daughter preferred the company of others and sadder that one of those people was Sakaam, who began taking Little Bit to church with Mary and Esel and sometimes Wildfire, though Schweeleh didn't approve. The priests were not only teaching them about the Christian way of behaving and believing but also how to appreciate peace with the neighboring Blackfeet, planting crops in the fields, and the written word as presented in the Bible.

Bet really couldn't complain about any of that. She liked the idea of peace with everyone and fresh food from a garden, and reading might be useful to Little Bit down the road because Bet knew her daughter would rather live with people in a town than with her mother in the mountains. But would it be an Indian village or a white man's town, for the latter would certainly appear in the valley one day? Would Little Bit one day marry, and would it be to an Indian such as Wildfire? Would Little Bit ever have babies, and would she want them? Would she ever insist on knowing who her own father was? Would she ever want to travel to St. Louis or the big Eastern cities? Would she be there for her mother when her mother became decrepit like Otter Woman? When she and Little Bit were living as a hermit team at Three Boulder, Bet had rarely contemplated such things. So, her worries were mostly about things that hadn't happened yet or might never happen, but they were still worries.

Not that Bet spent all her time worrying. She began gambling and smoking her pipe tomahawk again with the old men who had been friends with Left Hand. She was far from pretty now, and her age could be measured by the lines on her face, but her hair was still a shiny yellow and these gentlemen still didn't mind when she won these betting games. It was a secretive activity, for they knew the priests, particularly

De Smet, thought gambling was sinful and ruined a person's life spiritually if not financially. Also somewhat secretive were her meetings with Schweeleh, who sometimes just needed to get away from his pregnant wife and his crowded tepee to talk about things that made them both smile, or about nothing at all. If he wanted something more than talk, he never let on, and she resisted many urges to touch his strong arms, his black hair, and a certain distinct dimple she knew he had on his lower back. As much as she had loved raising a little girl, she was now close to fifty and couldn't bear to be with child again even if it were possible.

"Sometimes I can't remember how old I am," she admitted to Schweeleh at one of their evening meetings when she knew her Little Bit and his Wildfire were on the hill looking for the new moon. "I don't think I have ever felt my age. When I was young and wandering the West, I felt much older. Now settled in the Bitterroot, I feel much younger."

"You not old."

"Oh, I am, just not as old as you."

They both laughed. He touched her forehead. "Wise one. Think young. Feel young."

"But I don't look young, do I?"

"Always young to me."

"It's too dark for you to see all the lines on my face. It's damn good I don't own a mirror."

"I feel young, too. Still warrior. Still hunt buffalo good. Still fight Blackfeet."

"And still making feet for children's moccasins. It's easier for you to feel young with your two much younger wives and three little ones. Four, if everything works out. When is Spukani due?"

"Two moons, maybe three. Little Bit make five."

"It must feel like she's one of your own — she spends so much time in your tepee."

"All love Little Bit."

"Including Wildfire, it seems. I'm not sure when we'll ever get back to Three Boulder. I do miss it but maybe not as much as I thought I would. You are more fun to talk to than my camp bird, Jay Talker."

"Thank you. You more fun for talk than Sakaam." They shared a burst of laugher again, but Schweeleh abruptly stopped and kicked at the ground. "Sakaam talk like Black Robe."

"What about your first wife? You like talking to Spukani, don't you?"

"All baby talk." He reached out in the darkness and stroked her hair briefly the way Left Hand used to do. "Feel good." With that Schweeleh retired to his tepee, and Bet stood there for some time with her face tilted upward, trying to look around the stars to find a trace of moon.

Bet and Little Bit left for Three Boulder in July, just before De Smet returned to St. Mary's from Vancouver. It may only have been a coincidence, but Bet was glad to miss seeing the man who said she didn't belong among the Salish. Things, however, did not go well at home. Although there were berries to pick, Little Bit was in no mood to help and listlessly roamed the mountainside, thoughtlessly eating more huckleberries than she plucked from the bushes and even coming back to the tepee empty-handed at times. Bet finally had it out with her, and Little Bit confessed that she missed Wildfire terribly and his entire family as well. Not only that. She asserted that she had taken to Sunday services at the Jesuits' church and to reading the Bible, which "had some interesting parts," and wanted to get back to learning things her mother never could or would teach her. Bet told her daughter it was best if she stayed away from the boy and his family for a while and spent time with her own family, doing the work that needed to be done to get ready for a hard winter.

"But you by yourself are my whole entire family," Little Bit argued. "And the winter won't be nearly so hard if we are down below with the others in the warm village instead of up here alone on a cold mountain. Besides, you want me to learn to read and write, don't you?"

"No," Bet shouted. "I mean yes to reading and writing, but I can teach you those things myself. My mother taught me. I'll just have to get something for us to read, and paper and pen."

"They have those things in the village."

"Look, little one, you can't always have your way. Sometimes you have to . . . to listen to your mother."

"I have been listening to you my whole entire life. You aren't always right, you know."

"I know that, but . . ."

"I need to hear other voices."

"Is it really so bad here at our mountain home? Don't we share many things, including laughter?"

"I'm *not* like you, Mama. I don't want to run away from people."

"I'm not running away. I'm staying put at Three Boulder. I've made a home for us."

"Thank you. But I feel like . . . I don't know what. I feel old."

"Old? You have known less than a dozen years. It's me who is old, really old."

"I know that. But I don't want to grow old on this mountain."

In September, which Bet still thought of as the Moon of Drying Grass, they returned to the valley.

CHAPTER TWENTY-FIVE

Father De Smet was gone again when they got there. Being a man on a mission far greater than just showing the Salish the correct path to salvation, he was back on the road. After stopping at the buffalo grounds, where his fellow priest Point was observing a Salish summer hunt, he proceeded to St. Louis and from there to Europe to raise money and gather missionaries to help convert the Indians of the Northwest. His work to make the Salish subservient to the Church and the priests was not yet done, but De Smet would be gone from the valley for nearly three years.

During the time De Smet was away the Bitterroot transformed further, with new cabins built at the mission and vegetable gardens starting to thrive. But warfare had not been eliminated, in part because the Blackfeet had not been Christianized but also because Salish warriors like Schweeleh continued to fight for their right to use the buffalo grounds. No matter how many potatoes, turnips, beets, and peas the missionaries and their converts harvested, the people still wanted their buffalo meat. So war and hunting on the Plains continued, and some of the men, though not so much Schweeleh, protested the priests' abolishment of polygamy. Bet and Little Bit went back and forth between Three Boulder and the Salish village at St. Mary's Mission, but mother and daughter continued to drift apart in their thinking. They were equally stubborn in what each believed was right as far as living arrangements, family interaction, and matters of romance.

In January 1845, feeling full-grown and head over heels in love at age fourteen, Little Bit declared that she was leaving their mountain home for good and intended to marry the "exceptional and exceeding magnificent" (words she had discovered in the Bible) Wildfire, with or without Bet's consent. Trouble was, he hadn't asked her yet and, in any case, Spukani told her son and his white sweetheart to wait until they were sixteen and then have a church wedding presided over by a priest. Wildfire was his father's son when it came to fighting and hunting, but he listened to his mother, certainly far better than Little Bit listened to hers. Little Bit agreed that waiting was best because that was what her true love wanted, but in the meantime, she would not set foot in Three Boulder. Instead of an immediate wedding, she settled for a visit to a Salish women's lodge where she underwent belated puberty rites that she reluctantly told her mother about afterward.

"No need to keep secrets from me," Bet told her daughter. "I'm not blind to what's going on. This is a time of change for you. It happens to white girls just as it does to Indian girls. It's all natural."

"Of course, I know *that,* Mama," said Little Bit, rolling her eyes. "After *it* happens, Salish girls get married within two to four years."

"No need for you to rush things just because those other girls do. Marriage can wait."

"Says you who never married. You waited too long."

"Maybe so. But the world didn't come to an end."

"No, but when I have a baby, I want it to have a father, and I want him to be Wildfire."

"You didn't turn out so badly, did you, little one?"

"I'd prefer *not* to be called *little one* anymore, Mama. You think I haven't wished all these years to have a father? You know what that makes me, don't you — a by-blow."

"Jesus Christ! Where did you learn such a word?"

"I heard some of the fathers talking — you know, the Black Robes."

"Sometimes I wish I didn't. No need for you to listen to such talk."

"You don't want me to keep secrets from you, yet you keep so many secrets from me, including the big one: Who, Mama, is the man who fathered me?"

"It's nothing you need to know, little one. Sorry — but you are my little one, no matter what. As I've told you many times before, he doesn't matter, not even a little bit."

"Very well. Keep your deep dark secret. But Wildfire matters a whole lot, and in two years' time I shall marry him."

The uncomfortable subject was dropped.

When Father De Smet returned to St. Mary's that spring he brought with him Father Anthony Ravalli, a man of many skills and totally dedicated to converting the whole valley full of Salish. He encour-aged farming and raising livestock and taught the Salish how to use a hot iron to sear St. Mary's "Cross on a Hill" brand — the first brand used in what would become Montana — onto their cattle. He also operated what amounted to a drugstore and did some doctoring, though he hardly ever used the methods of the late Otter Woman. The valley would get its first sawmill and gristmill thanks to Ravalli. In 1846 he and the other fathers made full use of the sawmill to build a new, larger church and a dozen new wood dwellings for the Indians. And that wasn't all. The most energetic of the fathers was also big on baptism, which served as a healing ritual for the ill and elderly and as an induction ritual into the Christian community for the young Salish. He reminded them all that for a soul to not experience the fires of Hell, it must be baptized. Their so-called guardian spirits could be of no help in this matter.

On a sandy shoreline of the Bitterroot River, Little Bit stood first in line to be baptized, with Sakaam standing right behind her for moral support. Little Bit was a good swimmer and not afraid in the slightest when Father Ravalli himself immersed her in the still waters. She was glad to get that treatment instead of a mere sprinkling of water on her head that the priests reserved for the old and sick. Her mother was old and had a sore throat (from shouting too much at her, Little Bit thought) and wanted no part of any kind of baptism business. Bet was back at Three Boulder telling both her guardian Beaver Spirit and the living beavers in the lake how sad she was to have lost her precious little daughter. At about the time she suspected Ravalli was done "saving" Little Bit, Bet stripped naked and plunged into Beaverhead Lake. It wasn't her intention to drown herself, since she was only half miserable being alone and knew her daughter would come home someday. It was only her intention to strike at the cold water with both arms and legs in a personal anti-baptism gesture.

Tired of being called Little Bit as a young woman soon to marry and not wanting to be a Bet like her mother or a Betty like her mother's aunt or to have one of those Salish names like Spukani or Sakaam, Little Bit had chosen to be baptized under a Christian name. She had gone to the Bible and come up with Eve, Sarah, Esther, Ruth, Jezebel, and Delilah, but Wildfire weighed in on his favorite, so Little Bit chose Bathsheba. The name was a mouthful, but Father Ravalli had not objected to it and had even told her that Bathsheba was the mother of Solomon, who was full of wisdom.

Even after partially reconciling with her mother and admitting she was proud to have been baptized, Little Bit thought it wise not to reveal that in the eyes of God she was now *Bathsheba*. Even though Wildfire had talked her into that name, he immediately started using Sheba for short and sometimes when feeling particularly amorous he would call her "Bath Baby" and they would go bathe naked in the Bitterroot River. The first few times, she felt sinful frolicking in the same body of water where she had undergone baptism. But she got over it. Bet, though, never got over her daughter's new name, which she eventually learned from Sakaam, who thought Eve would have been a better choice. Bet didn't care for either Eve or Bathsheba, or any of the others. To her, Little Bit would be Little Bit till the end of time.

Whether Father De Smet approved of a white girl being baptized among *his* Indians, Bet had no idea. In the fall he departed again for the East, on the way stopping off on the Plains and conducting an open-air mass with not only the Salish hunters but also the Nez Perces, Gros Ventres, Blackfeet, and other tribes. Schweeleh was there with Wildfire, now a full-fledged buffalo hunter. Schweeleh later told Bet that many of his fellow Salish were upset that De Smet gave the enemy the Catholic medicine (prayers, baptisms, Hail Marys, etc.), but Schweeleh himself didn't believe that kind of medicine helped either his people or the Blackfeet. What did bother Schweeleh, and even more so the fiery young Wildfire, was that the buffalo herd was depleted, which was reason enough for increased warfare by the competing tribes on the buffalo grounds.

After De Smet continued on his journey, the Salish engaged in some of the old war dances and returned from their hunt in foul moods. Some of them were openly hostile to the priests, especially to the austere Father Gregorio Mengarini, who in De Smet's absence was in charge of St. Mary's Mission. It didn't help matters that more and more hard-living white trappers, hunters, and even cattlemen came to the area and almost never acted like good Christians. Some chose to stay awhile instead of just passing through the valley.

"I reckon they are all contaminating the Salish more than me," Bet told Schweeleh, because not even a new member of his family, a baby girl, could keep him too busy for a talk every few days.

"See anyone you know?" Schweeleh asked.

"By that I know you mean what's his name, Hawk — Eldridge Hawkinson. Even you said he was a nice guy for a mountain man."

"You bet. He like you."

"That was a long time ago. He had a Crow wife."

"And he want another."

"Yes. Two, like you."

"Humph. Maybe one enough."

"And are four children enough yet? What's the name of the fourth?"

"Eve."

"You mean like in Adam and Eve? Has Spukani started reading the Bible, too?

"Spukani have baby. Sakaam give name."

"And you didn't object to calling the little one Eve?"

"She Spukani's *first* girl. Spukani happy. Me happy. Sakaam happy. Mary happy. Esel happy."

"What about Spukani's first boy?"

"Wildfire happy, too. All family happy."

"And what about my daughter? She doesn't have time for her mother anymore. I hardly ever see her these days. I take it Wildfire still plans to marry her next year?"

"You bet."

"In that case, Little Bit must be happy as a lark."

"Yes, but she no Little Bit. She Sheba now."

"Not in my book, which by the way, isn't the Bible."

The big event in the church never happened as planned in 1847 or in the years that followed. Little Bit, at sixteen, was as ready to be married as any princess in a storybook would be to a handsome prince. Wildfire didn't necessarily get cold feet. But three days before he was to make his vows in front of Father Ravalli, he spent twelve hours in a sweat lodge and then in the middle of the night he went off on a vision quest. He chose Bald Mountain, which was out of the Bitterroot on the other side of the Clark Fork River, not far from the campsite where the redheaded mountain man had attacked Bet Hex and paid for it with his life.

What happened on Bald Mountain is not known. But Wildfire was never seen again. Schweeleh led two search parties that found no trace of the young man, and Schweeleh later went out alone and roamed Bald Mountain and the surrounding hills and hidden valleys for two weeks without any luck. The father and most everyone else ruled out an accident or a grizzly bear attack because no remains were ever found. They all came to the same conclusion: Wildfire had fallen into the hands of the Blackfeet and was taken from the scene to be tortured to death. The day before Wildfire set out on his first serious vision quest, a Blackfeet boy had come into the valley with a small group to steal Salish horses and cattle, and been shot through the belly and then tortured before he died and his body mutilated afterward. It was the same old vicious pattern. The Blackfeet had taken their revenge. The Black Robes had changed many things for the Salish in the Bitterroot Valley, but they could not negotiate a peace between the warring tribes.

The death of her intended husband naturally sent Little Bit into a frenzy of grief accompanied by notions to leap into the Bitterroot River and let the rapid spring runoff carry her away to drown so she could join Wildfire in a place far better than even their valley. After settling for cutting off most of her yellow hair instead of suicide, she could not bear to stay in Schweeleh's tepee any longer. She joined her mother in Otter Woman's old lodge for a week and then they returned to Three Boulder together.

For the rest of the year, mother and

daughter talked to each other only when absolutely necessary. Silence reigned in the tepee, and there was no Jay Talker anymore to break the silence outside. He had long ago flown away or died. Little Bit would often sit under Lonesome Pine and chew on bark and twigs while the tears flowed. Mostly she cried because she missed Wildfire so much, but almost anything made her cry, including the absence of that Steller's jay, the absence of a father she had never known, and the absence of hope for the future. She told her mother she would stop eating so she could wither away to nothing, but that didn't last longer than three days. Bet made a hash out of deer meat, boiled potatoes, and onions that Little Bit devoured as if she were a starving dog. She also told her mother she would never use the names Sheba or Bathsheba again because those names came from Wildfire, and she kept her word on that for years. Her last vow was to never marry as long as she lived, and she kept that vow to old age as if it were an heirloom.

Wildfire's death changed Schweeleh as well. He stopped talking to Bet about happiness — his own, his family's, or hers. Neglecting her was one thing, but he also often neglected his family, sometimes wandering as far south as the old Medicine Tree where Wildfire and Little Bit had both been cured of troublesome coughs when they were babies. He never told anyone what he did there, but Bet suspected he knelt on the tree roots, not to pray to any kind of God, but to tear at his hair and cry like a baby.

At the St. Mary's settlement, many Salish, both the converted and unconverted, rose up and spoke out against the teachings of Father De Smet and the other Jesuits. Although he had never taken to the Catholic mission, Schweeleh took no part in this bloodless rebellion. He revealed many years later that he had stopped caring about what his people believed in, what his people did, or how much the white race contaminated the Salish of the Bitterroot Valley. His despondency continued for the rest of the decade while relations between the people and the priests continued to deteriorate and Blackfeet marauders continually harassed the missionaries. In 1850, however, he couldn't help but see a ray of hope break through the gloom that still loomed over the jagged Bitterroot mountaintops: The Black Robes were closing St. Mary's Mission.

CHAPTER TWENTY-SIX

Bet Hex didn't mind a bit when the Black Robes gave up the mission. She took a certain pleasure in Father De Smet's failure in the valley. For a decade he had been trying to convert every Indian he could lay a hand on and to keep the pagan whites out. A white businessman named John Owen had bought the Jesuit property for $250 on November 5, 1850, and in a matter of a few days had transformed St. Mary's into Fort Owen, a trading post plus farm that served anyone who could barter or buy. Capitalism had bloodlessly overrun Catholicism. Not that Bet was any more eager to rub elbows with white people than red people. She had a heartbroken daughter to look after and had to deal with her own heartache over what had happened to Wildfire and how it had shattered Schweeleh. Isolation from the whole world was just fine. Three Boulder might not be heaven on Earth, but it was hers and she didn't have to share it with anybody but Little Bit, the beavers, and occasionally with four-legged or two-legged wild animals just passing through.

It was nearly two years before things started to change for mother and daughter. It was between berry-picking time on the mountain and ice-forming time on Beaverhead Lake that Schweeleh showed up at their tepee door with the carcass of a moose and his living second son. Nearly as tall as his father and nearly as thick through the chest and neck, Esel proudly announced that he had felled the moose with a trade rifle purchased at Fort Owen. He further boasted that it had taken only one shot and that he was the youngest man in the village ever to claim a moose kill. Schweeleh beamed as he listened to his son, not even suggesting the old man had played any part in stalking the bull moose, issuing moose calls, and then cornering the animal. Listening to the young man at first brought more tears to Little Bit's eyes because this hunter so full of himself was sixteen, the same age as his older brother the year Wildfire was to marry her but instead went on a vision quest that ended his vision permanently.

Little Bit recovered in time to help her mother cut the meat into thin strips and hang them over a slow fire to dry. Some of the strips were boiled for the evening meal while others were made into pemmican with berries and melted moose fat. She discovered that Esel was not a copy of his late brother. Esel grew bashful when Little Bit touched his father's arm and then his and declared that the boy had more muscle. He also took small bites and chewed carefully with his mouth closed where Wildfire would chomp with his mouth open. Unlike Wildfire, he also knew how to read English, and not just the Bible. Back in his home tepee he had a copy of English author Charles Dickens' *A Christmas Carol* that he had traded two deer hides for at the new trading post. Esel was all strong, lean, sun-kissed Indian, but he knew far more about England, Christmas, and books than Little Bit, a white girl not raised like one of her race.

All through the meal and long into the night, Schweeleh had much to say about life in the valley, although his English was only marginally better than it ever had been. From time to time, Esel would help him with words. The family was doing fine — Mary did most of the cooking because Spukani preferred to dote on young Eve, while Sakaam never wanted to stop reading the Bible that Father Ravalli gave her as a parting gift. All, however, took a hand in the traditional bitterroot and camas gatherings. Schweeleh admitted he had missed at least three buffalo hunts, but he intended to go again on the winter hunt and take Esel along now that he knew the boy was a good shot.

Schweeleh mentioned that the white missionaries were gone but whites without much Christianity had replaced them. It wasn't a bother to him because he felt much more comfortable around the coarse white nonbelievers than the smooth-talking holier-than-thou Jesuits. But other Salish complained that the replacement whites knew less than they did about the Great Spirit, Sunday prayer, and turning the other cheek. Schweeleh had overheard one chief tell John Owen that he feared the Salish people "will all be swallowed by the white tribe." Schweeleh finished off the evening with a long harangue about the Blackfeet without mentioning Wildfire's likely death at their hands. He said Fort Owen, with its log buildings surrounded by log palisades, hadn't stopped the Blackfeet from intruding any more than the mission had, though the fort itself had never been attacked. The black-moccasin raiders showed up with regularity to steal horses, not trade for them, and to kill cattle, not for eating but out of malice. John Owen had hired a man making his way to the California goldfields, but on just his second day of hauling hay, Blackfeet killed and scalped him in sight of the fort.

Schweeleh might have gone on in this anti-Blackfeet vein all evening, but Bet, who had said little up to that point, finally interrupted him. "Excuse me, mister," she said. "But wouldn't all those Salish fellows who resent the white intrusion into the valley not mind so much that the Blackfeet killed a white man instead of one of them?"

That caused Schweeleh to tilt his head as if he didn't understand. But after snarling a little to the amusement of all, he declared: "Whites can all go to Hell. Blackfeet worse but can't go to Hell. They never hear of it. Don't know where it is. Make own Hell on Earth."

"Mama and I should resent the first part you said about white people, Uncle Schweeleh," Little Bet said, but with a twinkle in her eye that Bet hadn't seen since Wildfire's disappearance at Bald Mountain. "You happen to be a guest, sitting in the tepee of two female pale-faced persons."

Silence followed. Schweeleh didn't apologize or say anything again. He was deep in thought about something. Bet wondered who was on his mind — his oldest son in the ever after, his very much alive first wife, or the white woman he had loved before those other two.

"My father is sorry even if he can't say so," said Esel. "He is an old man whose legs grew tired trying to keep up with son when chasing moose, and whose tongue now grows tired in your tepee from too much talk. We must allow the old man to rest."

That night Schweeleh and Esel slept soundly on one side of the warm tepee fire while Bet and Little Bet slept on the other but not so soundly, for they both listened long to the two men snoring. In the morning when Schweeleh and Esel took some of the moose meat back to the rest of their family in the village, Bet and Little Bit went with them. It was actually Little Bit's idea because she wanted to see Fort Owen herself and shop around for things they might need that winter at Three Boulder, as well as anything that caught her fancy that might not be necessary. Her mother was eager to make the trek herself, not because of the trading post but because she had seen some of Schweeleh's old spirit return and she wanted to spend more time with the one man she had always loved the most.

■ ■ ■ ■

On that somewhat happy note, I wish to end the story of Bet Hex, for the Woman who Roamed the Mountains would roam no more, and for me, the storyteller, her death makes for too sad an ending, as deaths often do. But, with your allowance, I shall reinsert myself into the proceedings — remember I am the once and forever (at least in the memory part of my brain) Little Bit — and try to quickly reach a conclusion for those of you who are curious to know the rest of the story.

Mama and I must have liked what we saw of Fort Owen because, while we did return to Three Boulder before the big snows (me with a white woman's hairbrush and John Owen's last copy of *A Christmas Carol*), we went back to the fort in the spring to live in one of the wood houses built by the Jesuits. We got to live there for free because Schweeleh brought much business to the trading post and John Owen and his Sho-shone wife Nancy paid him back by giving me my first job. I sometimes worked behind the counter, usually did the cleaning up, and when needed helped handle the fickle Salish women, such as Spukani and Sakaam, who thought they might want to make a deal. Mama became a homebody, but she made friends with several Salish women, Owen's wife, and even Mary and Eve, the daughters of Sakaam and Spukani. And of course there was Schweeleh, who always made time for her each week now that she was more conveniently located, just two or three stone throws from his home tepee.

Overall, business wasn't so good at the fort, however. John Owen left for a while and about gave up the store, so to speak, but he returned, and things picked up in 1854 when the U.S. Army came to the valley and established Cantonment Stevens (named for American military officer Isaac Stevens, who was governor of the Territory of Washington, which included the Bitterroot Valley) twelve miles south of Fort Owen. The soldiers were good customers, and their presence caused the Blackfeet to behave. That same year the Jesuits made a comeback with the Salish, but to the north just south of Flathead Lake where they built the St. Ignatius Mission, which attracted not only Salish but also Kootenais and Pend d'Oreilles. But the Salish in the Bitterroot weren't moving up that way . . . not yet.

Trade at Fort Owen was going better than

ever, and I was still gainfully employed, in 1856. That May many Salish fell sick and some of them died. The white medical men couldn't figure it out and neither could the shamans that still practiced in the old way. Some of the saddened survivors and their families blamed the growing white population for spreading diseases to the people. But the thing is, a white woman — Mama — got as sick as anyone. It might have been related to smallpox, because there were cases of that in the valley the next year, but it isn't certain. All I know is that I was worried sick about Mama. In her weakened state, she revealed to me that my father was one Rufus C. Dixon, a mountain man who forced himself upon her. She refused to take any of my questions but told me I could read all about it later in something she had written, something she titled "The Ignoble Incident."

Mama was in bed for four weeks and then seemed on her way to recovery. But one morning during the Moon When the Hot Weather Begins, as Mama called it since her time with the Arapahos, I was busy at the trading post when my reading friend Esel showed up looking afraid, as if there were Blackfeet in the area. It wasn't that at all. It was worse. Esel said he had gone to the Hex house to bring Aunt Bet, as he had started calling her, a pot of Mary's willow bark tea for her pain but she wasn't in bed or anywhere around.

It was hard for me to keep my head. "Mama!" I screamed. "Where are you?" I imagined her feeling good when she woke up, good enough to get out of bed and go for a walk, but then having her fatigued feet give out, her collapsing and now lying helpless on the ground.

I told John Owen I had to run because Mama came first in my life. He not only agreed I should go but told his wife to mind the store while he helped me look for missing Mama. Esel went home and got his mother and Sakaam to help search the village. Uncle Schweeleh happened to be fishing or sleeping along the Bitterroot River at the time. When he returned without any fish but looking well rested, he immediately began searching for tracks, as if he was one of those Indian scouts in the service of the U.S. Army. He found them soon enough.

"How can you be sure?" I asked.

"They right size. Leave from back door."

"All right. All right. In what direction do they go?"

"To fences with ponies behind."

"Yes, the Fort Owen corral. But why

would she go there?"

"To ride pony."

"But Mama hasn't ridden a horse as long as I've known her."

"Not forget how to ride."

"I suppose not, but . . ."

"I get my horse. Follow."

"Yes, go, go, Uncle Schweeleh. Mama never taught me to ride, but I can ride on the back of your horse, can't I?"

"You stay. I go faster alone. Find Bet."

"But I have to go. She's my mama."

He nodded. "We go."

And so we did. Schweeleh followed fresh horse tracks to the south, up the valley, with me behind him hanging on to his waist, looking from side to side and expecting at any moment to see Mama lying in the dirt. But we rode a long time and saw nothing. I asked him if he might not be mistaken, that perhaps we were following the wrong tracks. He didn't bother to answer me. Somewhere near a deserted Salish village campsite he pulled up abruptly and sprang off the pony, ran off a way, and turned his back on me. I thought the old man had to pass water. But he bent down (from my seat on the horse I heard his knees crack) and picked up something.

"What is it?" I shouted. "Tell me what

you've found."

Schweeleh no doubt didn't know the English word for it. He turned around and held the object high in the air. It was Mama's pipe tomahawk that she always carried when she went on a long trip.

"My God," I yelled. "She must have dropped it and . . . and not noticed it was missing."

"We go," he said. "On right track."

I remember that conversation so well, and of course I remember what happened after that, but there is no point in dwelling on it. Like I always say, *Every living thing must die.* That doesn't exactly help you, though, when the person who dies is the mother who raised you in the wilderness, so to speak, without the help of a father. Schweeleh noticed where the tracks left the valley floor and followed, but by then there was no need to follow tracks. Even I knew where Mama was going. At Beaverhead Lake we found a horse, one Schweeleh recognized as belonging to John Owen's Shoshone wife. The horse paid little attention to us. It just stood there looking out at the still water as if it expected at any moment to hear the whack of a beaver's tail.

"Maybe she came back to pick huckleberries," I muttered. "Mama always loved berry-picking season."

We rode on. Mama was on foot now, and her feet must have been giving her trouble, for twice, according to Schweeleh, she dropped to her knees before making herself stand and continue. She was still a tough lady at whatever she was, past sixty for sure, but she didn't quite make it to the home tepee at Three Boulder. She lay facedown on the familiar ground halfway between Lonesome Pine and the tepee door. When we reached her, there was a lot of chattering going on from one of the lower branches of *our* pine. It was a blue and black Steller's jay all right, probably a descendant of the original Jay Talker.

"Damn shit," said Uncle Schweeleh, using two English words I'd never heard him use before. "Pretty Pale Face come home to die."

"Gone Beaver," I said.

For land's sake. I can't quite end on that sad note either. It's hard to know quite what else to say, though. I can tell you that the settlement of St. Mary's got a new name in 1864 — Stevensville, in honor of the territorial governor. And in 1866 Father Ravalli, whose name in 1893 was given to the county embracing Three Boulder and

Stevensville, was back with another priest to reopen St. Mary's Mission. Uncle Schweeleh was probably glad *not* to live long enough to see that happen. He had died in the winter of 1863, not fighting the Blackfeet or getting crushed by a herd of stampeding buffalo, but peacefully in the Hex house, where he had come to live after Mama died because he said in his old age he loved the luxury of a soft white woman's bed. I was still working for the Owens at the fort in 1868, but Nancy died that year and John started drinking heavily and acting crazy. The authorities took him away and he ended up living out his last years with relatives in far-off Philadelphia.

By the early 1870s there were so many white settlers in the Bitterroot Valley that the U.S. government told the Salish chiefs they would have to move north to the Jocko Reservation unless they became landholding U.S. citizens. Subchiefs Arlee and Adolph made the move, and so did Schweeleh's widow Sakaam and her unmarried daughter Mary. Head Chief Charlo, though, remained in the Bitterroot, as did most of the people, including Spukani, Esel, and Eve. It wasn't until 1891 that Charlo and the other holdouts relented and left their beloved valley for the reservation to the north.

St. Mary's Mission closed for good. I stayed because my Christian name was Bathsheba Hex and I was white. And so here I am still in Stevensville, reading and writing as I live out my final years. I live quietly and nobody in this town pays much attention to little old me. I had to give myself my own nickname, and I chose a rather unwieldly one that sometimes even confounds me — Daughter of White Woman Who Never Dies and Who Herself Ain't Dead Yet.

ABOUT THE AUTHOR

Gregory Lalire majored in history at the University of New Mexico and worked at newspapers in New Mexico, Montana, New York, and Virginia. He was the editor of the history magazine *Wild West* from 1995 to October 2002 and is currently editor emeritus. His previous books include the children's book *The Red Sweater* (1982) and four historical Westerns from Five Star — *Captured: From the Frontier Diary of Infant Danny Duly* (2014), *Our Frontier Pastime: 1804–1815* (2019), *Man from Montana* (2021), and *The Call of McCall* (2022). He is a member of both the Western Writers of America and the Wild West History Association.